The Old Man
in the Corner

The Old Man in the Corner

Baroness Emmuska Orczy

MINT EDITIONS

The Old Man in the Corner was first published in 1908.

This edition published by Mint Editions 2021.

ISBN 9781513272160 | E-ISBN 9781513277165

Published by Mint Editions®

 **MINT
EDITIONS**

minteditionbooks.com

Publishing Director: Jennifer Newens
Design & Production: Rachel Lopez Metzger
Project Manager: Micaela Clark
Typesetting: Westchester Publishing Services

Contents

I

The Fenchurch Street Mystery

The man in the corner pushed aside his glass, and leant across the table.

"Mysteries!" he commented. "There is no such thing as a mystery in connection with any crime, provided intelligence is brought to bear upon its investigation."

Very much astonished Polly Burton looked over the top of her newspaper, and fixed a pair of very severe, coldly inquiring brown eyes upon him.

She had disapproved of the man from the instant when he shuffled across the shop and sat down opposite to her, at the same marble-topped table which already held her large coffee (3d.), her roll and butter (2d.), and plate of tongue (6d.).

Now this particular corner, this very same table, that special view of the magnificent marble hall—known as the Norfolk Street branch of the Aërated Bread Company's depôts—were Polly's own corner, table, and view. Here she had partaken of eleven pennyworth of luncheon and one pennyworth of daily information ever since that glorious never-to-be-forgotten day when she was enrolled on the staff of the *Evening Observer* (we'll call it that, if you please), and became a member of that illustrious and world-famed organization known as the British Press.

She was a personality, was Miss Burton of the *Evening Observer*. Her cards were printed thus:

She had interviewed Miss Ellen Terry and the Bishop of Madagascar, Mr. Seymour Hicks and the Chief Commissioner of Police. She had been present at the last Marlborough House garden party—in the cloak-room, that is to say, where she caught sight of Lady Thingummy's hat, Miss What-you-may-call's sunshade, and of various other things modistical or fashionable, all of which were duly described under the heading "Royalty and Dress" in the early afternoon edition of the *Evening Observer*.

(The article itself is signed M.J.B., and is to be found in the files of that leading halfpennyworth.)

For these reasons—and for various others, too—Polly felt irate with the man in the corner, and told him so with her eyes, as plainly as any pair of brown eyes can speak.

She had been reading an article in the *Daily Telegraph*. The article was palpitatingly interesting. Had Polly been commenting audibly upon it? Certain it is that the man over there had spoken in direct answer to her thoughts.

She looked at him and frowned; the next moment she smiled. Miss Burton (of the *Evening Observer)* had a keen sense of humour, which two years' association with the British Press had not succeeded in destroying, and the appearance of the man was sufficient to tickle the most ultra-morose fancy. Polly thought to herself that she had never seen any one so pale, so thin, with such funny light-coloured hair, brushed very smoothly across the top of a very obviously bald crown. He looked so timid and nervous as he fidgeted incessantly with a piece of string; his long, lean, and trembling fingers tying and untying it into knots of wonderful and complicated proportions.

Having carefully studied every detail of the quaint personality Polly felt more amiable.

"And yet," she remarked kindly but authoritatively, "this article, in an otherwise well-informed journal, will tell you that, even within the last year, no fewer than six crimes have completely baffled the police, and the perpetrators of them are still at large."

"Pardon me," he said gently, "I never for a moment ventured to suggest that there were no mysteries to the *police*; I merely remarked that there were none where intelligence was brought to bear upon the investigation of crime."

"Not even in the Fenchurch Street *mystery*. I suppose," she asked sarcastically.

"Least of all in the so-called Fenchurch Street *mystery*," he replied quietly.

Now the Fenchurch Street mystery, as that extraordinary crime had popularly been called, had puzzled—as Polly well knew—the brains of every thinking man and woman for the last twelve months. It had puzzled her not inconsiderably; she had been interested, fascinated; she had studied the case, formed her own theories, thought about it all often and often, had even written one or two letters to the Press on the subject—suggesting, arguing, hinting at possibilities and probabilities, adducing proofs which other amateur detectives were equally ready to refute. The attitude of that timid man in the corner, therefore, was peculiarly exasperating, and she retorted with sarcasm destined to completely annihilate her self-complacent interlocutor.

"What a pity it is, in that case, that you do not offer your priceless services to our misguided though well-meaning police."

"Isn't it?" he replied with perfect good-humour. "Well, you know, for one thing I doubt if they would accept them; and in the second place my inclinations and my duty would—were I to become an active member of the detective force—nearly always be in direct conflict. As often as not my sympathies go to the criminal who is clever and astute enough to lead our entire police force by the nose.

"I don't know how much of the case you remember," he went on quietly. "It certainly, at first, began even to puzzle me. On the 12th of last December a woman, poorly dressed, but with an unmistakable air of having seen better days, gave information at Scotland Yard of the disappearance of her husband, William Kershaw, of no occupation, and apparently of no fixed abode. She was accompanied by a friend—a fat, oily-looking German—and between them they told a tale which set the police immediately on the move.

"It appears that on the 10th of December, at about three o'clock in the afternoon, Karl Müller, the German, called on his friend, William Kershaw, for the purpose of collecting a small debt—some ten pounds or so—which the latter owed him. On arriving at the squalid lodging in Charlotte Street, Fitzroy Square, he found William Kershaw in a wild state of excitement, and his wife in tears. Müller attempted to state the object of his visit, but Kershaw, with wild gestures, waved him aside, and—in his own words—flabbergasted him by asking him point-blank for another loan of two pounds, which sum, he declared, would be the means of a speedy fortune for himself and the friend who would help him in his need.

"After a quarter of an hour spent in obscure hints, Kershaw, finding the cautious German obdurate, decided to let him into the secret plan, which, he averred, would place thousands into their hands."

Instinctively Polly had put down her paper; the mild stranger, with his nervous air and timid, watery eyes, had a peculiar way of telling his tale, which somehow fascinated her.

"I don't know," he resumed, "if you remember the story which the German told to the police, and which was corroborated in every detail by the wife or widow. Briefly it was this: Some thirty years previously,

Kershaw, then twenty years of age, and a medical student at one of the London hospitals, had a chum named Barker, with whom he roomed, together with another.

"The latter, so it appears, brought home one evening a very considerable sum of money, which he had won on the turf, and the following morning he was found murdered in his bed. Kershaw, fortunately for himself, was able to prove a conclusive *alibi*; he had spent the night on duty at the hospital; as for Barker, he had disappeared, that is to say, as far as the police were concerned, but not as far as the watchful eyes of his friend Kershaw were able to spy—at least, so the latter said. Barker very cleverly contrived to get away out of the country, and, after sundry vicissitudes, finally settled down at Vladivostok, in Eastern Siberia, where, under the assumed name of Smethurst, he built up an enormous fortune by trading in furs.

"Now, mind you, every one knows Smethurst, the Siberian millionaire. Kershaw's story that he had once been called Barker, and had committed a murder thirty years ago, was never proved, was it? I am merely telling you what Kershaw said to his friend the German and to his wife on that memorable afternoon of December the 10th.

"According to him Smethurst had made one gigantic mistake in his clever career—he had on four occasions written to his late friend, William Kershaw. Two of these letters had no bearing on the case, since they were written more than twenty-five years ago, and Kershaw, moreover, had lost them—so he said—long ago. According to him, however, the first of these letters was written when Smethurst, alias Barker, had spent all the money he had obtained from the crime, and found himself destitute in New York.

"Kershaw, then in fairly prosperous circumstances, sent him a £10 note for the sake of old times. The second, when the tables had turned, and Kershaw had begun to go downhill, Smethurst, as he then already called himself, sent his whilom friend £50. After that, as Müller gathered, Kershaw had made sundry demands on Smethurst's ever-increasing purse, and had accompanied these demands by various threats, which, considering the distant country in which the millionaire lived, were worse than futile.

"But now the climax had come, and Kershaw, after a final moment of hesitation, handed over to his German friend the two last letters purporting to have been written by Smethurst, and which, if you remember, played such an important part in the mysterious story of this extraordinary crime. I have a copy of both these letters here," added the man in the corner, as he took out a piece of paper from a very worn-out pocket-book, and, unfolding it very deliberately, he began to read:—

Sir,

Your preposterous demands for money are wholly unwarrantable. I have already helped you quite as much as you deserve. However, for the sake of old times, and because you once helped me when I was in a terrible difficulty, I am willing to once more let you impose upon my good nature. A friend of mine here, a Russian merchant, to whom I have sold my business, starts in a few days for an extended tour to many European and Asiatic ports in his yacht, and has invited me to accompany him as far as England. Being tired of foreign parts, and desirous of seeing the old country once again after thirty years' absence, I have decided to accept his invitation. I don't know when we may actually be in Europe, but I promise you that as soon as we touch a suitable port I will write to you again, making an appointment for you to see me in London. But remember that if your demands are too preposterous I will not for a moment listen to them, and that I am the last man in the world to submit to persistent and unwarrantable blackmail.

I am, sir,
Yours truly,
Francis Smethurst

"The second letter was dated from Southampton," continued the old man in the corner calmly, "and, curiously enough, was the only letter which Kershaw professed to have received from Smethurst of which he had kept the envelope, and which was dated. It was quite brief," he added, referring once more to his piece of paper.

Dear Sir,

Referring to my letter of a few weeks ago, I wish to inform you that the *Tsarskoe Selo* will touch at Tilbury on Tuesday next, the 10th. I shall land there, and immediately go up to London by the first train I can get. If you like, you may meet me at Fenchurch Street Station, in the first-class waiting-room, in the late afternoon. Since I surmise that after thirty years' absence my face may not be familiar to you, I may as well tell you that you will recognize me by a heavy Astrakhan fur coat, which I shall wear, together with a cap of the same. You may then introduce yourself to me, and I will personally listen to what you may have to say.

Yours faithfully,
Francis Smethurst

"It was this last letter which had caused William Kershaw's excitement and his wife's tears. In the German's own words, he was walking up and down the room like a wild beast, gesticulating wildly, and muttering sundry exclamations. Mrs. Kershaw, however, was full of apprehension. She mistrusted the man from foreign parts—who, according to her husband's story, had already one crime upon his conscience—who might, she feared, risk another, in order to be rid of a dangerous enemy. Woman-like, she thought the scheme a dishonourable one, for the law, she knew, is severe on the blackmailer.

"The assignation might be a cunning trap, in any case it was a curious one; why, she argued, did not Smethurst elect to see Kershaw at his hotel the following day? A thousand whys and wherefores made her anxious, but the fat German had been won over by Kershaw's visions of untold gold, held tantalisingly before his eyes. He had lent the necessary £2, with which his friend intended to tidy himself up a bit before he went to meet his friend the millionaire. Half an hour afterwards Kershaw had left his lodgings, and that was the last the unfortunate woman saw of her husband, or Müller, the German, of his friend.

"Anxiously his wife waited that night, but he did not return; the next day she seems to have spent in making purposeless and futile inquiries about the neighbourhood of Fenchurch Street; and on the 12th she went to Scotland Yard, gave what particulars she knew, and placed in the hands of the police the two letters written by Smethurst."

II

A Millionaire in the Dock

The man in the corner had finished his glass of milk. His watery blue eyes looked across at Miss Polly Burton's eager little face, from which all traces of severity had now been chased away by an obvious and intense excitement.

"It was only on the 31st," he resumed after a while, "that a body, decomposed past all recognition, was found by two lightermen in the bottom of a disused barge. She had been moored at one time at the foot of one of those dark flights of steps which lead down between tall warehouses to the river in the East End of London. I have a photograph of the place here," he added, selecting one out of his pocket, and placing it before Polly.

"The actual barge, you see, had already been removed when I took this snapshot, but you will realize what a perfect place this alley is for the purpose of one man cutting another's throat in comfort, and without fear of detection. The body, as I said, was decomposed beyond all recognition; it had probably been there eleven days, but sundry articles, such as a silver ring and a tie pin, were recognizable, and were identified by Mrs. Kershaw as belonging to her husband.

"She, of course, was loud in denouncing Smethurst, and the police had no doubt a very strong case against him, for two days after the discovery of the body in the barge, the Siberian millionaire, as he was already popularly called by enterprising interviewers, was arrested in his luxurious suite of rooms at the Hotel Cecil.

"To confess the truth, at this point I was not a little puzzled. Mrs. Kershaw's story and Smethurst's letters had both found their way into the papers, and following my usual method—mind you, I am only an amateur, I try to reason out a case for the love of the thing—I sought about for a motive for the crime, which the police declared Smethurst had committed. To effectually get rid of a dangerous blackmailer was the generally accepted theory. Well! did it ever strike you how paltry that motive really was?"

Miss Polly had to confess, however, that it had never struck her in that light.

"Surely a man who had succeeded in building up an immense fortune by his own individual efforts, was not the sort of fool to believe that he had anything to fear from a man like Kershaw. He must have *known* that Kershaw held no damning proofs against him—not enough to hang him, anyway. Have you ever seen Smethurst?" he added, as he once more fumbled in his pocket-book.

Polly replied that she had seen Smethurst's picture in the illustrated papers at the time. Then he added, placing a small photograph before her:

"What strikes you most about the face?"

"Well, I think its strange, astonished expression, due to the total absence of eyebrows, and the funny foreign cut of the hair."

"So close that it almost looks as if it had been shaved. Exactly. That is what struck me most when I elbowed my way into the court that morning and first caught sight of the millionaire in the dock. He was a tall, soldierly-looking man, upright in stature, his face very bronzed and tanned. He wore neither moustache nor beard, his hair was cropped quite close to his head, like a Frenchman's; but, of course, what was so very remarkable about him was that total absence of eyebrows and even eyelashes, which gave the face such a peculiar appearance—as you say, a perpetually astonished look.

"He seemed, however, wonderfully calm; he had been accommodated with a chair in the dock—being a millionaire—and chatted pleasantly with his lawyer, Sir Arthur Inglewood, in the intervals between the calling of the several witnesses for the prosecution; whilst during the examination of these witnesses he sat quite placidly, with his head shaded by his hand.

"Müller and Mrs. Kershaw repeated the story which they had already told to the police. I think you said that you were not able, owing to pressure of work, to go to the court that day, and hear the case, so perhaps you have no recollection of Mrs. Kershaw. No? Ah, well! Here is a snapshot I managed to get of her once. That is her. Exactly as she stood in the box—over-dressed—in elaborate crape, with a bonnet which once had contained pink roses, and to which a remnant of pink petals still clung obtrusively amidst the deep black.

"She would not look at the prisoner, and turned her head resolutely towards the magistrate. I fancy she had been fond of that vagabond husband of hers: an enormous wedding-ring encircled her finger, and that, too, was swathed in black. She firmly believed that Kershaw's murderer sat there in the dock, and she literally flaunted her grief before him.

"I was indescribably sorry for her. As for Müller, he was just fat, oily, pompous, conscious of his own importance as a witness; his fat fingers, covered with brass rings, gripped the two incriminating letters, which he had identified. They were his passports, as it were, to a delightful land of importance and notoriety. Sir Arthur Inglewood, I think, disappointed him by stating that he had no questions to ask of him. Müller had been brimful of answers, ready with the most perfect indictment, the most elaborate accusations against the bloated millionaire who had decoyed his dear friend Kershaw, and murdered him in Heaven knows what an out-of-the-way corner of the East End.

"After this, however, the excitement grew apace. Müller had been dismissed, and had retired from the court altogether, leading away Mrs. Kershaw, who had completely broken down.

"Constable D 21 was giving evidence as to the arrest in the meanwhile. The prisoner, he said, had seemed completely taken by surprise, not understanding the cause or history of the accusation against him; however, when put in full possession of the facts, and realizing, no doubt, the absolute futility of any resistance, he had quietly enough followed the constable into the cab. No one at the fashionable and crowded Hotel Cecil had even suspected that anything unusual had occurred.

"Then a gigantic sigh of expectancy came from every one of the spectators. The 'fun' was about to begin. James Buckland, a porter at Fenchurch Street railway station, had just sworn to tell all the truth, etc. After all, it did not amount to much. He said that at six o'clock in the afternoon of December the 10th, in the midst of one of the densest fogs he ever remembers, the 5.5 from Tilbury steamed into the station, being just about an hour late. He was on the arrival platform, and was hailed by a passenger in a first-class carriage. He could see very little of him beyond an enormous black fur coat and a travelling cap of fur also.

"The passenger had a quantity of luggage, all marked F.S., and he directed James Buckland to place it all upon a four-wheel cab, with the exception of a small hand-bag, which he carried himself. Having seen that all his luggage was safely bestowed, the stranger in the fur coat paid the porter, and, telling the cabman to wait until he returned, he walked away in the direction of the waiting-rooms, still carrying his small hand-bag.

"'I stayed for a bit,' added James Buckland, 'talking to the driver about the fog and that; then I went about my business, seein' that the local from Southend 'ad been signalled.'

"The prosecution insisted most strongly upon the hour when the stranger in the fur coat, having seen to his luggage, walked away towards the waiting-rooms. The porter was emphatic. 'It was not a minute later than 6.15,' he averred.

"Sir Arthur Inglewood still had no questions to ask, and the driver of the cab was called.

"He corroborated the evidence of James Buckland as to the hour when the gentleman in the fur coat had engaged him, and having filled his cab in and out with luggage, had told him to wait. And cabby did wait. He waited in the dense fog—until he was tired, until he seriously thought of depositing all the luggage in the lost property office, and of looking out for another fare—waited until at last, at a quarter before nine, whom should he see walking hurriedly towards his cab but the gentleman in the fur coat and cap, who got in quickly and told the driver to take him at once to the Hotel Cecil. This, cabby declared, had occurred at a quarter before nine. Still Sir Arthur Inglewood made no comment, and Mr. Francis Smethurst, in the crowded, stuffy court, had calmly dropped to sleep.

"The next witness, Constable Thomas Taylor, had noticed a shabbily dressed individual, with shaggy hair and beard, loafing about the station and waiting-rooms in the afternoon of December the 10th. He seemed to be watching the arrival platform of the Tilbury and Southend trains.

"Two separate and independent witnesses, cleverly unearthed by the police, had seen this same shabbily dressed individual stroll into the first-class waiting-room at about 6.15 on Wednesday, December the 10th, and go straight up to a gentleman in a heavy fur coat and cap, who had also just come into the room. The two talked together for a while; no one heard what they said, but presently they walked off together. No one seemed to know in which direction.

"Francis Smethurst was rousing himself from his apathy; he whispered to his lawyer, who nodded with a bland smile of encouragement. The employés of the Hotel Cecil gave evidence as to the arrival of Mr. Smethurst at about 9.30 P.M. on Wednesday, December the 10th, in a cab, with a quantity of luggage; and this closed the case for the prosecution.

"Everybody in that court already *saw* Smethurst mounting the gallows. It was uninterested curiosity which caused the elegant audience to wait and hear what Sir Arthur Inglewood had to say. He, of course, is the most fashionable man in the law at the present moment. His lolling attitudes, his drawling speech, are quite the rage, and imitated by the gilded youth of society.

"Even at this moment, when the Siberian millionaire's neck literally and metaphorically hung in the balance, an expectant titter went round the fair spectators as Sir Arthur stretched out his long loose limbs and lounged across the table. He waited to make his effect—Sir Arthur is a born actor—and there is no doubt that he made it, when in his slowest, most drawly tones he said quietly;

"'With regard to this alleged murder of one William Kershaw, on Wednesday, December the 10th, between 6.15 and 8.45 P.M., your Honour, I now propose to call two witnesses, who saw this same William Kershaw alive on Tuesday afternoon, December the 16th, that is to say, six days after the supposed murder.'

"It was as if a bombshell had exploded in the court. Even his Honour was aghast, and I am sure the lady next to me only recovered from the shock of the surprise in order to wonder whether she need put off her dinner party after all.

"As for me," added the man in the corner, with that strange mixture of nervousness and self-complacency which had set Miss Polly Burton wondering, "well, you see, *I* had made up my mind long ago where the hitch lay in this particular case, and I was not so surprised as some of the others.

"Perhaps you remember the wonderful development of the case, which so completely mystified the police—and in fact everybody except myself. Torriani and a waiter at his hotel in the Commercial Road both deposed that at about 3.30 P.M. on December the 10th a shabbily dressed individual lolled into the coffee-room and ordered some tea. He was pleasant enough and talkative, told the waiter that his name was William Kershaw, that very soon all London would be talking about him, as he was about, through an unexpected stroke of good fortune, to become a very rich man, and so on, and so on, nonsense without end.

"When he had finished his tea he lolled out again, but no sooner had he disappeared down a turning of the road than the waiter discovered an old umbrella, left behind accidentally by the shabby, talkative individual. As is the custom in his highly respectable restaurant, Signor Torriani put the umbrella carefully away in his office, on the chance of his customer calling to claim it when he had discovered his loss. And sure enough nearly a week later, on Tuesday, the 16th, at about 1 P.M., the same shabbily dressed individual called and asked for his umbrella. He had some lunch, and chatted once again to the waiter. Signor Torriani and the waiter gave a description of William Kershaw, which coincided exactly with that given by Mrs. Kershaw of her husband.

"Oddly enough he seemed to be a very absent-minded sort of person, for on this second occasion, no sooner had he left than the waiter found a pocket-book in the coffee-room, underneath the table. It contained sundry letters and bills, all addressed to William Kershaw. This pocket-book was produced, and Karl Müller, who had returned to the court, easily identified it as having belonged to his dear and lamented friend 'Villiam.'

"This was the first blow to the case against the accused. It was a pretty stiff one, you will admit. Already it had begun to collapse like a house of cards. Still, there was the assignation, and the undisputed meeting between Smethurst and Kershaw, and those two and a half hours of a foggy evening to satisfactorily account for."

The man in the corner made a long pause, keeping the girl on tenterhooks. He had fidgeted with his bit of string till there was not an inch of it free from the most complicated and elaborate knots.

"I assure you," he resumed at last, "that at that very moment the whole mystery was, to me, as clear as daylight. I only marvelled how his Honour could waste his time and mine by putting what he thought were searching questions to the accused relating to his past. Francis Smethurst, who had quite shaken off his somnolence, spoke with a curious nasal twang, and with an almost imperceptible soupçon of foreign accent, He calmly denied Kershaw's version of his past; declared that he had never been called Barker, and had certainly never been mixed up in any murder case thirty years ago.

"'But you knew this man Kershaw,' persisted his Honour, 'since you wrote to him?'

"'Pardon me, your Honour,' said the accused quietly, 'I have never, to my knowledge, seen this man Kershaw, and I can swear that I never wrote to him.'

"'Never wrote to him?' retorted his Honour warningly. 'That is a strange assertion to make when I have two of your letters to him in my hands at the present moment.'

"'I never wrote those letters, your Honour,' persisted the accused quietly, 'they are not in my handwriting.'

"'Which we can easily prove,' came in Sir Arthur Inglewood's drawly tones, as he handed up a packet to his Honour; 'here are a number of letters written by my client since he has landed in this country, and some of which were written under my very eyes.'

"As Sir Arthur Inglewood had said, this could be easily proved, and the prisoner, at his Honour's request, scribbled a few lines, together with his signature, several times upon a sheet of note-paper. It was easy to read upon the magistrate's astounded countenance, that there was not the slightest similarity in the two handwritings.

"A fresh mystery had cropped up. Who, then, had made the assignation with William Kershaw at Fenchurch Street railway station? The prisoner gave a fairly satisfactory account of the employment of his time since his landing in England.

"'I came over on the *Tsarskoe Selo*,' he said, 'a yacht belonging to a friend of mine. When we arrived at the mouth of the Thames there was such a dense fog that it was twenty-four hours before it was thought safe for me to land. My friend, who is a Russian, would not land at all; he was regularly frightened at this land of fogs. He was going on to Madeira immediately.

"'I actually landed on Tuesday, the 10th, and took a train at once for town. I did see to my luggage and a cab, as the porter and driver told your Honour; then I tried to find my way to a refreshment-room, where I could get a glass of wine. I drifted into the waiting-room, and there I was accosted by a shabbily dressed individual, who began telling me a piteous tale. Who he was I do not know. He *said* he was an old soldier who had served his country faithfully, and then been left to starve. He begged of me to accompany him to his lodgings, where I could see his wife and starving children, and verify the truth and piteousness of his tale.

"'Well, your Honour,' added the prisoner with noble frankness, 'it was my first day in the old country. I had come back after thirty years with my pockets full of gold, and this was the first sad tale I had heard; but I am a business man, and did not want to be exactly "done" in the eye. I followed my man through the fog, out into the streets. He walked silently by my side for a time. I had not a notion where I was.

"'Suddenly I turned to him with some question, and realized in a moment that my gentleman had given me the slip. Finding, probably, that I would not part with my money till I *had* seen the starving wife and children, he left me to my fate, and went in search of more willing bait.

"'The place where I found myself was dismal and deserted. I could see no trace of cab or omnibus. I retraced my steps and tried to find my way back to the station, only to find myself in worse and more deserted neighbourhoods. I became hopelessly lost and fogged. I don't wonder that two and a half hours elapsed while I thus wandered on in the dark and deserted streets; my sole astonishment is that I ever found the station at all that night, or rather close to it a policeman, who showed me the way.'

"'But how do you account for Kershaw knowing all your movements?' still persisted his Honour, 'and his knowing the exact date of your arrival in England? How do you account for these two letters, in fact?'

"'I cannot account for it or them, your Honour,' replied the prisoner quietly. 'I have proved to you, have I not, that I never wrote those letters, and that the man—er—Kershaw is his name?—was not murdered by me?'

"'Can you tell me of anyone here or abroad who might have heard of your movements, and of the date of your arrival?'

"'My late employés at Vladivostok, of course, knew of my departure, but none of them could have written these letters, since none of them know a word of English.'

"'Then you can throw no light upon these mysterious letters? You cannot help the police in any way towards the clearing up of this strange affair?'

"'The affair is as mysterious to me as to your Honour, and to the police of this country.'

"Francis Smethurst was discharged, of course; there was no semblance of evidence against him sufficient to commit him for trial. The two overwhelming points of his defence which had completely routed the prosecution were, firstly, the proof that he had never written the letters making the assignation, and secondly, the fact that the man supposed to have been murdered on the 10th was seen to be alive and well on the 16th. But then, who in the world was the mysterious individual who had apprised Kershaw of the movements of Smethurst, the millionaire?"

III

His Deduction

The man in the corner cocked his funny thin head on one side and looked at Polly; then he took up his beloved bit of string and deliberately untied every knot he had made in it. When it was quite smooth he laid it out upon the table.

"I will take you, if you like, point by point along the line of reasoning which I followed myself, and which will inevitably lead you, as it led me, to the only possible solution of the mystery.

"First take this point," he said with nervous restlessness, once more taking up his bit of string, and forming with each point raised a series of knots which would have shamed a navigating instructor, "obviously it was *impossible* for Kershaw not to have been acquainted with Smethurst, since he was fully apprised of the latter's arrival in England by two letters. Now it was clear to me from the first that *no one* could have written those two letters except Smethurst. You will argue that those letters were proved not to have been written by the man in the dock. Exactly. Remember, Kershaw was a careless man—he had lost both envelopes. To him they were insignificant. Now it was never *disproved* that those letters were written by Smethurst."

"But—" suggested Polly.

"Wait a minute," he interrupted, while knot number two appeared upon the scene, "it was proved that six days after the murder, William Kershaw was alive, and visited the Torriani Hotel, where already he was known, and where he conveniently left a pocket-book behind, so that there should be no mistake as to his identity; but it was never questioned where Mr. Francis Smethurst, the millionaire, happened to spend that very same afternoon."

"Surely, you don't mean?" gasped the girl.

"One moment, please," he added triumphantly. "How did it come about that the landlord of the Torriani Hotel was brought into court at all? How did Sir Arthur Inglewood, or rather his client, know that William Kershaw had on those two memorable occasions visited the hotel, and that its landlord could bring such convincing evidence forward that would for ever exonerate the millionaire from the imputation of murder?"

"Surely," I argued, "the usual means, the police—"

"The police had kept the whole affair very dark until the arrest at the Hotel Cecil. They did not put into the papers the usual: 'If anyone happens to know of the whereabouts, etc. etc'. Had the landlord of that hotel heard of the disappearance of Kershaw through the usual channels, he would have put himself in communication with the police. Sir Arthur Inglewood produced him. How did Sir Arthur Inglewood come on his track?"

"Surely, you don't mean?"

"Point number four," he resumed imperturbably, "Mrs. Kershaw was never requested to produce a specimen of her husband's handwriting. Why? Because the police, clever as you say they are, never started on the right tack. They believed William Kershaw to have been murdered; they looked for William Kershaw.

"On December the 31st, what was presumed to be the body of William Kershaw was found by two lightermen: I have shown you a photograph of the place where it was found. Dark and deserted it is in all conscience, is it not? Just the place where a bully and a coward would decoy an unsuspecting stranger, murder him first, then rob him of his valuables, his papers, his very identity, and leave him there to rot. The body was found in a disused barge which had been moored some time against the wall, at the foot of these steps. It was in the last stages of decomposition, and, of course, could not be identified; but the police would have it that it was the body of William Kershaw.

"It never entered their heads that it was the body of *Francis Smethurst, and that William Kershaw was his murderer*.

"Ah! it was cleverly, artistically conceived! Kershaw is a genius. Think of it all! His disguise! Kershaw had a shaggy beard, hair, and moustache. He shaved up to his very eyebrows! No wonder that even his wife did not recognize him across the court; and remember she never saw much of his face while he stood in the dock. Kershaw was shabby, slouchy, he stooped. Smethurst, the millionaire, might have served in the Prussian army.

"Then that lovely trait about going to revisit the Torriani Hotel. Just a few days' grace, in order to purchase moustache and beard and wig, exactly similar to what he had himself shaved off. Making up to look like himself! Splendid! Then leaving the pocket-book behind! He! he! he! Kershaw was not murdered! Of course not. He called at the Torriani Hotel six days after the murder, whilst Mr. Smethurst, the millionaire, hobnobbed in the park with duchesses! Hang such a man! Fie!"

He fumbled for his hat. With nervous, trembling fingers he held it deferentially in his hand whilst he rose from the table. Polly watched him as he strode up to the desk, and paid twopence for his glass of milk and his bun. Soon he disappeared through the shop, whilst she still found herself hopelessly bewildered, with a number of snap-shot photographs before her, still staring at a long piece of string, smothered from end to end in a series of knots, as bewildering, as irritating, as puzzling as the man who had lately sat in the corner.

IV

The Robbery in Phillimore Terrace

Whether Miss Polly Burton really did expect to see the man in the corner that Saturday afternoon, 'twere difficult to say; certain it is that when she found her way to the table close by the window and realized that he was not there, she felt conscious of an overwhelming sense of disappointment. And yet during the whole of the week she had, with more pride than wisdom, avoided this particular A.B.C. shop.

"I thought you would not keep away very long," said a quiet voice close to her ear.

She nearly lost her balance—where in the world had he come from? She certainly had not heard the slightest sound, and yet there he sat, in the corner, like a veritable Jack-in-the-box, his mild blue eyes staring apologetically at her, his nervous fingers toying with the inevitable bit of string.

The waitress brought him his glass of milk and a cheese-cake. He ate it in silence, while his piece of string lay idly beside him on the table. When he had finished he fumbled in his capacious pockets, and drew out the inevitable pocket-book.

Placing a small photograph before the girl, he said quietly:

"That is the back of the houses in Phillimore Terrace, which overlook Adam and Eve Mews."

She looked at the photograph, then at him, with a kindly look of indulgent expectancy.

"You will notice that the row of back gardens have each an exit into the mews. These mews are built in the shape of a capital F. The photograph is taken looking straight down the short horizontal line, which ends, as you see, in a *cul-de-sac*. The bottom of the vertical line turns into Phillimore Terrace, and the end of the upper long horizontal line into High Street, Kensington. Now, on that particular night, or rather early morning, of January 15th, Constable D 21, having turned into the mews from Phillimore Terrace, stood for a moment at the angle formed by the long vertical artery of the mews and the short horizontal one which, as I observed before, looks on to the back gardens of the Terrace houses, and ends in a *cul-de-sac*.

"How long D 21 stood at that particular corner he could not exactly say, but he thinks it must have been three or four minutes before he noticed a suspicious-looking individual shambling along under the shadow of the garden walls. He was working his way cautiously in the direction of the *cul-de-sac*, and D 21, also keeping well within the shadow, went noiselessly after him.

"He had almost overtaken him—was, in fact, not more than thirty yards from him—when from out of one of the two end houses—No. 22, Phillimore Terrace, in fact—a man, in nothing but his night-shirt, rushed out excitedly, and, before D 21 had time to intervene, literally threw himself upon the suspected individual, rolling over and over with him on the hard cobble-stones, and frantically shrieking, 'Thief! Thief! Police!'

"It was some time before the constable succeeded in rescuing the tramp from the excited grip of his assailant, and several minutes before he could make himself heard.

"'There! there! that'll do!' he managed to say at last, as he gave the man in the shirt a vigorous shove, which silenced him for the moment. 'Leave the man alone now, you mustn't make that noise this time o' night, wakin' up all the folks.' The unfortunate tramp, who in the meanwhile had managed to get onto his feet again, made no attempt to get away; probably he thought he would stand but a poor chance. But the man in the shirt had partly recovered his power of speech, and was now blurting out jerky, half—intelligible sentences:

"'I have been robbed—robbed—I—that is—my master—Mr. Knopf. The desk is open—the diamonds gone—all in my charge—and—now they are stolen! That's the thief—I'll swear—I heard him—not three minutes ago—rushed downstairs—the door into the garden was smashed—I ran across the garden—he was sneaking about here still—Thief! Thief! Police! Diamonds! Constable, don't let him go—I'll make you responsible if you let him go—'

"'Now then—that'll do!' admonished D 21 as soon as he could get a word in, 'stop that row, will you?'

"The man in the shirt was gradually recovering from his excitement.

"'Can I give this man in charge?' he asked.

"'What for?'

"'Burglary and housebreaking. I heard him, I tell you. He must have Mr. Knopf's diamonds about him at this moment.'

"'Where is Mr. Knopf?'

"'Out of town,' groaned the man in the shirt. 'He went to Brighton last night, and left me in charge, and now this thief has been and—'

"The tramp shrugged his shoulders and suddenly, without a word, he quietly began taking off his coat and waistcoat. These he handed across to the constable. Eagerly the man in the shirt fell on them, and turned the ragged pockets inside out. From one of the windows a hilarious voice made some facetious remark, as the tramp with equal solemnity began divesting himself of his nether garments.

"'Now then, stop that nonsense,' pronounced D 21 severely, 'what were you doing here this time o' night, anyway?'

"'The streets o' London is free to the public, ain't they?' queried the tramp.

"'This don't lead nowhere, my man.'

"'Then I've lost my way, that's all,' growled the man surlily, 'and p'raps you'll let me get along now.'

"By this time a couple of constables had appeared upon the scene. D 21 had no intention of losing sight of his friend the tramp, and the man in the shirt had again made a dash for the latter's collar at the bare idea that he should be allowed to 'get along.'

"I think D 21 was alive to the humour of the situation. He suggested that Robertson (the man in the night-shirt) should go in and get some clothes on, whilst he himself would wait for the inspector and the detective, whom D 15 would send round from the station immediately.

"Poor Robertson's teeth were chattering with cold. He had a violent fit of sneezing as D 21 hurried him into the house. The latter, with another constable, remained to watch the burglared premises both back and front, and D 15 took the wretched tramp to the station with a view to sending an inspector and a detective round immediately.

"When the two latter gentlemen arrived at No. 22, Phillimore Terrace, they found poor old Robertson in bed, shivering, and still quite blue. He had got himself a hot drink, but his eyes were streaming and his voice was terribly husky. D 21 had stationed himself in the dining-room, where Robertson had pointed the desk out to him, with its broken lock and scattered contents.

"Robertson, between his sneezes, gave what account he could of the events which happened immediately before the robbery.

"His master, Mr. Ferdinand Knopf, he said, was a diamond merchant, and a bachelor. He himself had been in Mr. Knopf's employ over fifteen years, and was his only indoor servant. A charwoman came every day to do the housework.

"Last night Mr. Knopf dined at the house of Mr. Shipman, at No. 26, lower down. Mr. Shipman is the great jeweller who has his place of business in South Audley Street. By the last post there came a letter with the Brighton postmark, and marked 'urgent,' for Mr. Knopf, and he (Robertson) was just wondering if he should run over to No. 26 with it, when his master returned. He gave one glance at the contents of the letter, asked for his A.B.C. Railway Guide, and ordered him (Robertson) to pack his bag at once and fetch him a cab.

"'I guessed what it was,' continued Robertson after another violent fit of sneezing. 'Mr. Knopf has a brother, Mr. Emile Knopf, to whom he is very much attached, and who is a great invalid. He generally goes about from one seaside place to another. He is now at Brighton, and has recently been very ill.

"'If you will take the trouble to go downstairs I think you will still find the letter lying on the hall table.

"'I read it after Mr. Knopf left; it was not from his brother, but from a gentleman who signed himself J. Collins, M.D. I don't remember the exact words, but, of course, you'll be able to read the letter— Mr. J. Collins said he had been called in very suddenly to see Mr. Emile Knopf, who, he added, had not many hours to live, and had begged of the doctor to communicate at once with his brother in London.

"'Before leaving, Mr. Knopf warned me that there were some valuables in his desk—diamonds mostly, and told me to be particularly careful about locking up the house. He often has left me like this in charge of his premises, and usually there have been diamonds in his desk, for Mr. Knopf has no regular City office as he is a commercial traveller.'

"This, briefly, was the gist of the matter which Robertson related to the inspector with many repetitions and persistent volubility.

"The detective and inspector, before returning to the station with their report, thought they would call at No. 26, on Mr. Shipman, the great jeweller.

"You remember, of course," added the man in the corner, dreamily contemplating his bit of string, "the exciting developments of this extraordinary case. Mr. Arthur Shipman is the head of the firm of Shipman and Co., the wealthy jewellers. He is a widower, and lives very quietly by himself in his own old-fashioned way in the small

Kensington house, leaving it to his two married sons to keep up the style and swagger befitting the representatives of so wealthy a firm.

"'I have only known Mr. Knopf a very little while,' he explained to the detectives. 'He sold me two or three stones once or twice, I think; but we are both single men, and we have often dined together. Last night he dined with me. He had that afternoon received a very fine consignment of Brazilian diamonds, as he told me, and knowing how beset I am with callers at my business place, he had brought the stones with him, hoping, perhaps, to do a bit of trade over the nuts and wine.

"'I bought £25,000 worth of him,' added the jeweller, as if he were speaking of so many farthings, 'and gave him a cheque across the dinner table for that amount. I think we were both pleased with our bargain, and we had a final bottle of '48 port over it together. Mr. Knopf left me at about 9.30, for he knows I go very early to bed, and I took my new stock upstairs with me, and locked it up in the safe. I certainly heard nothing of the noise in the mews last night. I sleep on the second floor, in the front of the house, and this is the first I have heard of poor Mr. Knopf's loss—'

"At this point of his narrative Mr. Shipman very suddenly paused, and his face became very pale. With a hasty word of excuse he unceremoniously left the room, and the detective heard him running quickly upstairs.

"Less than two minutes later Mr. Shipman returned. There was no need for him to speak; both the detective and the inspector guessed the truth in a moment by the look upon his face.

"'The diamonds!' he gasped. 'I have been robbed.'"

V

A Night's Adventure

N ow I must tell you," continued the man in the corner, "that after I had read the account of the double robbery, which appeared in the early afternoon papers, I set to work and had a good think— yes!" he added with a smile, noting Polly's look at the bit of string, on which he was still at work, "yes! aided by this small adjunct to continued thought—I made notes as to how I should proceed to discover the clever thief, who had carried off a small fortune in a single night. Of course, my methods are not those of a London detective; he has his own way of going to work. The one who was conducting this case questioned the unfortunate jeweller very closely about his servants and his household generally.

"'I have three servants,' explained Mr. Shipman, two of whom have been with me for many years; one, the housemaid, is a fairly new comer—she has been here about six months. She came recommended by a friend, and bore an excellent character. She and the parlourmaid room together. The cook, who knew me when I was a schoolboy, sleeps alone; all three servants sleep on the floor above. I locked the jewels up in the safe which stands in the dressing-room. My keys and watch I placed, as usual, beside my bed. As a rule, I am a fairly light sleeper.

"'I cannot understand how it could have happened—but—you had better come up and have a look at the safe. The key must have been abstracted from my bedside, the safe opened, and the keys replaced— all while I was fast asleep. Though I had no occasion to look into the safe until just now, I should have discovered my loss before going to business, for I intended to take the diamonds away with me—'

"The detective and the inspector went up to have a look at the safe. The lock had in no way been tampered with—it had been opened with its own key. The detective spoke of chloroform, but Mr. Shipman declared that when he woke in the morning at about half-past seven there was no smell of chloroform in the room. However, the proceedings of the daring thief certainly pointed to the use of an anaesthetic. An examination of the premises brought to light the fact that the burglar had, as in Mr. Knopf's house, used the glass-panelled door from the garden as a means of entrance, but in this instance he had carefully cut out the pane of glass with a diamond, slipped the bolts, turned the key, and walked in.

"'Which among your servants knew that you had the diamonds in your house last night, Mr. Shipman?' asked the detective.

"'Not one, I should say,' replied the jeweller, 'though, perhaps, the parlourmaid, whilst waiting at table, may have heard me and Mr. Knopf discussing our bargain.'

"'Would you object to my searching all your servants' boxes?'

"'Certainly not. They would not object, either, I am sure. They are perfectly honest.'

"The searching of servants' belongings is invariably a useless proceeding," added the man in the corner, with a shrug of the shoulders. "No one, not even a latter-day domestic, would be fool enough to keep stolen property in the house. However, the usual farce was gone through, with more or less protest on the part of Mr. Shipman's servants, and with the usual result.

"The jeweller could give no further information; the detective and inspector, to do them justice, did their work of investigation minutely and, what is more, intelligently. It seemed evident, from their deductions, that the burglar had commenced proceedings on No. 26, Phillimore Terrace, and had then gone on, probably climbing over the garden walls between the houses to No. 22, where he was almost caught in the act by Robertson. The facts were simple enough, but the mystery remained as to the individual who had managed to glean the information of the presence of the diamonds in both the houses, and the means which he had adopted to get that information. It was obvious that the thief or thieves knew more about Mr. Knopf's affairs than Mr. Shipman's, since they had known how to use Mr. Emile Knopf's name in order to get his brother out of the way.

"It was now nearly ten o'clock, and the detectives, having taken leave of Mr. Shipman, went back to No. 22, in order to ascertain whether Mr. Knopf had come back; the door was opened by the old charwoman, who said that her master had returned, and was having some breakfast in the dining-room.

"Mr. Ferdinand Knopf was a middle-aged man, with sallow complexion, black hair and beard, of obviously Hebrew extraction. He spoke with a marked foreign accent, but very courteously, to the two officials, who, he begged, would excuse him if he went on with his breakfast.

"'I was fully prepared to hear the bad news,' he explained, 'which my man Robertson told me when I arrived. The letter I got last night was a bogus one; there is no such person as J. Collins, M.D. My brother had never felt better in his life. You will, I am sure, very soon trace the cunning writer of that epistle—ah! but I was in a rage, I can tell you, when I got to the Metropole at Brighton, and found that Emile, my brother, had never heard of any Doctor Collins.

"'The last train to town had gone, although I raced back to the station as hard as I could. Poor old Robertson, he has a terrible cold. Ah yes! my loss! it is for me a very serious one; if I had not made that lucky bargain with Mr. Shipman last night I should, perhaps, at this moment be a ruined man.

"'The stones I had yesterday were, firstly, some magnificent Brazilians; these I sold to Mr. Shipman mostly. Then I had some very good Cape diamonds—all gone; and some quite special Parisians, of wonderful work and finish, entrusted to me for sale by a great French house. I tell you, sir, my loss will be nearly £10,000 altogether. I sell on commission, and, of course, have to make good the loss.'

"He was evidently trying to bear up manfully, and as a business man should, under his sad fate. He refused in any way to attach the slightest blame to his old and faithful servant Robertson, who had caught, perhaps, his death of cold in his zeal for his absent master. As for any hint of suspicion falling even remotely upon the man, the very idea appeared to Mr. Knopf absolutely preposterous.

"With regard to the old charwoman, Mr. Knopf certainly knew nothing about her, beyond the fact that she had been recommended to him by one of the tradespeople in the neighbourhood, and seemed perfectly honest, respectable, and sober.

"About the tramp Mr. Knopf knew still less, nor could he imagine how he, or in fact anybody else, could possibly know that he happened to have diamonds in his house that night.

"This certainly seemed the great hitch in the case.

"Mr. Ferdinand Knopf, at the instance of the police, later on went to the station and had a look at the suspected tramp. He declared that he had never set eyes on him before.

"Mr. Shipman, on his way home from business in the afternoon, had done likewise, and made a similar statement.

"Brought before the magistrate, the tramp gave but a poor account of himself. He gave a name and address, which latter, of course, proved to be false. After that he absolutely refused to speak. He seemed not to care whether he was kept in custody or not. Very soon even the police realized that, for the present, at any rate, nothing could be got out of the suspected tramp.

"Mr. Francis Howard, the detective, who had charge of the case, though he would not admit it even to himself, was at his wits' ends. You must remember that the burglary, through its very simplicity, was an exceedingly mysterious affair. The constable, D 21, who had stood in Adam and Eve Mews, presumably while Mr. Knopf's house was being robbed, had seen no one turn out from the *cul-de-sac* into the main passage of the mews.

"The stables, which immediately faced the back entrance of the Phillimore Terrace houses, were all private ones belonging to residents in the neighbourhood. The coachmen, their families, and all the grooms who slept in the stablings were rigidly watched and questioned. One and all had seen nothing, heard nothing, until Robertson's shrieks had roused them from their sleep.

"As for the letter from Brighton, it was absolutely commonplace, and written upon note-paper which the detective, with Machiavellian cunning, traced to a stationer's shop in West Street. But the trade at that particular shop was a very brisk one; scores of people had bought note-paper there, similar to that on which the supposed doctor had written his tricky letter. The handwriting was cramped, perhaps a disguised one; in any case, except under very exceptional circumstances, it could afford no clue to the identity of the thief. Needless to say, the tramp, when told to write his name, wrote a totally different and absolutely uneducated hand.

"Matters stood, however, in the same persistently mysterious state when a small discovery was made, which suggested to Mr. Francis Howard an idea, which, if properly carried out, would, he hoped, inevitably bring the cunning burglar safely within the grasp of the police.

"That was the discovery of a few of Mr. Knopf's diamonds," continued the man in the corner after a slight pause, "evidently trampled into the ground by the thief whilst making his hurried exit through the garden of No. 22, Phillimore Terrace.

"At the end of this garden there is a small studio which had been built by a former owner of the house, and behind it a small piece of waste ground about seven feet square which had once been a rockery, and is still filled with large loose stones, in the shadow of which earwigs and woodlice innumerable have made a happy hunting ground.

"It was Robertson who, two days after the robbery, having need of a large stone, for some household purpose or other, dislodged one from that piece of waste ground, and found a few shining pebbles beneath it. Mr. Knopf took them round to the police-station himself immediately, and identified the stones as some of his Parisian ones.

"Later on the detective went to view the place where the find had been made, and there conceived the plan upon which he built big cherished hopes.

"Acting upon the advice of Mr. Francis Howard, the police decided to let the anonymous tramp out of his safe retreat within the station, and to allow him to wander whithersoever he chose. A good idea, perhaps—the presumption being that, sooner or later, if the man was in any way mixed up with the cunning thieves, he would either rejoin his comrades or even lead the police to where the remnant of his hoard lay hidden; needless to say, his footsteps were to be literally dogged.

"The wretched tramp, on his discharge, wandered out of the yard, wrapping his thin coat round his shoulders, for it was a bitterly cold afternoon. He began operations by turning into the Town Hall Tavern for a good feed and a copious drink. Mr. Francis Howard noted that he seemed to eye every passer-by with suspicion, but he seemed to enjoy his dinner, and sat some time over his bottle of wine.

"It was close upon four o'clock when he left the tavern, and then began for the indefatigable Mr. Howard one of the most wearisome and uninteresting chases, through the mazes of the London streets, he ever remembers to have made. Up Notting Hill, down the slums of Notting Dale, along the High Street, beyond Hammersmith, and through Shepherd's Bush did that anonymous tramp lead the unfortunate detective, never hurrying himself, stopping every now and then at a public-house to get a drink, whither Mr. Howard did not always care to follow him.

"In spite of his fatigue, Mr. Francis Howard's hopes rose with every half-hour of this weary tramp. The man was obviously striving to kill time; he seemed to feel no weariness, but walked on and on, perhaps suspecting that he was being followed.

"At last, with a beating heart, though half perished with cold, and with terribly sore feet, the detective began to realize that the tramp was gradually working his way back towards Kensington. It was then close upon eleven o'clock at night; once or twice the man had walked up and down the High Street, from St. Paul's School to Derry and Toms' shops and back again, he had looked down one or two of the side streets and—at last—he turned into Phillimore Terrace. He seemed in no hurry, he oven stopped once in the middle of the road, trying to light a pipe, which, as there was a high east wind, took him some considerable time. Then he leisurely sauntered down the street, and turned into Adam and Eve Mews, with Mr. Francis Howard now close at his heels.

"Acting upon the detective's instructions, there were several men in plain clothes ready to his call in the immediate neighbourhood. Two stood within the shadow of the steps of the Congregational Church at the corner of the mews, others were stationed well within a soft call.

"Hardly, therefore, had the hare turned into the *cul-de-sac* at the back of Phillimore Terrace than, at a slight sound from Mr. Francis Howard, every egress was barred to him, and he was caught like a rat in a trap.

"As soon as the tramp had advanced some thirty yards or so (the whole length of this part of the mews is about one hundred yards) and was lost in the shadow, Mr. Francis Howard directed four or five of his men to proceed cautiously up the mews, whilst the same number were to form a line all along the front of Phillimore Terrace between the mews and the High Street.

"Remember, the back-garden walls threw long and dense shadows, but the silhouette of the man would be clearly outlined if he made any attempt at climbing over them. Mr. Howard felt quite sure that the thief was bent on recovering the stolen goods, which, no doubt, he had hidden in the rear of one of the houses. He would be caught *in flagrante delicto*, and, with a heavy sentence hovering over him, he would probably be induced to name his accomplice. Mr. Francis Howard was thoroughly enjoying himself.

"The minutes sped on; absolute silence, in spite of the presence of so many men, reigned in the dark and deserted mews.

"Of course, this night's adventure was never allowed to get into the papers," added the man in the corner with his mild smile. "Had the plan been successful, we should have heard all about it, with a long eulogistic article as to the astuteness of our police; but as it was—well, the tramp sauntered up the mews—and—there he remained for aught Mr. Francis Howard or the other constables could ever explain. The earth or the shadows swallowed him up. No one saw him climb one of the garden walls, no one heard him break open a door; he had retreated within the shadow of the garden walls, and was seen or heard of no more."

"One of the servants in the Phillimore Terrace houses must have belonged to the gang," said Polly with quick decision.

"Ah, yes! but which?" said the man in the corner, making a beautiful knot in his bit of string. "I can assure you that the police left not a stone unturned once more to catch sight of that tramp whom they had had in custody for two days, but not a trace of him could they find, nor of the diamonds, from that day to this."

VI

All He Knew

The tramp was missing," continued the man in the corner, "and Mr. Francis Howard tried to find the missing tramp. Going round to the front, and seeing the lights at No. 26 still in, he called upon Mr. Shipman. The jeweller had had a few friends to dinner, and was giving them whiskies-and-sodas before saying good night. The servants had just finished washing up, and were waiting to go to bed; neither they nor Mr. Shipman nor his guests had seen or heard anything of the suspicious individual.

"Mr. Francis Howard went on to see Mr. Ferdinand Knopf. This gentleman was having his warm bath, preparatory to going to bed. So Robertson told the detective. However, Mr. Knopf insisted on talking to Mr. Howard through his bath-room door. Mr. Knopf thanked him for all the trouble he was taking, and felt sure that he and Mr. Shipman would soon recover possession of their diamonds, thanks to the persevering detective.

"He! he! he!" laughed the man in the corner. "Poor Mr. Howard. He persevered—but got no farther; no, nor anyone else, for that matter. Even I might not be able to convict the thieves if I told all I knew to the police.

"Now, follow my reasoning, point by point," he added eagerly.

"Who knew of the presence of the diamonds in the house of Mr. Shipman and Mr. Knopf? Firstly," he said, putting up an ugly claw-like finger, "Mr. Shipman, then Mr. Knopf, then, presumably, the man Robertson."

"And the tramp?" said Polly.

"Leave the tramp alone for the present since he has vanished, and take point number two. Mr. Shipman was drugged. That was pretty obvious; no man under ordinary circumstances would, without waking, have his keys abstracted and then replaced at his own bedside. Mr. Howard suggested that the thief was armed with some anaesthetic; but how did the thief get into Mr. Shipman's room without waking him from his natural sleep? Is it not simpler to suppose that the thief had taken the precaution to drug the jeweller *before* the latter went to bed?"

"But—"

"Wait a moment, and take point number three. Though there was every proof that Mr. Shipman had been in possession of £25,000 worth of goods since Mr. Knopf had a cheque from him for that amount, there was no proof that in Mr. Knopf's house there was even an odd stone worth a sovereign.

"And then again," went on the scarecrow, getting more and more excited, "did it ever strike you, or anybody else, that at *no* time, while the tramp was in custody, while all that searching examination was being gone on with, no one ever saw Mr. Knopf and his man Robertson together at the same time?

"Ah!" he continued, whilst suddenly the young girl seemed to see the whole thing as in a vision, "they did not forget a single detail—follow them with me, point by point. Two cunning scoundrels—geniuses they should be called—well provided with some ill-gotten funds—but determined on a grand *coup*. They play at respectability, for six months, say. One is the master, the other the servant; they take a house in the same street as their intended victim, make friends with him, accomplish one or two creditable but very small business transactions, always drawing on the reserve funds, which might even have amounted to a few hundreds—and a bit of credit.

"Then the Brazilian diamonds, and the Parisians—which, remember, were so perfect that they required chemical testing to be detected. The Parisian stones are sold—not in business, of course—in the evening, after dinner and a good deal of wine. Mr. Knopf's Brazilians were beautiful; perfect! Mr. Knopf was a well-known diamond merchant.

"Mr. Shipman bought—but with the morning would have come sober sense, the cheque stopped before it could have been presented, the swindler caught. No! those exquisite Parisians were never intended to rest in Mr. Shipman's safe until the morning. That last bottle of '48 port, with the aid of a powerful soporific, ensured that Mr. Shipman would sleep undisturbed during the night.

"Ah! remember all the details, they were so admirable! the letter posted in Brighton by the cunning rogue to himself, the smashed desk, the broken pane of glass in his own house. The man Robertson on the watch, while Knopf himself in ragged clothing found his way into No. 26. If Constable D 21 had not appeared upon the scene that exciting comedy in the early morning would not have been enacted. As it was, in the supposed fight, Mr. Shipman's diamonds passed from the hands of the tramp into those of his accomplice.

"Then, later on, Robertson, ill in bed, while his master was supposed to have returned—by the way, it never struck anybody that no one saw Mr. Knopf come home, though he surely would have driven up in a cab. Then the double part played by one man for the next two days. It certainly never struck either the police or the inspector. Remember they only saw Robertson when in bed with a streaming cold. But Knopf had to be got out of gaol as soon as possible; the dual *rôle* could not have been kept up for long. Hence the story of the diamonds found in the garden of No. 22. The cunning rogues guessed that the usual plan would be acted upon, and the suspected thief allowed to visit the scene where his hoard lay hidden.

"It had all been foreseen, and Robertson must have been constantly on the watch. The tramp stopped, mind you, in Phillimore Terrace for some moments, lighting a pipe. The accomplice, then, was fully on the alert; he slipped the bolts of the back garden gate. Five minutes later Knopf was in the house, in a hot bath, getting rid of the disguise of our friend the tramp. Remember that again here the detective did not actually see him.

"The next morning Mr. Knopf, black hair and beard and all, was himself again. The whole trick lay in one simple art, which those two cunning rascals knew to absolute perfection, the art of impersonating one another.

"They are brothers, presumably—twin brothers, I should say."

"But Mr. Knopf—" suggested Polly.

"Well, look in the Trades' Directory; you will see F. Knopf & Co., diamond merchants, of some City address. Ask about the firm among the trade; you will hear that it is firmly established on a sound financial basis. He! he! he! and it deserves to be," added the man in the corner, as, calling for the waitress, he received his ticket, and taking up his shabby hat, took himself and his bit of string rapidly out of the room.

VII

The York Mystery

The man in the corner looked quite cheerful that morning; he had had two glasses of milk and had even gone to the extravagance of an extra cheese-cake. Polly knew that he was itching to talk police and murders, for he cast furtive glances at her from time to time, produced a bit of string, tied and untied it into scores of complicated knots, and finally, bringing out his pocket-book, he placed two or three photographs before her.

"Do you know who that is?" he asked, pointing to one of these.

The girl looked at the face on the picture. It was that of a woman, not exactly pretty, but very gentle and childlike, with a strange pathetic look in the large eyes which was wonderfully appealing.

"That was Lady Arthur Skelmerton," he said, and in a flash there flitted before Polly's mind the weird and tragic history which had broken this loving woman's heart. Lady Arthur Skelmerton! That name recalled one of the most bewildering, most mysterious passages in the annals of undiscovered crimes.

"Yes. It was sad, wasn't it?" he commented, in answer to Polly's thoughts. "Another case which but for idiotic blunders on the part of the police must have stood clear as daylight before the public and satisfied general anxiety. Would you object to my recapitulating its preliminary details?"

She said nothing, so he continued without waiting further for a reply.

"It all occurred during the York racing week, a time which brings to the quiet cathedral city its quota of shady characters, who congregate wherever money and wits happen to fly away from their owners. Lord Arthur Skelmerton, a very well-known figure in London society and in racing circles, had rented one of the fine houses which overlook the racecourse. He had entered Peppercorn, by St. Armand—Notre Dame, for the Great Ebor Handicap. Peppercorn was the winner of the Newmarket, and his chances for the Ebor were considered a practical certainty.

"If you have ever been to York you will have noticed the fine houses which have their drive and front entrances in the road called 'The Mount.'

and the gardens of which extend as far as the racecourse, commanding a lovely view over the entire track. It was one of these houses, called 'The Elms,' which Lord Arthur Skelmerton had rented for the summer.

"Lady Arthur came down some little time before the racing week with her servants—she had no children; but she had many relatives and friends in York, since she was the daughter of old Sir John Etty, the cocoa manufacturer, a rigid Quaker, who, it was generally said, kept the tightest possible hold on his own purse-strings and looked with marked disfavour upon his aristocratic son-in-law's fondness for gaming tables and betting books.

"As a matter of fact, Maud Etty had married the handsome young lieutenant in the Hussars, quite against her father's wishes. But she was an only child, and after a good deal of demur and grumbling, Sir John, who idolized his daughter, gave way to her whim, and a reluctant consent to the marriage was wrung from him.

"But, as a Yorkshireman, he was far too shrewd a man of the world not to know that love played but a very small part in persuading a Duke's son to marry the daughter of a cocoa manufacturer, and as long as he lived he determined that since his daughter was being wed because of her wealth, that wealth should at least secure her own happiness. He refused to give Lady Arthur any capital, which, in spite of the most carefully worded settlements, would inevitably, sooner or later, have found its way into the pockets of Lord Arthur's racing friends. But he made his daughter a very handsome allowance, amounting to over £3000 a year, which enabled her to keep up an establishment befitting her new rank.

"A great many of these facts, intimate enough as they are, leaked out, you see, during that period of intense excitement which followed the murder of Charles Lavender, and when the public eye was fixed searchingly upon Lord Arthur Skelmerton, probing all the inner details of his idle, useless life.

"It soon became a matter of common gossip that poor little Lady Arthur continued to worship her handsome husband in spite of his obvious neglect, and not having as yet presented him with an heir, she settled herself down into a life of humble apology for her plebeian existence, atoning for it by condoning all his faults and forgiving all his vices, even to the extent of cloaking them before the prying eyes of Sir John, who was persuaded to look upon his son-in-law as a paragon of all the domestic virtues and a perfect model of a husband.

"Among Lord Arthur Skelmerton's many expensive tastes there was certainly that for horseflesh and cards. After some successful betting at the beginning of his married life, he had started a racing-stable which it was generally believed—as he was very lucky—was a regular source of income to him.

"Peppercorn, however, after his brilliant performances at Newmarket did not continue to fulfil his master's expectations. His collapse at York was attributed to the hardness of the course and to various other causes, but its immediate effect was to put Lord Arthur Skelmerton in what is popularly called a tight place, for he had backed his horse for all he was worth, and must have stood to lose considerably over £5000 on that one day.

"The collapse of the favourite and the grand victory of King Cole, a rank outsider, on the other hand, had proved a golden harvest for the bookmakers, and all the York hotels were busy with dinners and suppers given by the confraternity of the Turf to celebrate the happy occasion. The next day was Friday, one of few important racing events, after which the brilliant and the shady throng which had flocked into the venerable city for the week would fly to more congenial climes, and leave it, with its fine old Minster and its ancient walls, as sleepy, as quiet as before.

"Lord Arthur Skelmerton also intended to leave York on the Saturday, and on the Friday night he gave a farewell bachelor dinner party at 'The Elms,' at which Lady Arthur did not appear. After dinner the gentlemen settled down to bridge, with pretty stiff points, you may be sure. It had just struck eleven at the Minster Tower, when constables McNaught and Murphy, who were patrolling the racecourse, were startled by loud cries of 'murder' and 'police.'

"Quickly ascertaining whence these cries proceeded, they hurried on at a gallop, and came up—quite close to the boundary of Lord Arthur Skelmerton's grounds—upon a group of three men, two of whom seemed to be wrestling vigorously with one another, whilst the third was lying face downwards on the ground. As soon as the constables drew near, one of the wrestlers shouted more vigorously, and with a certain tone of authority:

"'Here, you fellows, hurry up, sharp; the brute is giving me the slip!'

"But the brute did not seem inclined to do anything of the sort; he certainly extricated himself with a violent jerk from his assailant's grasp, but made no attempt to run away. The constables had quickly dismounted, whilst he who had shouted for help originally added more quietly:

"'My name is Skelmerton. This is the boundary of my property. I was smoking a cigar at the pavilion over there with a friend when I heard loud voices, followed by a cry and a groan. I hurried down the steps, and saw this poor fellow lying on the ground, with a knife sticking between his shoulder-blades, and his murderer,' he added, pointing to the man who stood quietly by with Constable McNaught's firm grip upon his shoulder, 'still stooping over the body of his victim. I was too late, I fear, to save the latter, but just in time to grapple with the assassin—"

"'It's a lie!' here interrupted the man hoarsely. 'I didn't do it, constable; I swear I didn't do it. I saw him fall—I was coming along a couple of hundred yards away, and I tried to see if the poor fellow was dead. I swear I didn't do it.'

"'You'll have to explain that to the inspector presently, my man,' was Constable McNaught's quiet comment, and, still vigorously protesting his innocence, the accused allowed himself to be led away, and the body was conveyed to the station, pending fuller identification.

"The next morning the papers were full of the tragedy; a column and a half of the *York Herald* was devoted to an account of Lord Arthur Skelmerton's plucky capture of the assassin. The latter had continued to declare his innocence, but had remarked, it appears, with grim humour, that he quite saw he was in a tight place, out of which, however, he would find it easy to extricate himself. He had stated to the police that the deceased's name was Charles Lavender, a well-known bookmaker, which fact was soon verified, for many of the murdered man's 'pals' were still in the city.

"So far the most pushing of newspaper reporters had been unable to glean further information from the police; no one doubted, however, but that the man in charge, who gave his name as George Higgins, had killed the bookmaker for purposes of robbery. The inquest had been fixed for the Tuesday after the murder.

"Lord Arthur had been obliged to stay in York a few days, as his evidence would be needed. That fact gave the case, perhaps, a certain amount of interest as far as York and London 'society' were concerned. Charles Lavender, moreover, was well known on the turf; but no bombshell exploding beneath the walls of the ancient cathedral city could more have astonished its inhabitants than the news which, at about five in the afternoon on the day of the inquest, spread like wildfire

BARONESS EMMUSKA ORCZY

throughout the town. That news was that the inquest had concluded at three o'clock with a verdict of 'Wilful murder against some person or persons unknown,' and that two hours later the police had arrested Lord Arthur Skelmerton at his private residence, 'The Elms,' and charged him on a warrant with the murder of Charles Lavender, the bookmaker."

VIII

The Capital Charge

The police, it appears, instinctively feeling that some mystery lurked round the death of the bookmaker and his supposed murderer's quiet protestations of innocence, had taken a very considerable amount of trouble in collecting all the evidence they could for the inquest which might throw some light upon Charles Lavender's life, previous to his tragic end. Thus it was that a very large array of witnesses was brought before the coroner, chief among whom was, of course, Lord Arthur Skelmerton.

"The first witnesses called were the two constables, who deposed that, just as the church clocks in the neighbourhood were striking eleven, they had heard the cries for help, had ridden to the spot whence the sounds proceeded, and had found the prisoner in the tight grasp of Lord Arthur Skelmerton, who at once accused the man of murder, and gave him in charge. Both constables gave the same version of the incident, and both were positive as to the time when it occurred.

"Medical evidence went to prove that the deceased had been stabbed from behind between the shoulder-blades whilst he was walking, that the wound was inflicted by a large hunting knife, which was produced, and which had been left sticking in the wound.

"Lord Arthur Skelmerton was then called and substantially repeated what he had already told the constables. He stated, namely, that on the night in question he had some gentlemen friends to dinner, and afterwards bridge was played. He himself was not playing much, and at a few minutes before eleven he strolled out with a cigar as far as the pavilion at the end of his garden; he then heard the voices, the cry and the groan previously described by him, and managed to hold the murderer down until the arrival of the constables.

"At this point the police proposed to call a witness, James Terry by name and a bookmaker by profession, who had been chiefly instrumental in identifying the deceased, a 'pal' of his. It was his evidence which first introduced that element of sensation into the case which culminated in the wildly exciting arrest of a Duke's son upon a capital charge.

"It appears that on the evening after the Ebor, Terry and Lavender were in the bar of the Black Swan Hotel having drinks.

"'I had done pretty well over Peppercorn's fiasco,' he explained, 'but poor old Lavender was very much down in the dumps; he had held only a few very small bets against the favourite, and the rest of the day had been a poor one with him. I asked him if he had any bets with the owner of Peppercorn, and he told me that he only held one for less than £500.

"'I laughed and said that if he held one for £5000 it would make no difference, as from what I had heard from the other fellows, Lord Arthur Skelmerton must be about stumped. Lavender seemed terribly put out at this, and swore he would get that £500 out of Lord Arthur, if no one else got another penny from him.

"'It's the only money I've made to-day,' he says to me. 'I mean to get it.'

"'You won't,' I says.

"'I will,' he says.

"'You will have to look pretty sharp about it then,' I says, 'for every one will be wanting to get something, and first come first served.'

"'Oh! He'll serve me right enough, never you mind!' says Lavender to me with a laugh. 'If he don't pay up willingly, I've got that in my pocket which will make him sit up and open my lady's eyes and Sir John Etty's too about their precious noble lord.'

"'Then he seemed to think he had gone too far, and wouldn't say anything more to me about that affair. I saw him on the course the next day. I asked him if he had got his £500. He said: "No, but I shall get it to-day."'

"Lord Arthur Skelmerton, after having given his own evidence, had left the court; it was therefore impossible to know how he would take this account, which threw so serious a light upon an association with the dead man, of which he himself had said nothing.

"Nothing could shake James Terry's account of the facts he had placed before the jury, and when the police informed the coroner that they proposed to place George Higgins himself in the witness-box, as his evidence would prove, as it were, a complement and corollary of that of Terry, the jury very eagerly assented.

"If James Terry, the bookmaker, loud, florid, vulgar, was an unprepossessing individual, certainly George Higgins, who was still under the accusation of murder, was ten thousand times more so.

"None too clean, slouchy, obsequious yet insolent, he was the very personification of the cad who haunts the racecourse and who lives not so much by his own wits as by the lack of them in others. He described himself as a turf commission agent, whatever that may be.

"He stated that at about six o'clock on the Friday afternoon, when the racecourse was still full of people, all hurrying after the day's excitements, he himself happened to be standing close to the hedge which marks the boundary of Lord Arthur Skelmerton's grounds. There is a pavilion there at the end of the garden, he explained, on slightly elevated ground, and he could hear and see a group of ladies and gentlemen having tea. Some steps lead down a little to the left of the garden on to the course, and presently he noticed at the bottom of these steps Lord Arthur Skelmerton and Charles Lavender standing talking together. He knew both gentlemen by sight, but he could not see them very well as they were both partly hidden by the hedge. He was quite sure that the gentlemen had not seen him, and he could not help overhearing some of their conversation.

"'That's my last word, Lavender,' Lord Arthur was saying very quietly. 'I haven't got the money and I can't pay you now. You'll have to wait.'

"'Wait? I can't wait,' said old Lavender in reply. 'I've got my engagements to meet, same as you. I'm not going to risk being posted up as a defaulter while you hold £500 of my money. You'd better give it me now or—'

"But Lord Arthur interrupted him very quietly, and said:

"'Yes, my good man. . . or?'

"'Or I'll let Sir John have a good look at that little bill I had of yours a couple of years ago. If you'll remember, my lord, it has got at the bottom of it Sir John's signature in *your* handwriting. Perhaps Sir John, or perhaps my lady, would pay me something for that little bill. If not, the police can have a squint at it. I've held my tongue long enough, and—'

"'Look here, Lavender,' said Lord Arthur, 'do you know what this little game of yours is called in law?'

"'Yes, and I don't care,' says Lavender. 'If I don't have that £500 I am a ruined man. If you ruin me I'll do for you, and we shall be quits. That's my last word.'

"He was talking very loudly, and I thought some of Lord Arthur's friends up in the pavilion must have heard. He thought so, too, I think, for he said quickly:

"'If you don't hold your confounded tongue, I'll give you in charge for blackmail this instant.'

"'You wouldn't dare,' says Lavender, and he began to laugh. But just then a lady from the top of the steps said: 'Your tea is getting cold,' and Lord Arthur turned to go; but just before he went Lavender says to him: 'I'll come back to-night. You'll have the money then.'

"George Higgins, it appears, after he had heard this interesting conversation, pondered as to whether he could not turn what he knew into some sort of profit. Being a gentleman who lives entirely by his wits, this type of knowledge forms his chief source of income. As a preliminary to future moves, he decided not to lose sight of Lavender for the rest of the day.

"'Lavender went and had dinner at The Black Swan,' explained Mr. George Higgins, 'and I, after I had had a bite myself, waited outside till I saw him come out. At about ten o'clock I was rewarded for my trouble. He told the hall porter to get him a fly and he jumped into it. I could not hear what direction he gave the driver, but the fly certainly drove off towards the racecourse.

"'Now, I was interested in this little affair,' continued the witness, 'and I couldn't afford a fly. I started to run. Of course, I couldn't keep up with it, but I thought I knew which way my gentleman had gone. I made straight for the racecourse, and for the hedge at the bottom of Lord Arthur Skelmerton's grounds.

"'It was rather a dark night and there was a slight drizzle. I couldn't see more than about a hundred yards before me. All at once it seemed to me as if I heard Lavender's voice talking loudly in the distance. I hurried forward, and suddenly saw a group of two figures—mere blurs in the darkness—for one instant, at a distance of about fifty yards from where I was.

"'The next moment one figure had fallen forward and the other had disappeared. I ran to the spot, only to find the body of the murdered man lying on the ground. I stooped to see if I could be of any use to him, and immediately I was collared from behind by Lord Arthur himself.'

"You may imagine," said the man in the corner, "how keen was the excitement of that moment in court. Coroner and jury alike literally hung breathless on every word that shabby, vulgar individual uttered. You see, by itself his evidence would have been worth very little, but coming on the top of that given by James Terry, its significance—more, its truth—had become glaringly apparent. Closely cross-examined, he adhered strictly to his statement; and having finished his evidence, George Higgins remained in charge of the constables, and the next witness of importance was called up.

"This was Mr. Chipps, the senior footman in the employment of Lord Arthur Skelmerton. He deposed that at about 10.30 on the Friday evening a 'party' drove up to 'The Elms' in a fly, and asked to see Lord Arthur. On being told that his lordship had company he seemed terribly put out.

"'I hasked the party to give me 'is card,' continued Mr. Chipps, 'as I didn't know, perhaps, that 'is lordship might wish to see 'im, but I kept 'im standing at the 'all door, as I didn't altogether like his looks. I took the card in. His lordship and the gentlemen was playin' cards in the smoking-room, and as soon as I could do so without disturbing 'is lordship, I give him the party's card.'

"'What name was there on the card?' here interrupted the coroner.

"'I couldn't say now, sir,' replied Mr. Chipps; 'I don't really remember. It was a name I had never seen before. But I see so many visiting cards one way and the other in 'is lordship's 'all that I can't remember all the names.'

"'Then, after a few minutes' waiting, you gave his lordship the card? What happened then?'

"'Is lordship didn't seem at all pleased,' said Mr. Chipps with much guarded dignity; but finally he said: "Show him into the library, Chipps, I'll see him," and he got up from the card table, saying to the gentlemen: "Go on without me; I'll be back in a minute or two."

"'I was about to open the door for 'is lordship when my lady came into the room, and then his lordship suddenly changed his mind like, and said to me: "Tell that man I'm busy and can't see him," and 'e sat down again at the card table. I went back to the 'all, and told the party 'is lordship wouldn't see 'im. 'E said: "Oh! it doesn't matter," and went away quite quiet like.'

"'Do you recollect at all at what time that was?' asked one of the jury.

"'Yes, sir, while I was waiting to speak to 'is lordship I looked at the clock, sir; it was twenty past ten, sir.'

"There was one more significant fact in connection with the case, which tended still more to excite the curiosity of the public at the time, and still further to bewilder the police later on, and that fact was mentioned by Chipps in his evidence. The knife, namely, with which Charles Lavender had been stabbed, and which, remember, had been left in the wound, was now produced in court. After a little hesitation

Chipps identified it as the property of his master, Lord Arthur Skelmerton.

"Can you wonder, then, that the jury absolutely refused to bring in a verdict against George Higgins? There was really, beyond Lord Arthur Skelmerton's testimony, not one particle of evidence against him, whilst, as the day wore on and witness after witness was called up, suspicion ripened in the minds of all those present that the murderer could be no other than Lord Arthur Skelmerton himself.

"The knife was, of course, the strongest piece of circumstantial evidence, and no doubt the police hoped to collect a great deal more now that they held a clue in their hands. Directly after the verdict, therefore, which was guardedly directed against some person unknown, the police obtained a warrant and later on arrested Lord Arthur in his own house."

"The sensation, of course, was tremendous. Hours before he was brought up before the magistrate the approach to the court was thronged. His friends, mostly ladies, were all eager, you see, to watch the dashing society man in so terrible a position. There was universal sympathy for Lady Arthur, who was in a very precarious state of health. Her worship of her worthless husband was well known; small wonder that his final and awful misdeed had practically broken her heart. The latest bulletin issued just after his arrest stated that her ladyship was not expected to live. She was then in a comatose condition, and all hope had perforce to be abandoned.

"At last the prisoner was brought in. He looked very pale, perhaps, but otherwise kept up the bearing of a high-bred gentleman. He was accompanied by his solicitor, Sir Marmaduke Ingersoll, who was evidently talking to him in quiet, reassuring tones.

"Mr. Buchanan prosecuted for the Treasury, and certainly his indictment was terrific. According to him but one decision could be arrived at, namely, that the accused in the dock had, in a moment of passion, and perhaps of fear, killed the blackmailer who threatened him with disclosures which might for ever have ruined him socially, and, having committed the deed and fearing its consequences, probably realizing that the patrolling constables might catch sight of his retreating figure, he had availed himself of George Higgins's presence on the spot to loudly accuse him of the murder.

"Having concluded his able speech, Mr. Buchanan called his witnesses, and the evidence, which on second hearing seemed more damning than ever, was all gone through again.

"Sir Marmaduke had no question to ask of the witnesses for the prosecution; he stared at them placidly through his gold-rimmed spectacles. Then he was ready to call his own for the defence. Colonel McIntosh, R.A., was the first. He was present at the bachelors' party given by Lord Arthur the night of the murder. His evidence tended at first to corroborate that of Chipps the footman with regard to Lord Arthur's orders to show the visitor into the library, and his counter-order as soon as his wife came into the room.

"'Did you not think it strange, Colonel?' asked Mr. Buchanan, 'that Lord Arthur should so suddenly have changed his mind about seeing his visitor?'

"'Well, not exactly strange,' said the Colonel, a fine, manly, soldierly figure who looked curiously out of his element in the witness-box. 'I don't think that it is a very rare occurrence for racing men to have certain acquaintances whom they would not wish their wives to know anything about.'

"'Then it did not strike you that Lord Arthur Skelmerton had some reason for not wishing his wife to know of that particular visitor's presence in his house?'

"'I don't think that I gave the matter the slightest serious consideration,' was the Colonel's guarded reply.

"Mr. Buchanan did not press the point, and allowed the witness to conclude his statements.

"'I had finished my turn at bridge,' he said, 'and went out into the garden to smoke a cigar. Lord Arthur Skelmerton joined me a few minutes later, and we were sitting in the pavilion when I heard a loud and, as I thought, threatening voice from the other side of the hedge.

"'I did not catch the words, but Lord Arthur said to me: "There seems to be a row down there. I'll go and have a look and see what it is." I tried to dissuade him, and certainly made no attempt to follow him, but not more than half a minute could have elapsed before I heard a cry and a groan, then Lord Arthur's footsteps hurrying down the wooden stairs which lead on to the racecourse.'

"You may imagine," said the man in the corner, "what severe cross-examination the gallant Colonel had to undergo in order that his assertions might in some way be shaken by the prosecution, but with military precision and frigid calm he repeated his important statements amidst a general silence, through which you could have heard the proverbial pin.

"He had heard the threatening voice *while* sitting with Lord Arthur Skelmerton; then came the cry and groan, and, *after that*, Lord Arthur's steps down the stairs. He himself thought of following to see what had happened, but it was a very dark night and he did not know the grounds very well. While trying to find his way to the garden steps he heard Lord Arthur's cry for help, the tramp of the patrolling constables' horses, and subsequently the whole scene between Lord Arthur, the man Higgins, and the constables. When he finally found his way to the stairs, Lord Arthur was returning in order to send a groom for police assistance.

"The witness stuck to his points as he had to his guns at Beckfontein a year ago; nothing could shake him, and Sir Marmaduke looked triumphantly across at his opposing colleague.

"With the gallant Colonel's statements the edifice of the prosecution certainly began to collapse. You see, there was not a particle of evidence to show that the accused had met and spoken to the deceased after the latter's visit at the front door of 'The Elms.' He told Chipps that he wouldn't see the visitor, and Chipps went into the hall directly and showed Lavender out the way he came. No assignation could have been made, no hint could have been given by the murdered man to Lord Arthur that he would go round to the back entrance and wished to see him there.

"Two other guests of Lord Arthur's swore positively that after Chipps had announced the visitor, their host stayed at the card-table until a quarter to eleven, when evidently he went out to join Colonel McIntosh in the garden. Sir Marmaduke's speech was clever in the extreme. Bit by bit he demolished that tower of strength, the case against the accused, basing his defence entirely upon the evidence of Lord Arthur Skelmerton's guests that night.

"Until 10.45 Lord Arthur was playing cards; a quarter of an hour later the police were on the scene, and the murder had been committed. In the meanwhile Colonel McIntosh's evidence proved conclusively that the accused had been sitting with him, smoking a cigar. It was obvious, therefore, clear as daylight, concluded the great lawyer, that his client was entitled to a full discharge; nay, more, he thought that the police should have been more careful before they harrowed up public feeling by arresting a high-born gentleman on such insufficient evidence as they had brought forward.

"The question of the knife remained certainly, but Sir Marmaduke passed over it with guarded eloquence, placing that strange question in the category of those inexplicable coincidences which tend to puzzle the ablest detectives, and cause them to commit such unpardonable blunders as the present one had been. After all, the footman may have been mistaken. The pattern of that knife was not an exclusive one, and he, on behalf of his client, flatly denied that it had ever belonged to him.

"Well," continued the man in the corner, with the chuckle peculiar to him in moments of excitement, "the noble prisoner was discharged. Perhaps it would be invidious to say that he left the court without a stain on his character, for I daresay you know from experience that the crime known as the York Mystery has never been satisfactorily cleared up.

"Many people shook their heads dubiously when they remembered that, after all, Charles Lavender was killed with a knife which one witness had sworn belonged to Lord Arthur; others, again, reverted to the original theory that George Higgins was the murderer, that he and James Terry had concocted the story of Lavender's attempt at blackmail on Lord Arthur, and that the murder had been committed for the sole purpose of robbery.

"Be that as it may, the police have not so far been able to collect sufficient evidence against Higgins or Terry, and the crime has been classed by press and public alike in the category of so-called impenetrable mysteries."

IX

A Broken-Hearted Woman

The man in the corner called for another glass of milk, and drank it down slowly before he resumed:

"Now Lord Arthur lives mostly abroad," he said. "His poor, suffering wife died the day after he was liberated by the magistrate. She never recovered consciousness even sufficiently to hear the joyful news that the man she loved so well was innocent after all.

"Mystery!" he added as if in answer to Polly's own thoughts. "The murder of that man was never a mystery to me. I cannot understand how the police could have been so blind when every one of the witnesses, both for the prosecution and defence, practically pointed all the time to the one guilty person. What do you think of it all yourself?"

"I think the whole case so bewildering," she replied, "that I do not see one single clear point in it."

"You don't?" he said excitedly, while the bony fingers fidgeted again with that inevitable bit of string. "You don't see that there is one point clear which to me was the key of the whole thing?

"Lavender was murdered, wasn't he? Lord Arthur did not kill him. He had, at least, in Colonel McIntosh an unimpeachable witness to prove that he could not have committed that murder—and yet," he added with slow, excited emphasis, marking each sentence with a knot, "and yet he deliberately tries to throw the guilt upon a man who obviously was also innocent. Now why?"

"He may have thought him guilty."

"Or wished to shield or cover the retreat of *one he knew to be guilty*."

"I don't understand."

"Think of someone," he said excitedly, "someone whose desire would be as great as that of Lord Arthur to silence a scandal round that gentleman's name. Someone who, unknown perhaps to Lord Arthur, had overheard the same conversation which George Higgins related to the police and the magistrate, someone who, whilst Chipps was taking Lavender's card in to his master, had a few minutes' time wherein to make an assignation with Lavender, promising him money, no doubt, in exchange for the compromising bills."

"Surely you don't mean—" gasped Polly.

"Point number one," he interrupted quietly, "utterly missed by the police. George Higgins in his deposition stated that at the most animated stage of Lavender's conversation with Lord Arthur, and when the bookmaker's tone of voice became loud and threatening, a voice from the top of the steps interrupted that conversation, saying: 'Your tea is getting cold.'"

"Yes—but—" she argued.

"Wait a moment, for there is point number two. That voice was a lady's voice. Now, I did exactly what the police should have done, but did not do. I went to have a look from the racecourse side at those garden steps which to my mind are such important factors in the discovery of this crime. I found only about a dozen rather low steps; anyone standing on the top must have heard every word Charles Lavender uttered the moment he raised his voice."

"Even then—"

"Very well, you grant that," he said excitedly. "Then there was the great, the all-important point which, oddly enough, the prosecution never for a moment took into consideration. When Chipps, the footman, first told Lavender that Lord Arthur could not see him the bookmaker was terribly put out; Chipps then goes to speak to his master; a few minutes elapse, and when the footman once again tells Lavender that his lordship won't see him, the latter says 'Very well,' and seems to treat the matter with complete indifference.

"Obviously, therefore, something must have happened in between to alter the bookmaker's frame of mind. Well! What had happened? Think over all the evidence, and you will see that one thing only had occurred in the interval, namely, Lady Arthur's advent into the room.

"In order to go into the smoking-room she must have crossed the hall; she must have seen Lavender. In that brief interval she must have realized that the man was persistent, and therefore a living danger to her husband. Remember, women have done strange things; they are a far greater puzzle to the student of human nature than the sterner, less complex sex has ever been. As I argued before—as the police should have argued all along—why did Lord Arthur deliberately accuse an innocent man of murder if not to shield the guilty one?

"Remember, Lady Arthur may have been discovered; the man, George Higgins, may have caught sight of her before she had time to make good her retreat. His attention, as well us that of the constables, had to be diverted. Lord Arthur acted on the blind impulse of saving his wife at any cost."

"She may have been met by Colonel McIntosh," argued Polly.

"Perhaps she was," he said. "Who knows? The gallant colonel had to swear to his friend's innocence. He could do that in all conscience—after that his duty was accomplished. No innocent man was suffering for the guilty. The knife which had belonged to Lord Arthur would always save George Higgins. For a time it had pointed to the husband; fortunately never to the wife. Poor thing, she died probably of a broken heart, but women when they love, think only of one object on earth—the one who is beloved.

"To me the whole thing was clear from the very first. When I read the account of the murder—the knife! stabbing!—bah! Don't I know enough of *English* crime not to be certain at once that no English*man*, be he ruffian from the gutter or be he Duke's son, ever stabs his victim in the back. Italians, French, Spaniards do it, if you will, and women of most nations. An Englishman's instinct is to strike and not to stab. George Higgins or Lord Arthur Skelmerton would have knocked their victim down; the woman only would lie in wait till the enemy's back was turned. She knows her weakness, and she does not mean to miss.

"Think it over. There is not one flaw in my argument, but the police never thought the matter out—perhaps in this case it was as well."

He had gone and left Miss Polly Burton still staring at the photograph of a pretty, gentle-looking woman, with a decided, wilful curve round the mouth, and a strange, unaccountable look in the large pathetic eyes; and the little journalist felt quite thankful that in this case the murder of Charles Lavender the bookmaker—cowardly, wicked as it was—had remained a mystery to the police and the public.

X

The Mysterious Death on the Underground Railway

It was all very well for Mr. Richard Frobisher (of the *London Mail*) to cut up rough about it. Polly did not altogether blame him.

She liked him all the better for that frank outburst of manlike ill-temper which, after all said and done, was only a very flattering form of masculine jealousy.

Moreover, Polly distinctly felt guilty about the whole thing. She had promised to meet Dickie—that is Mr. Richard Frobisher—at two o'clock sharp outside the Palace Theatre, because she wanted to go to a Maud Allan *matinée*, and because he naturally wished to go with her.

But at two o'clock sharp she was still in Norfolk Street, Strand, inside an A.B.C. shop, sipping cold coffee opposite a grotesque old man who was fiddling with a bit of string.

How could she be expected to remember Maud Allan or the Palace Theatre, or Dickie himself for a matter of that? The man in the corner had begun to talk of that mysterious death on the underground railway, and Polly had lost count of time, of place, and circumstance.

She had gone to lunch quite early, for she was looking forward to the *matinée* at the Palace.

The old scarecrow was sitting in his accustomed place when she came into the A.B.C. shop, but he had made no remark all the time that the young girl was munching her scone and butter. She was just busy thinking how rude he was not even to have said "Good morning," when an abrupt remark from him caused her to look up.

"Will you be good enough," he said suddenly, "to give me a description of the man who sat next to you just now, while you were having your cup of coffee and scone."

Involuntarily Polly turned her head towards the distant door, through which a man in a light overcoat was even now quickly passing. That man had certainly sat at the next table to hers, when she first sat down to her coffee and scone: he had finished his luncheon—whatever it was—moment ago, had paid at the desk and gone out. The incident did not appear to Polly as being of the slightest consequence.

Therefore she did not reply to the rude old man, but shrugged her shoulders, and called to the waitress to bring her bill.

"Do you know if he was tall or short, dark or fair?" continued the man in the corner, seemingly not the least disconcerted by the young girl's indifference. "Can you tell me at all what he was like?"

"Of course I can," rejoined Polly impatiently, "but I don't see that my description of one of the customers of an A.B.C. shop can have the slightest importance."

He was silent for a minute, while his nervous fingers fumbled about in his capacious pockets in search of the inevitable piece of string. When he had found this necessary "adjunct to thought," he viewed the young girl again through his half-closed lids, and added maliciously:

"But supposing it were of paramount importance that you should give an accurate description of a man who sat next to you for half an hour to-day, how would you proceed?"

"I should say that he was of medium height—"

"Five foot eight, nine, or ten?" he interrupted quietly.

"How can one tell to an inch or two?" rejoined Polly crossly. "He was between colours."

"What's that?" he inquired blandly.

"Neither fair nor dark—his nose—"

"Well, what was his nose like? Will you sketch it?"

"I am not an artist. His nose was fairly straight—his eyes—"

"Were neither dark nor light—his hair had the same striking peculiarity—he was neither short nor tall—his nose was neither aquiline nor snub—" he recapitulated sarcastically.

"No," she retorted; "he was just ordinary looking."

"Would you know him again—say to-morrow, and among a number of other men who were 'neither tall nor short, dark nor fair, aquiline nor snub-nosed,' etc.?"

"I don't know—I might—he was certainly not striking enough to be specially remembered."

"Exactly," he said, while he leant forward excitedly, for all the world like a Jack-in-the-box let loose. "Precisely; and you are a journalist—call yourself one, at least—and it should be part of your business to notice and describe people. I don't mean only the wonderful personage with the clear Saxon features, the fine blue eyes, the noble brow and classic face, but the ordinary person—the person who represents ninety out of every hundred of his own kind—the average Englishman, say, of the middle classes, who is neither very tall nor very short, who wears a moustache which is neither fair nor dark, but which masks his mouth, and a top hat which hides the shape of his head and brow, a man, in fact, who dresses like hundreds of his fellow-creatures, moves like them, speaks like them, has no peculiarity.

"Try to describe *him*, to recognize him, say a week hence, among his other eighty-nine doubles; worse still, to swear his life away, if he happened to be implicated in some crime, wherein *your* recognition of him would place the halter round his neck.

"Try that, I say, and having utterly failed you will more readily understand how one of the greatest scoundrels unhung is still at large, and why the mystery on the Underground Railway was never cleared up.

"I think it was the only time in my life that I was seriously tempted to give the police the benefit of my own views upon the matter. You see, though I admire the brute for his cleverness, I did not see that his being unpunished could possibly benefit any one.

"In these days of tubes and motor traction of all kinds, the old-fashioned 'best, cheapest, and quickest route to City and West End' is often deserted, and the good old Metropolitan Railway carriages cannot at any time be said to be overcrowded. Anyway, when that particular train steamed into Aldgate at about 4 P.M. on March 18th last, the first-class carriages were all but empty.

"The guard marched up and down the platform looking into all the carriages to see if anyone had left a halfpenny evening paper behind for him, and opening the door of one of the first-class compartments, he noticed a lady sitting in the further corner, with her head turned away towards the window, evidently oblivious of the fact that on this line Aldgate is the terminal station.

"'Where are you for, lady?' he said.

"The lady did not move, and the guard stepped into the carriage, thinking that perhaps the lady was asleep. He touched her arm lightly and looked into her face. In his own poetic language, he was 'struck all of a 'eap.' In the glassy eyes, the ashen colour of the cheeks, the rigidity of the head, there was the unmistakable look of death.

"Hastily the guard, having carefully locked the carriage door, summoned a couple of porters, and sent one of them off to the police-station, and the other in search of the station-master.

"Fortunately at this time of day the up platform is not very crowded, all the traffic tending westward in the afternoon. It was only when an

BARONESS EMMUSKA ORCZY

inspector and two police constables, accompanied by a detective in plain clothes and a medical officer, appeared upon the scene, and stood round a first-class railway compartment, that a few idlers realized that something unusual had occurred, and crowded round, eager and curious.

"Thus it was that the later editions of the evening papers, under the sensational heading, 'Mysterious Suicide on the Underground Railway,' had already an account of the extraordinary event. The medical officer had very soon come to the decision that the guard had not been mistaken, and that life was indeed extinct.

"The lady was young, and must have been very pretty before the look of fright and horror had so terribly distorted her features. She was very elegantly dressed, and the more frivolous papers were able to give their feminine readers a detailed account of the unfortunate woman's gown, her shoes, hat, and gloves.

"It appears that one of the latter, the one on the right hand, was partly off, leaving the thumb and wrist bare. That hand held a small satchel, which the police opened, with a view to the possible identification of the deceased, but which was found to contain only a little loose silver, some smelling-salts, and a small empty bottle, which was handed over to the medical officer for purposes of analysis.

"It was the presence of that small bottle which had caused the report to circulate freely that the mysterious case on the Underground Railway was one of suicide. Certain it was that neither about the lady's person, nor in the appearance of the railway carriage, was there the slightest sign of struggle or even of resistance. Only the look in the poor woman's eyes spoke of sudden terror, of the rapid vision of an unexpected and violent death, which probably only lasted an infinitesimal fraction of a second, but which had left its indelible mark upon the face, otherwise so placid and so still."

"The body of the deceased was conveyed to the mortuary. So far, of course, not a soul had been able to identify her, or to throw the slightest light upon the mystery which hung around her death.

"Against that, quite a crowd of idlers—genuinely interested or not—obtained admission to view the body, on the pretext of having lost or mislaid a relative or a friend. At about 8.30 P.M. a young man, very well dressed, drove up to the station in a hansom, and sent in his card to the superintendent. It was Mr. Hazeldene, shipping agent, of 11, Crown Lane, E.C., and No. 19, Addison Row, Kensington.

"The young man looked in a pitiable state of mental distress; his hand clutched nervously a copy of the *St. James's Gazette*, which contained the fatal news. He said very little to the superintendent except that a person who was very dear to him had not returned home that evening.

"He had not felt really anxious until half an hour ago, when suddenly he thought of looking at his paper. The description of the deceased lady, though vague, had terribly alarmed him. He had jumped into a hansom, and now begged permission to view the body, in order that his worst fears might be allayed.

"You know what followed, of course," continued the man in the corner, "the grief of the young man was truly pitiable. In the woman lying there in a public mortuary before him, Mr. Hazeldene had recognized his wife.

"I am waxing melodramatic," said the man in the corner, who looked up at Polly with a mild and gentle smile, while his nervous fingers vainly endeavoured to add another knot on the scrappy bit of string with which he was continually playing, "and I fear that the whole story savours of the penny novelette, but you must admit, and no doubt you remember, that it was an intensely pathetic and truly dramatic moment.

"The unfortunate young husband of the deceased lady was not much worried with questions that night. As a matter of fact, he was not in a fit condition to make any coherent statement. It was at the coroner's inquest on the following day that certain facts came to light, which for the time being seemed to clear up the mystery surrounding Mrs. Hazeldene's death, only to plunge that same mystery, later on, into denser gloom than before.

"The first witness at the inquest was, of course, Mr. Hazeldene himself. I think every one's sympathy went out to the young man as he stood before the coroner and tried to throw what light he could upon the mystery. He was well dressed, as he had been the day before, but he looked terribly ill and worried, and no doubt the fact that he had not shaved gave his face a careworn and neglected air.

"It appears that he and the deceased had been married some six years or so, and that they had always been happy in their married life. They had no children. Mrs. Hazeldene seemed to enjoy the best of health till lately, when she had had a slight attack of influenza, in which Dr. Arthur Jones had attended her. The doctor was present at this moment, and would no doubt explain to the coroner and the jury whether he thought that Mrs. Hazeldene had the slightest tendency to heart disease, which might have had a sudden and fatal ending.

"The coroner was, of course, very considerate to the bereaved husband. He tried by circumlocution to get at the point he wanted, namely, Mrs. Hazeldene's mental condition lately. Mr. Hazeldene seemed loath to talk about this. No doubt he had been warned as to the existence of the small bottle found in his wife's satchel.

"'It certainly did seem to me at times,' he at last reluctantly admitted, 'that my wife did not seem quite herself. She used to be very gay and bright, and lately I often saw her in the evening sitting, as if brooding over some matters, which evidently she did not care to communicate to me.'

"Still the coroner insisted, and suggested the small bottle.

"'I know, I know,' replied the young man, with a short, heavy sigh. 'You mean—the question of suicide—I cannot understand it at all—it seems so sudden and so terrible—she certainly had seemed listless and troubled lately—but only at times—and yesterday morning, when I went to business, she appeared quite herself again, and I suggested that we should go to the opera in the evening. She was delighted, I know, and told me she would do some shopping, and pay a few calls in the afternoon.'

"'Do you know at all where she intended to go when she got into the Underground Railway?'

"'Well, not with certainty. You see, she may have meant to get out at Baker Street, and go down to Bond Street to do her shopping. Then, again, she sometimes goes to a shop in St. Paul's Churchyard, in which case she would take a ticket to Aldersgate Street; but I cannot say.'

"'Now, Mr. Hazeldene,' said the coroner at last very kindly, 'will you try to tell me if there was anything in Mrs. Hazeldene's life which you know of, and which might in some measure explain the cause of the distressed state of mind, which you yourself had noticed? Did there exist any financial difficulty which might have preyed upon Mrs. Hazeldene's mind; was there any friend—to whose intercourse with Mrs. Hazeldene—you—er—at any time took exception? In fact,' added the coroner, as if thankful that he had got over an unpleasant moment, 'can you give me the slightest indication which would tend to confirm the suspicion that the unfortunate lady, in a moment of mental anxiety or derangement, may have wished to take her own life?'

"There was silence in the court for a few moments. Mr. Hazeldene seemed to every one there present to be labouring under some terrible moral doubt. He looked very pale and wretched, and twice attempted to speak before he at last said in scarcely audible tones:

"'No; there were no financial difficulties of any sort. My wife had an independent fortune of her own—she had no extravagant tastes—'

"'Nor any friend you at any time objected to?' insisted the coroner.

"'Nor any friend, I—at any time objected to,' stammered the unfortunate young man, evidently speaking with an effort.

"I was present at the inquest," resumed the man in the corner, after he had drunk a glass of milk and ordered another, "and I can assure you that the most obtuse person there plainly realized that Mr. Hazeldene was telling a lie. It was pretty plain to the meanest intelligence that the unfortunate lady had not fallen into a state of morbid dejection for nothing, and that perhaps there existed a third person who could throw more light on her strange and sudden death than the unhappy, bereaved young widower.

"That the death was more mysterious even than it had at first appeared became very soon apparent. You read the case at the time, no doubt, and must remember the excitement in the public mind caused by the evidence of the two doctors. Dr. Arthur Jones, the lady's usual medical man, who had attended her in a last very slight illness, and who had seen her in a professional capacity fairly recently, declared most emphatically that Mrs. Hazeldene suffered from no organic complaint which could possibly have been the cause of sudden death. Moreover, he had assisted Mr. Andrew Thornton, the district medical officer, in making a postmortem examination, and together they had come to the conclusion that death was due to the action of prussic acid, which had caused instantaneous failure of the heart, but how the drug had been administered neither he nor his colleague were at present able to state.

"'Do I understand, then, Dr. Jones, that the deceased died, poisoned with prussic acid?'

"'Such is my opinion,' replied the doctor.

"'Did the bottle found in her satchel contain prussic acid?'

"'It had contained some at one time, certainly.'

"'In your opinion, then, the lady caused her own death by taking a dose of that drug?'

"'Pardon me, I never suggested such a thing; the lady died poisoned by the drug, but how the drug was administered we cannot say. By injection of some sort, certainly. The drug certainly was not swallowed; there was not a vestige of it in the stomach.'

"'Yes,' added the doctor in reply to another question from the coroner, 'death had probably followed the injection in this case almost immediately; say within a couple of minutes, or perhaps three. It was quite possible that the body would not have more than one quick and sudden convulsion, perhaps not that; death in such cases is absolutely sudden and crushing.'

"I don't think that at the time any one in the room realized how important the doctor's statement was, a statement which, by the way, was confirmed in all its details by the district medical officer, who had conducted the postmortem. Mrs. Hazeldene had died suddenly from an injection of prussic acid, administered no one knew how or when. She had been travelling in a first-class railway carriage in a busy time of the day. That young and elegant woman must have had singular nerve and coolness to go through the process of a self-inflicted injection of a deadly poison in the presence of perhaps two or three other persons.

"Mind you, when I say that no one there realized the importance of the doctor's statement at that moment, I am wrong; there were three persons, who fully understood at once the gravity of the situation, and the astounding development which the case was beginning to assume.

"Of course, I should have put myself out of the question," added the weird old man, with that inimitable self-conceit peculiar to himself. "I guessed then and there in a moment where the police were going wrong, and where they would go on going wrong until the mysterious death on the Underground Railway had sunk into oblivion, together with the other cases which they mismanage from time to time.

"I said there were three persons who understood the gravity of the two doctors' statements—the other two were, firstly, the detective who had originally examined the railway carriage, a young man of energy and plenty of misguided intelligence, the other was Mr. Hazeldene.

"At this point the interesting element of the whole story was first introduced into the proceedings, and this was done through the humble channel of Emma Funnel, Mrs. Hazeldene's maid, who, as far as was known then, was the last person who had seen the unfortunate lady alive and had spoken to her.

"'Mrs. Hazeldene lunched at home,' explained Emma, who was shy, and spoke almost in a whisper; 'she seemed well and cheerful. She went out at about half-past three, and told me she was going to

Spence's, in St. Paul's Churchyard, to try on her new tailor-made gown. Mrs. Hazeldene had meant to go there in the morning, but was prevented as Mr. Errington called.'

"'Mr. Errington?' asked the coroner casually. 'Who is Mr. Errington?'

"But this Emma found difficult to explain. Mr. Errington was— Mr. Errington, that's all.

"'Mr. Errington was a friend of the family. He lived in a flat in the Albert Mansions. He very often came to Addison Row, and generally stayed late.'

"Pressed still further with questions, Emma at last stated that latterly Mrs. Hazeldene had been to the theatre several times with Mr. Errington, and that on those nights the master looked very gloomy, and was very cross.

"Recalled, the young widower was strangely reticent. He gave forth his answers very grudgingly, and the coroner was evidently absolutely satisfied with himself at the marvellous way in which, after a quarter of an hour of firm yet very kind questionings, he had elicited from the witness what information he wanted.

"Mr. Errington was a friend of his wife. He was a gentleman of means, and seemed to have a great deal of time at his command. He himself did not particularly care about Mr. Errington, but he certainly had never made any observations to his wife on the subject.

"'But who is Mr. Errington?' repeated the coroner once more. 'What does he do? What is his business or profession?'

"'He has no business or profession.

"'What is his occupation, then?

"'He has no special occupation. He has ample private means. But he has a great and very absorbing hobby.'

"'What is that?'

"'He spends all his time in chemical experiments, and is, I believe, as an amateur, a very distinguished toxicologist.'"

XI

Mr. Errington

Did you ever see Mr. Errington, the gentleman so closely connected with the mysterious death on the Underground Railway?" asked the man in the corner as he placed one or two of his little snap-shot photos before Miss Polly Burton.

"There he is, to the very life. Fairly good-looking, a pleasant face enough, but ordinary, absolutely ordinary.

"It was this absence of any peculiarity which very nearly, but not quite, placed the halter round Mr. Errington's neck.

"But I am going too fast, and you will lose the thread.

"The public, of course, never heard how it actually came about that Mr. Errington, the wealthy bachelor of Albert Mansions, of the Grosvenor, and other young dandies' clubs, one fine day found himself before the magistrates at Bow Street, charged with being concerned in the death of Mary Beatrice Hazeldene, late of No. 19, Addison Row.

"I can assure you both press and public were literally flabbergasted. You see, Mr. Errington was a well-known and very popular member of a certain smart section of London society. He was a constant visitor at the opera, the racecourse, the Park, and the Carlton, he had a great many friends, and there was consequently quite a large attendance at the police court that morning.

"What had transpired was this:

"After the very scrappy bits of evidence which came to light at the inquest, two gentlemen bethought themselves that perhaps they had some duty to perform towards the State and the public generally. Accordingly they had come forward, offering to throw what light they could upon the mysterious affair on the Underground Railway.

"The police naturally felt that their information, such as it was, came rather late in the day, but as it proved of paramount importance, and the two gentlemen, moreover, were of undoubtedly good position in the world, they were thankful for what they could get, and acted accordingly; they accordingly brought Mr. Errington up before the magistrate on a charge of murder.

"The accused looked pale and worried when I first caught sight of him in the court that day, which was not to be wondered at, considering the terrible position in which he found himself.

"He had been arrested at Marseilles, where he was preparing to start for Colombo.

"I don't think he realized how terrible his position really was until later in the proceedings, when all the evidence relating to the arrest had been heard, and Emma Funnel had repeated her statement as to Mr. Errington's call at 19, Addison Row, in the morning, and Mrs. Hazeldene starting off for St. Paul's Churchyard at 3.30 in the afternoon.

"Mr. Hazeldene had nothing to add to the statements he had made at the coroner's inquest. He had last seen his wife alive on the morning of the fatal day. She had seemed very well and cheerful.

"I think every one present understood that he was trying to say as little as possible that could in any way couple his deceased wife's name with that of the accused.

"And yet, from the servant's evidence, it undoubtedly leaked out that Mrs. Hazeldene, who was young, pretty, and evidently fond of admiration, had once or twice annoyed her husband by her somewhat open, yet perfectly innocent, flirtation with Mr. Errington.

"I think every one was most agreeably impressed by the widower's moderate and dignified attitude. You will see his photo there, among this bundle. That is just how he appeared in court. In deep black, of course, but without any sign of ostentation in his mourning. He had allowed his beard to grow lately, and wore it closely cut in a point.

"After his evidence, the sensation of the day occurred. A tall, dark-haired man, with the word 'City' written metaphorically all over him, had kissed the book, and was waiting to tell the truth, and nothing but the truth.

"He gave his name as Andrew Campbell, head of the firm of Campbell & Co., brokers, of Throgmorton Street.

"In the afternoon of March 18th Mr. Campbell, travelling on the Underground Railway, had noticed a very pretty woman in the same carriage as himself. She had asked him if she was in the right train for Aldersgate. Mr. Campbell replied in the affirmative, and then buried himself in the Stock Exchange quotations of his evening paper.

"At Gower Street, a gentleman in a tweed suit and bowler hat got into the carriage, and took a seat opposite the lady.

"She seemed very much astonished at seeing him, but Mr. Andrew Campbell did not recollect the exact words she said.

"The two talked to one another a good deal, and certainly the lady appeared animated and cheerful. Witness took no notice of them; he was very much engrossed in some calculations, and finally got out at Farringdon Street. He noticed that the man in the tweed suit also got out close behind him, having shaken hands with the lady, and said in a pleasant way: '*Au revoir*! Don't be late to-night.' Mr. Campbell did not hear the lady's reply, and soon lost sight of the man in the crowd.

"Every one was on tenter-hooks, and eagerly waiting for the palpitating moment when witness would describe and identify the man who last had seen and spoken to the unfortunate woman, within five minutes probably of her strange and unaccountable death.

"Personally I knew what was coming before the Scotch stockbroker spoke.

"I could have jotted down the graphic and lifelike description he would give of a probable murderer. It would have fitted equally well the man who sat and had luncheon at this table just now; it would certainly have described five out of every ten young Englishmen you know.

"The individual was of medium height, he wore a moustache which was not very fair nor yet very dark, his hair was between colours. He wore a bowler hat, and a tweed suit—and—and—that was all—Mr. Campbell might perhaps know him again, but then again, he might not—he was not paying much attention—the gentleman was sitting on the same side of the carriage as himself—and he had his hat on all the time. He himself was busy with his newspaper—yes—he might know him again—but he really could not say.

"Mr. Andrew Campbell's evidence was not worth very much, you will say. No, it was not in itself, and would not have justified any arrest were it not for the additional statements made by Mr. James Verner, manager of Messrs. Rodney & Co., colour printers.

"Mr. Verner is a personal friend of Mr. Andrew Campbell, and it appears that at Farringdon Street, where he was waiting for his train, he saw Mr. Campbell get out of a first-class railway carriage. Mr. Verner spoke to him for a second, and then, just as the train was moving off, he stepped into the same compartment which had just been vacated by the stockbroker and the man in the tweed suit. He vaguely recollects a lady sitting in the opposite corner to his own, with her face turned away from him, apparently asleep, but he paid no special attention to her. He was like nearly all business men when they are travelling—engrossed in his paper. Presently a special quotation interested him; he wished to make a note of it, took out a pencil from his waistcoat pocket, and seeing a clean piece of paste-board on the floor, he picked it up, and scribbled on it the memorandum, which he wished to keep. He then slipped the card into his pocket-book.

"'It was only two or three days later,' added Mr. Verner in the midst of breathless silence, 'that I had occasion to refer to these same notes again.

"'In the meanwhile the papers had been full of the mysterious death on the Underground Railway, and the names of those connected with it were pretty familiar to me. It was, therefore, with much astonishment that on looking at the paste-board which I had casually picked up in the railway carriage I saw the name on it, "Frank Errington."'

"There was no doubt that the sensation in court was almost unprecedented. Never since the days of the Fenchurch Street mystery, and the trial of Smethurst, had I seen so much excitement. Mind you, I was not excited—I knew by now every detail of that crime as if I had committed it myself. In fact, I could not have done it better, although I have been a student of crime for many years now. Many people there—his friends, mostly—believed that Errington was doomed. I think he thought so, too, for I could see that his face was terribly white, and he now and then passed his tongue over his lips, as if they were parched.

"You see he was in the awful dilemma—a perfectly natural one, by the way—of being absolutely incapable of *proving* an *alibi*. The crime—if crime there was—had been committed three weeks ago. A man about town like Mr. Frank Errington might remember that he spent certain hours of a special afternoon at his club, or in the Park, but it is very doubtful in nine cases out of ten if he can find a friend who could positively swear as to having seen him there. No! no! Mr. Errington was in a tight corner, and he knew it. You see, there were—besides the evidence—two or three circumstances which did not improve matters for him. His hobby in the direction of toxicology, to begin with. The police had found in his room every description of poisonous substances, including prussic acid.

"Then, again, that journey to Marseilles, the start for Colombo, was, though perfectly innocent, a very unfortunate one. Mr. Errington had gone on an aimless voyage, but the public thought that he had fled, terrified at his own crime. Sir Arthur Inglewood, however, here again displayed his marvellous skill on behalf of his client by the masterly way in which he literally turned all the witnesses for the Crown inside out.

"Having first got Mr. Andrew Campbell to state positively that in the accused he certainly did *not* recognize the man in the tweed suit, the eminent lawyer, after twenty minutes' cross-examination, had so completely upset the stockbroker's equanimity that it is very likely he would not have recognized his own office-boy.

"But through all his flurry and all his annoyance Mr. Andrew Campbell remained very sure of one thing; namely, that the lady was alive and cheerful, and talking pleasantly with the man in the tweed suit up to the moment when the latter, having shaken hands with her, left her with a pleasant '*Au revoir*! Don't be late to-night.' He had heard neither scream nor struggle, and in his opinion, if the individual in the tweed suit had administered a dose of poison to his companion, it must have been with her own knowledge and free will; and the lady in the train most emphatically neither looked nor spoke like a woman prepared for a sudden and violent death.

"Mr. James Verner, against that, swore equally positively that he had stood in full view of the carriage door from the moment that Mr. Campbell got out until he himself stepped into the compartment, that there was no one else in that carriage between Farringdon Street and Aldgate, and that the lady, to the best of his belief, had made no movement during the whole of that journey.

"No; Frank Errington was *not* committed for trial on the capital charge," said the man in the corner with one of his sardonic smiles, "thanks to the cleverness of Sir Arthur Inglewood, his lawyer. He absolutely denied his identity with the man in the tweed suit, and swore he had not seen Mrs. Hazeldene since eleven o'clock in the morning of that fatal day. There was no *proof* that he had; moreover, according to Mr. Campbell's opinion, the man in the tweed suit was in all probability not the murderer. Common sense would not admit that a woman could have a deadly poison injected into her without her knowledge, while chatting pleasantly to her murderer.

"Mr. Errington lives abroad now. He is about to marry. I don't think any of his real friends for a moment believed that he committed the dastardly crime. The police think they know better. They do know this much, that it could not have been a case of suicide, that if the man who undoubtedly travelled with Mrs. Hazeldene on that fatal afternoon had no crime upon his conscience he would long ago have come forward and thrown what light he could upon the mystery.

"As to who that man was, the police in their blindness have not the faintest doubt. Under the unshakable belief that Errington is guilty they have spent the last few months in unceasing labour to try and find further and stronger proofs of his guilt. But they won't find them, because there are none. There are no positive proofs against the actual murderer, for he was one of those clever blackguards who think of everything, foresee every eventuality, who know human nature well, and can foretell exactly what evidence will be brought against them, and act accordingly.

"This blackguard from the first kept the figure, the personality, of Frank Errington before his mind. Frank Errington was the dust which the scoundrel threw metaphorically in the eyes of the police, and you must admit that he succeeded in blinding them—to the extent even of making them entirely forget the one simple little sentence, overheard by Mr. Andrew Campbell, and which was, of course, the clue to the whole thing—the only slip the cunning rogue made—'Au revoir! Don't be late to-night.' Mrs. Hazeldene was going that night to the opera with her husband—

"You are astonished?" he added with a shrug of the shoulders, "you do not see the tragedy yet, as I have seen it before me all along. The frivolous young wife, the flirtation with the friend?—all a blind, all pretence. I took the trouble which the police should have taken immediately, of finding out something about the finances of the Hazeldene *ménage*. Money is in nine cases out of ten the keynote to a crime.

"I found that the will of Mary Beatrice Hazeldene had been proved by the husband, her sole executor, the estate being sworn at £15,000. I found out, moreover, that Mr. Edward Sholto Hazeldene was a poor shipper's clerk when he married the daughter of a wealthy builder in Kensington—and then I made note of the fact that the disconsolate widower had allowed his beard to grow since the death of his wife.

"There's no doubt that he was a clever rogue," added the strange creature, leaning excitedly over the table, and peering into Polly's face. "Do you know how that deadly poison was injected into the poor woman's system? By the simplest of all means, one known to every scoundrel in Southern Europe. A ring—yes! a ring, which has a tiny hollow needle capable of holding a sufficient quantity of prussic acid to have killed two persons instead of one. The man in the tweed suit shook

BARONESS EMMUSKA ORCZY

hands with his fair companion—probably she hardly felt the prick, not sufficiently in any case to make her utter a scream. And, mind you, the scoundrel had every facility, through his friendship with Mr. Errington, of procuring what poison he required, not to mention his friend's visiting card. We cannot gauge how many months ago he began to try and copy Frank Errington in his style of dress, the cut of his moustache, his general appearance, making the change probably so gradual, that no one in his own *entourage* would notice it. He selected for his model a man his own height and build, with the same coloured hair."

"But there was the terrible risk of being identified by his fellow-traveller in the Underground," suggested Polly.

"Yes, there certainly was that risk; he chose to take it, and he was wise. He reckoned that several days would in any case elapse before that person, who, by the way, was a business man absorbed in his newspaper, would actually see him again. The great secret of successful crime is to study human nature," added the man in the corner, as he began looking for his hat and coat. "Edward Hazeldene knew it well."

"But the ring?"

"He may have bought that when he was on his honeymoon," he suggested with a grim chuckle; "the tragedy was not planned in a week, it may have taken years to mature. But you will own that there goes a frightful scoundrel unhung. I have left you his photograph as he was a year ago, and as he is now. You will see he has shaved his beard again, but also his moustache. I fancy he is a friend now of Mr. Andrew Campbell."

He left Miss Polly Burton wondering, not knowing what to believe.

And that is why she missed her appointment with Mr. Richard Frobisher (of the *London Mail*) to go and see Maud Allan dance at the Palace Theatre that afternoon.

XII

The Liverpool Mystery

"A title—a foreign title, I mean—is always very useful for purposes of swindles and frauds," remarked the man in the corner to Polly one day. "The cleverest robberies of modern times were perpetrated lately in Vienna by a man who dubbed himself Lord Seymour; whilst over here the same class of thief calls himself Count Something ending in 'o,' or Prince the other, ending in 'off.'"

"Fortunately for our hotel and lodging-house keepers over here," she replied, "they are beginning to be more alive to the ways of foreign swindlers, and look upon all titled gentry who speak broken English as possible swindlers or thieves."

"The result sometimes being exceedingly unpleasant to the real *grands seigneurs* who honour this country at times with their visits," replied the man in the corner. "Now, take the case of Prince Semionicz, a man whose sixteen quarterings are duly recorded in Gotha, who carried enough luggage with him to pay for the use of every room in an hotel for at least a week, whose gold cigarette case with diamond and turquoise ornament was actually stolen without his taking the slightest trouble to try and recover it; that same man was undoubtedly looked upon with suspicion by the manager of the Liverpool North-Western Hotel from the moment that his secretary—a dapper, somewhat vulgar little Frenchman—bespoke on behalf of his employer, with himself and a valet, the best suite of rooms the hotel contained.

"Obviously those suspicions were unfounded, for the little secretary, as soon as Prince Semionicz had arrived, deposited with the manager a pile of bank notes, also papers and bonds, the value of which would exceed tenfold the most outrageous bill that could possibly be placed before the noble visitor. Moreover, M. Albert Lambert explained that the Prince, who only meant to stay in Liverpool a few days, was on his way to Chicago, where he wished to visit Princess Anna Semionicz, his sister, who was married to Mr. Girwan, the great copper king and multi-millionaire.

"Yet, as I told you before, in spite of all these undoubted securities, suspicion of the wealthy Russian Prince lurked in the minds of most

Liverpudlians who came in business contact with him. He had been at the North-Western two days when he sent his secretary to Window and Vassall, the jewellers of Bold Street, with a request that they would kindly send a representative round to the hotel with some nice pieces of jewellery, diamonds and pearls chiefly, which he was desirous of taking as a present to his sister in Chicago.

"Mr. Winslow took the order from M. Albert with a pleasant bow. Then he went to his inner office and consulted with his partner, Mr. Vassall, as to the best course to adopt. Both the gentlemen were desirous of doing business, for business had been very slack lately: neither wished to refuse a possible customer, or to offend Mr. Pettitt, the manager of the North-Western, who had recommended them to the Prince. But that foreign title and the vulgar little French secretary stuck in the throats of the two pompous and worthy Liverpool jewellers, and together they agreed, firstly, that no credit should be given; and, secondly, that if a cheque or even a banker's draft were tendered, the jewels were not to be given up until that cheque or draft was cashed.

"Then came the question as to who should take the jewels to the hotel. It was altogether against business etiquette for the senior partners to do such errands themselves; moreover, it was thought that it would be easier for a clerk to explain, without giving undue offence, that he could not take the responsibility of a cheque or draft, without having cashed it previously to giving up the jewels.

"Then there was the question of the probable necessity of conferring in a foreign tongue. The head assistant, Charles Needham, who had been in the employ of Winslow and Vassall for over twelve years, was, in true British fashion, ignorant of any language save his own; it was therefore decided to dispatch Mr. Schwarz, a young German clerk lately arrived, on the delicate errand.

"Mr. Schwarz was Mr. Winslow's nephew and godson, a sister of that gentleman having married the head of the great German firm of Schwarz & Co., silversmiths, of Hamburg and Berlin.

"The young man had soon become a great favourite with his uncle, whose heir he would presumably be, as Mr. Winslow had no children.

"At first Mr. Vassall made some demur about sending Mr. Schwarz with so many valuable jewels alone in a city which he had not yet had the time to study thoroughly; but finally he allowed himself to be persuaded by his senior partner, and a fine selection of necklaces, pendants, bracelets, and rings, amounting in value to over £16,000, having been made, it was decided that Mr. Schwarz should go to the North-Western in a cab the next day at about three o'clock in the afternoon. This he accordingly did, the following day being a Thursday.

"Business went on in the shop as usual under the direction of the head assistant, until about seven o'clock, when Mr. Winslow returned from his club, where he usually spent an hour over the papers every afternoon, and at once asked for his nephew. To his astonishment Mr. Needham informed him that Mr. Schwarz had not yet returned. This seemed a little strange, and Mr. Winslow, with a slightly anxious look in his face, went into the inner office in order to consult his junior partner. Mr. Vassall offered to go round to the hotel and interview Mr. Pettitt.

"'I was beginning to get anxious myself,' he said, 'but did not quite like to say so. I have been in over half an hour, hoping every moment that you would come in, and that perhaps you could give me some reassuring news. I thought that perhaps you had met Mr. Schwarz, and were coming back together.'

"However, Mr. Vassall walked round to the hotel and interviewed the hall porter. The latter perfectly well remembered Mr. Schwarz sending in his card to Prince Semionicz.

"'At what time was that?' asked Mr. Vassall.

"'About ten minutes past three, sir, when he came; it was about an hour later when he left.'

"'When he left?' gasped, more than said, Mr. Vassall.

"'Yes, sir. Mr. Schwarz left here about a quarter before four, sir.'

"'Are you quite sure?'

"'Quite sure. Mr. Pettitt was in the hall when he left, and he asked him something about business. Mr. Schwarz laughed and said, "not bad." I hope there's nothing wrong, sir,' added the man.

"'Oh—er—nothing—thank you. Can I see Mr. Pettitt?'

"'Certainly, sir.'

"Mr. Pettitt, the manager of the hotel, shared Mr. Vassall's anxiety, immediately he heard that the young German had not yet returned home.

"'I spoke to him a little before four o'clock. We had just switched on the electric light, which we always do these winter months at that hour. But I shouldn't worry myself, Mr. Vassall; the young man may have seen to some business on his way home. You'll probably find him in when you go back.'

"Apparently somewhat reassured, Mr. Vassall thanked Mr. Pettitt and hurried back to the shop, only to find that Mr. Schwarz had not returned, though it was now close on eight o'clock.

"Mr. Winslow looked so haggard and upset that it would have been cruel to heap reproaches upon his other troubles or to utter so much as the faintest suspicion that young Schwarz's permanent disappearance with £16,000 in jewels and money was within the bounds of probability.

"There was one chance left, but under the circumstances a very slight one indeed. The Winslows' private house was up the Birkenhead end of the town. Young Schwarz had been living with them ever since his arrival in Liverpool, and he may have—either not feeling well or for some other reason—gone straight home without calling at the shop. It was unlikely, as valuable jewellery was never kept at the private house, but—it just might have happened.

"It would be useless," continued the man in the corner, "and decidedly uninteresting, were I to relate to you Messrs. Winslow's and Vassall's further anxieties with regard to the missing young man. Suffice it to say that on reaching his private house Mr. Winslow found that his godson had neither returned nor sent any telegraphic message of any kind.

"Not wishing to needlessly alarm his wife, Mr. Winslow made an attempt at eating his dinner, but directly after that he hurried back to the North-Western Hotel, and asked to see Prince Semionicz. The Prince was at the theatre with his secretary, and probably would not be home until nearly midnight.

"Mr. Winslow, then, not knowing what to think, nor yet what to fear, and in spite of the horror he felt of giving publicity to his nephew's disappearance, thought it his duty to go round to the police-station and interview the inspector. It is wonderful how quickly news of that type travels in a large city like Liverpool. Already the morning papers of the following day were full of the latest sensation: 'Mysterious disappearance of a well-known tradesman.'

"Mr. Winslow found a copy of the paper containing the sensational announcement on his breakfast-table. It lay side by side with a letter addressed to him in his nephew's handwriting, which had been posted in Liverpool.

"Mr. Winslow placed that letter, written to him by his nephew, into the hands of the police. Its contents, therefore, quickly became public property. The astounding statements made therein by Mr. Schwarz created, in quiet, businesslike Liverpool, a sensation which has seldom been equalled.

"It appears that the young fellow did call on Prince Semionicz at a quarter past three on Wednesday, December 10th, with a bag full of jewels, amounting in value to some £16,000. The Prince duly admired, and finally selected from among the ornaments a necklace, pendant, and bracelet, the whole being priced by Mr. Schwarz, according to his instructions, at £10,500. Prince Semionicz was most prompt and businesslike in his dealings.

"'You will require immediate payment for these, of course,' he said in perfect English, 'and I know you business men prefer solid cash to cheques, especially when dealing with foreigners. I always provide myself with plenty of Bank of England notes in consequence,' he added with a pleasant smile, 'as £10,500 in gold would perhaps be a little inconvenient to carry. If you will kindly make out the receipt, my secretary, M. Lambert, will settle all business matters with you.'

"He thereupon took the jewels he had selected and locked them up in his dressing-case, the beautiful silver fillings of which Mr. Schwarz just caught a short glimpse of. Then, having been accommodated with paper and ink, the young jeweller made out the account and receipt, whilst M. Lambert, the secretary, counted out before him 105 crisp Bank of England notes of £100 each. Then, with a final bow to his exceedingly urbane and eminently satisfactory customer, Mr. Schwarz took his leave. In the hall he saw and spoke to Mr. Pettitt, and then he went out into the street.

"He had just left the hotel and was about to cross towards St. George's Hall when a gentleman, in a magnificent fur coat, stepped quickly out of a cab which had been stationed near the kerb, and, touching him lightly upon the shoulder, said with an unmistakable air of authority, at the same time handing him a card:

"'That is my name. I must speak with you immediately.'"

"Schwarz glanced at the card, and by the light of the arc lamps above his head read on it the name of 'Dimitri Slaviansky Burgreneff, de la IIIe Section de la Police Imperial de S.M. le Czar.'

"Quickly the owner of the unpronounceable name and the significant title pointed to the cab from which he had just alighted, and Schwarz, whose every suspicion with regard to his princely customer bristled up in one moment, clutched his bag and followed his imposing interlocutor;

as soon as they were both comfortably seated in the cab the latter began, with courteous apology in broken but fluent English:

"'I must ask your pardon, sir, for thus trespassing upon your valuable time, and I certainly should not have done so but for the certainty that our interests in a certain matter which I have in hand are practically identical, in so far that we both should wish to outwit a clever rogue.'

"Instinctively, and his mind full of terrible apprehension, Mr. Schwarz's hand wandered to his pocket-book, filled to overflowing with the bank-notes which he had so lately received from the Prince.

"'Ah, I see,' interposed the courteous Russian with a smile, 'he has played the confidence trick on you, with the usual addition of so many so-called bank-notes.'

"'So-called,' gasped the unfortunate young man.

"'I don't think I often err in my estimate of my own countrymen,' continued M. Burgreneff; 'I have vast experience, you must remember. Therefore, I doubt if I am doing M.—er—what does he call himself?—Prince something—an injustice if I assert, even without handling those crisp bits of paper you have in your pocket-book, that no bank would exchange them for gold.'

"Remembering his uncle's suspicions and his own, Mr. Schwarz cursed himself for his blindness and folly in accepting notes so easily without for a moment imagining that they might be false. Now, with every one of those suspicions fully on the alert, he felt the bits of paper with nervous, anxious fingers, while the imperturbable Russian calmly struck a match.

"'See here,' he said, pointing to one of the notes, 'the shape of that "w" in the signature of the chief cashier. I am not an English police officer, but I could pick out that spurious "w" among a thousand genuine ones. You see, I have seen a good many.'

"Now, of course, poor young Schwarz had not seen very many Bank of England notes. He could not have told whether one 'w' in Mr. Bowen's signature is better than another, but, though he did not speak English nearly as fluently as his pompous interlocutor, he understood every word of the appalling statement the latter had just made.

"'Then that Prince,' he said, 'at the hotel—'

"'Is no more Prince than you and I, my dear sir,' concluded the gentleman of His Imperial Majesty's police calmly.

"'And the jewels? Mr. Winslow's jewels?'

"'With the jewels there may be a chance—oh! a mere chance. These forged bank-notes, which you accepted so trustingly, may prove the means of recovering your property.'

"'How?'

"'The penalty of forging and circulating spurious bank-notes is very heavy. You know that. The fear of seven years' penal servitude will act as a wonderful sedative upon the—er—Prince's joyful mood. He will give up the jewels to me all right enough, never you fear. He knows,' added the Russian officer grimly, 'that there are plenty of old scores to settle up, without the additional one of forged bank-notes. Our interests, you see, are identical. May I rely on your co-operation?'

"'Oh, I will do as you wish,' said the delighted young German. 'Mr. Winslow and Mr. Vassall, they trusted me, and I have been such a fool. I hope it is not too late.'

"'I think not,' said M. Burgreneff, his hand already on the door of the cab. 'Though I have been talking to you I have kept an eye on the hotel, and our friend the Prince has not yet gone out. We are accustomed, you know, to have eyes everywhere, we of the Russian secret police. I don't think that I will ask you to be present at the confrontation. Perhaps you will wait for me in the cab. There is a nasty fog outside, and you will be more private. Will you give me those beautiful bank-notes? Thank you! Don't be anxious. I won't be long.'

"He lifted his hat, and slipped the notes into the inner pocket of his magnificent fur coat. As he did so, Mr. Schwarz caught sight of a rich uniform and a wide sash, which no doubt was destined to carry additional moral weight with the clever rogue upstairs.

"Then His Imperial Majesty's police officer stepped quickly out of the cab, and Mr. Schwarz was left alone."

XIII

A Cunning Rascal

Yes, left severely alone," continued the man in the corner with a sarcastic chuckle. "So severely alone, in fact, that one quarter of an hour after another passed by and still the magnificent police officer in the gorgeous uniform did not return. Then, when it was too late, Schwarz cursed himself once again for the double-dyed idiot that he was. He had been only too ready to believe that Prince Semionicz was a liar and a rogue, and under these unjust suspicions he had fallen an all too easy prey to one of the most cunning rascals he had ever come across.

"An inquiry from the hall porter at the North-Western elicited the fact that no such personage as Mr. Schwarz described had entered the hotel. The young man asked to see Prince Semionicz, hoping against hope that all was not yet lost. The Prince received him most courteously; he was dictating some letters to his secretary, while the valet was in the next room preparing his master's evening clothes. Mr. Schwarz found it very difficult to explain what he actually did want.

"There stood the dressing-case in which the Prince had locked up the jewels, and there the bag from which the secretary had taken the bank-notes. After much hesitation on Schwarz's part and much impatience on that of the Prince, the young man blurted out the whole story of the so-called Russian police officer whose card he still held in his hand.

"The Prince, it appears, took the whole thing wonderfully good-naturedly; no doubt he thought the jeweller a hopeless fool. He showed him the jewels, the receipt he held, and also a large bundle of bank-notes similar to those Schwarz had with such culpable folly given up to the clever rascal in the cab.

"'I pay all my bills with Bank of England notes, Mr. Schwarz. It would have been wiser, perhaps, if you had spoken to the manager of the hotel about me before you were so ready to believe any cock-and-bull story about my supposed rogueries.'

"Finally he placed a small 16mo volume before the young jeweller, and said with a pleasant smile:

"'If people in this country who are in a large way of business, and are therefore likely to come in contact with people of foreign nationality, were to study these little volumes before doing business with any foreigner who claims a title, much disappointment and a great loss would often be saved. Now in this case had you looked up page 797 of this little volume of Gotha's Almanach you would have seen my name in it and known from the first that the so-called Russian detective was a liar.'

"There was nothing more to be said, and Mr. Schwarz left the hotel. No doubt, now that he had been hopelessly duped he dared not go home, and half hoped by communicating with the police that they might succeed in arresting the thief before he had time to leave Liverpool. He interviewed Detective-Inspector Watson, and was at once confronted with the awful difficulty which would make the recovery of the bank-notes practically hopeless. He had never had the time or opportunity of jotting down the numbers of the notes.

"Mr. Winslow, though terribly wrathful against his nephew, did not wish to keep him out of his home. As soon as he had received Schwarz's letter, he traced him, with Inspector Watson's help, to his lodgings in North Street, where the unfortunate young man meant to remain hidden until the terrible storm had blown over, or perhaps until the thief had been caught red-handed with the booty still in his hands.

"This happy event, needless to say, never did occur, though the police made every effort to trace the man who had decoyed Schwarz into the cab. His appearance was such an uncommon one; it seemed most unlikely that no one in Liverpool should have noticed him after he left that cab. The wonderful fur coat, the long beard, all must have been noticeable, even though it was past four o'clock on a somewhat foggy December afternoon.

"But every investigation proved futile; no one answering Schwarz's description of the man had been seen anywhere. The papers continued to refer to the case as 'the Liverpool Mystery.' Scotland Yard sent Mr. Fairburn down—the celebrated detective—at the request of the Liverpool police, to help in the investigations, but nothing availed.

"Prince Semionicz, with his suite, left Liverpool, and he who had attempted to blacken his character, and had succeeded in robbing Messrs. Winslow and Vassall of £10,500, had completely disappeared."

The man in the corner readjusted his collar and necktie, which, during the narrative of this interesting mystery, had worked its way up his long, crane-like neck under his large flappy ears. His costume of checked tweed of a peculiarly loud pattern had tickled the fancy of some of the waitresses, who were standing gazing at him and giggling in one corner. This evidently made him nervous. He gazed up very meekly at Polly, looking for all the world like a bald-headed adjutant dressed for a holiday.

"Of course, all sorts of theories of the theft got about at first. One of the most popular, and at the same time most quickly exploded, being that young Schwarz had told a cock-and-bull story, and was the actual thief himself.

"However, as I said before, that was very quickly exploded, as Mr. Schwarz senior, a very wealthy merchant, never allowed his son's carelessness to be a serious loss to his kind employers. As soon as he thoroughly grasped all the circumstances of the extraordinary case, he drew a cheque for £10,500 and remitted it to Messrs. Winslow and Vassall. It was just, but it was also high-minded.

"All Liverpool knew of the generous action, as Mr. Winslow took care that it should; and any evil suspicion regarding young Mr. Schwarz vanished as quickly as it had come.

"Then, of course, there was the theory about the Prince and his suite, and to this day I fancy there are plenty of people in Liverpool, and also in London, who declare that the so-called Russian police officer was a confederate. No doubt that theory was very plausible, and Messrs. Winslow and Vassall spent a good deal of money in trying to prove a case against the Russian Prince.

"Very soon, however, that theory was also bound to collapse. Mr. Fairburn, whose reputation as an investigator of crime waxes in direct inverted ratio to his capacities, did hit upon the obvious course of interviewing the managers of the larger London and Liverpool *agents de change*. He soon found that Prince Semionicz had converted a great deal of Russian and French money into English bank-notes since his arrival in this country. More than £30,000 in good solid, honest money was traced to the pockets of the gentleman with the sixteen quarterings. It seemed, therefore, more than improbable that a man who was obviously fairly wealthy would risk imprisonment and hard labour, if not worse, for the sake of increasing his fortune by £10,000.

"However, the theory of the Prince's guilt has taken firm root in the dull minds of our police authorities. They have had every information with regard to Prince Semionicz's antecedents from Russia; his position, his wealth, have been placed above suspicion, and yet they suspect and go on suspecting him or his secretary. They have communicated with the police of every European capital; and while they still hope to obtain sufficient evidence against those they suspect, they calmly allow the guilty to enjoy the fruit of his clever roguery."

"The guilty?" said Polly. "Who do you think—"

"Who do I think knew at that moment that young Schwarz had money in his possession?" he said excitedly, wriggling in his chair like a Jack-in-the-box. "Obviously some one was guilty of that theft who knew that Schwarz had gone to interview a rich Russian, and would in all probability return with a large sum of money in his possession?"

"Who, indeed, but the Prince and his secretary?" she argued. "But just now you said—"

"Just now I said that the police were determined to find the Prince and his secretary guilty; they did not look further than their own stumpy noses. Messrs. Winslow and Vassall spent money with a free hand in those investigations. Mr. Winslow, as the senior partner, stood to lose over £9000 by that robbery. Now, with Mr. Vassall it was different.

"When I saw how the police went on blundering in this case I took the trouble to make certain inquiries, the whole thing interested me so much, and I learnt all that I wished to know. I found out, namely, that Mr. Vassall was very much a junior partner in the firm, that he only drew ten per cent of the profits, having been promoted lately to a partnership from having been senior assistant.

"Now, the police did not take the trouble to find that out."

"But you don't mean that—"

"I mean that in all cases where robbery affects more than one person the first thing to find out is whether it affects the second party equally with the first. I proved that to you, didn't I, over that robbery in Phillimore Terrace? There, as here, one of the two parties stood to lose very little in comparison with the other—"

"Even then—" she began.

"Wait a moment, for I found out something more. The moment I had ascertained that Mr. Vassall was not drawing more than about £500 a year from the business profits I tried to ascertain at what rate he lived and what were his chief vices. I found that he kept a fine house in Albert Terrace. Now, the rents of those houses are £250 a year. Therefore speculation, horse-racing or some sort of gambling, must help to keep up that establishment. Speculation and most forms of gambling are synonymous with debt and ruin. It is only a question of time. Whether Mr. Vassall was in debt or not at the time, that I cannot say, but this I do know, that ever since that unfortunate loss to him of about £1000 he has kept his house in nicer style than before, and he now has a good banking account at the Lancashire and Liverpool bank, which he opened a year after his 'heavy loss.'"

"But it must have been very difficult—" argued Polly.

"What?" he said. "To have planned out the whole thing? For carrying it out was mere child's play. He had twenty-four hours in which to put his plan into execution. Why, what was there to do? Firstly, to go to a local printer in some out-of-the-way part of the town and get him to print a few cards with the high-sounding name. That, of course, is done 'while you wait.' Beyond that there was the purchase of a good second-hand uniform, fur coat, and a beard and a wig from a costumier's.

"No, no, the execution was not difficult; it was the planning of it all, the daring that was so fine. Schwarz, of course, was a foreigner; he had only been in England a little over a fortnight. Vassall's broken English misled him; probably he did not know the junior partner very intimately. I have no doubt that but for his uncle's absurd British prejudice and suspicions against the Russian Prince, Schwarz would not have been so ready to believe in the latter's roguery. As I said, it would be a great boon if English tradesmen studied Gotha more; but it was clever, wasn't it? I couldn't have done it much better myself."

That last sentence was so characteristic. Before Polly could think of some plausible argument against his theory he was gone, and she was trying vainly to find another solution to the Liverpool mystery.

XIV

The Edinburgh Mystery

The man in the corner had not enjoyed his lunch. Miss Polly Burton could see that he had something on his mind, for, even before he began to talk that morning, he was fidgeting with his bit of string, and setting all her nerves on the jar.

"Have you ever felt real sympathy with a criminal or a thief?" he asked her after a while.

"Only once, I think," she replied, "and then I am not quite sure that the unfortunate woman who did enlist my sympathies was the criminal you make her out to be."

"You mean the heroine of the York mystery?" he replied blandly. "I know that you tried very hard that time to discredit the only possible version of that mysterious murder, the version which is my own. Now, I am equally sure that you have at the present moment no more notion as to who killed and robbed poor Lady Donaldson in Charlotte Square, Edinburgh, than the police have themselves, and yet you are fully prepared to pooh-pooh my arguments, and to disbelieve my version of the mystery. Such is the lady journalist's mind."

"If you have some cock-and-bull story to explain that extraordinary case," she retorted, "of course I shall disbelieve it. Certainly, if you are going to try and enlist my sympathies on behalf of Edith Crawford, I can assure you you won't succeed."

"Well, I don't know that that is altogether my intention. I see you are interested in the case, but I dare say you don't remember all the circumstances. You must forgive me if I repeat that which you know already. If you have ever been to Edinburgh at all, you will have heard of Graham's bank, and Mr. Andrew Graham, the present head of the firm, is undoubtedly one of the most prominent notabilities of 'modern Athens.'"

The man in the corner took two or three photos from his pocket-book and placed them before the young girl; then, pointing at them with his long bony finger—

"That," he said, "is Mr. Elphinstone Graham, the eldest son, a typical young Scotchman, as you see, and this is David Graham, the second son."

Polly looked more closely at this last photo, and saw before her a young face, upon which some lasting sorrow seemed already to have left its mark. The face was delicate and thin, the features pinched, and the eyes seemed almost unnaturally large and prominent.

"He was deformed," commented the man in the corner in answer to the girl's thoughts, "and, as such, an object of pity and even of repugnance to most of his friends. There was also a good deal of talk in Edinburgh society as to his mental condition, his mind, according to many intimate friends of the Grahams, being at times decidedly unhinged. Be that as it may, I fancy that his life must have been a very sad one; he had lost his mother when quite a baby, and his father seemed, strangely enough, to have an almost unconquerable dislike towards him.

"Every one got to know presently of David Graham's sad position in his father's own house, and also of the great affection lavished upon him by his godmother, Lady Donaldson, who was a sister of Mr. Graham's.

"She was a lady of considerable wealth, being the widow of Sir George Donaldson, the great distiller; but she seems to have been decidedly eccentric. Latterly she had astonished all her family—who were rigid Presbyterians—by announcing her intention of embracing the Roman Catholic faith, and then retiring to the convent of St. Augustine's at Newton Abbot in Devonshire.

"She had sole and absolute control of the vast fortune which a doting husband had bequeathed to her. Clearly, therefore, she was at liberty to bestow it upon a Devonshire convent if she chose. But this evidently was not altogether her intention.

"I told you how fond she was of her deformed godson, did I not? Being a bundle of eccentricities, she had many hobbies, none more pronounced than the fixed determination to see—before retiring from the world altogether—David Graham happily married.

"Now, it appears that David Graham, ugly, deformed, half-demented as he was, had fallen desperately in love with Miss Edith Crawford, daughter of the late Dr. Crawford, of Prince's Gardens. The young lady, however—very naturally, perhaps—fought shy of David Graham, who, about this time, certainly seemed very queer and morose, but Lady Donaldson, with characteristic determination, seems to have made up her mind to melt Miss Crawford's heart towards her unfortunate nephew.

"On October the 2nd last, at a family party given by Mr. Graham in his fine mansion in Charlotte Square, Lady Donaldson openly announced her intention of making over, by deed of gift, to her nephew, David Graham, certain property, money, and shares, amounting in total value to the sum of £100,000, and also her magnificent diamonds, which were worth £50,000, for the use of the said David's wife. Keith Macfinlay, a lawyer of Prince's Street, received the next day instructions for drawing up the necessary deed of gift, which she pledged herself to sign the day of her godson's wedding.

"A week later *The Scotsman* contained the following paragraph:—

"'A marriage is arranged and will shortly take place between David, younger son of Andrew Graham, Esq., of Charlotte Square, Edinburgh, and Dochnakirk, Perthshire, and Edith Lillian, only surviving daughter of the late Dr. Kenneth Crawford, of Prince's Gardens.'

"In Edinburgh society comments were loud and various upon the forthcoming marriage, and, on the whole, these comments were far from complimentary to the families concerned. I do not think that the Scotch are a particularly sentimental race, but there was such obvious buying, selling, and bargaining about this marriage that Scottish chivalry rose in revolt at the thought.

"Against that the three people most concerned seemed perfectly satisfied. David Graham was positively transformed; his moroseness was gone from him, he lost his queer ways and wild manners, and became gentle and affectionate in the midst of this great and unexpected happiness. Miss Edith Crawford ordered her trousseau, and talked of the diamonds to her friends, and Lady Donaldson was only waiting for the consummation of this marriage—her heart's desire—before she finally retired from the world, at peace with it and with herself.

"The deed of gift was ready for signature on the wedding day, which was fixed for November 7th, and Lady Donaldson took up her abode temporarily in her brother's house in Charlotte Square.

"Mr. Graham gave a large ball on October 23rd. Special interest is attached to this ball, from the fact that for this occasion Lady Donaldson insisted that David's future wife should wear the magnificent diamonds which were soon to become hers.

"They were, it seems, superb, and became Miss Crawford's stately beauty to perfection. The ball was a brilliant success, the last guest leaving at four A.M. The next day it was the universal topic of conversation, and the day after that, when Edinburgh unfolded the late editions of its morning papers, it learned with horror and dismay that Lady Donaldson had been found murdered in her room, and that the celebrated diamonds had been stolen.

"Hardly had the beautiful little city, however, recovered from this awful shock, than its newspapers had another thrilling sensation ready for their readers.

"Already all Scotch and English papers had mysteriously hinted at 'startling information' obtained by the Procurator Fiscal, and at an 'impending sensational arrest.'

"Then the announcement came, and every one in Edinburgh read, horror-struck and aghast, that the 'sensational arrest' was none other than that of Miss Edith Crawford, for murder and robbery, both so daring and horrible that reason refused to believe that a young lady, born and bred in the best social circle, could have conceived, much less executed, so heinous a crime. She had been arrested in London at the Midland Hotel, and brought to Edinburgh, where she was judicially examined, bail being refused."

XV

A Terrible Plight

Little more than a fortnight after that, Edith Crawford was duly committed to stand her trial before the High Court of Justiciary. She had pleaded 'Not Guilty' at the pleading diet, and her defence was entrusted to Sir James Fenwick, one of the most eminent advocates at the Criminal Bar.

"Strange to say," continued the man in the corner after a while, "public opinion from the first went dead against the accused. The public is absolutely like a child, perfectly irresponsible and wholly illogical; it argued that since Miss Crawford had been ready to contract a marriage with a half-demented, deformed creature for the sake of his £100,000 she must have been equally ready to murder and rob an old lady for the sake of £50,000 worth of jewellery, without the encumbrance of so undesirable a husband.

"Perhaps the great sympathy aroused in the popular mind for David Graham had much to do with this ill-feeling against the accused. David Graham had, by this cruel and dastardly murder, lost the best—if not the only—friend he possessed. He had also lost at one fell swoop the large fortune which Lady Donaldson had been about to assign to him.

"The deed of gift had never been signed, and the old lady's vast wealth, instead of enriching her favourite nephew, was distributed—since she had made no will—amongst her heirs-at-law. And now to crown this long chapter of sorrow David Graham saw the girl he loved accused of the awful crime which had robbed him of friend and fortune.

"It was, therefore, with an unmistakable thrill of righteous satisfaction that Edinburgh society saw this 'mercenary girl' in so terrible a plight.

"I was immensely interested in the case, and journeyed down to Edinburgh in order to get a good view of the chief actors in the thrilling drama which was about to be unfolded there.

"I succeeded—I generally do—in securing one of the front seats among the audience, and was already comfortably installed in my place in court when through the trap door I saw the head of the prisoner emerge. She was very becomingly dressed in deep black, and, led by two policemen, she took her place in the dock. Sir James Fenwick shook hands with her very warmly, and I could almost hear him instilling words of comfort into her.

"The trial lasted six clear days, during which time more than forty persons were examined for the prosecution, and as many for the defence. But the most interesting witnesses were certainly the two doctors, the maid Tremlett, Campbell, the High Street jeweller, and David Graham.

"There was, of course, a great deal of medical evidence to go through. Poor Lady Donaldson had been found with a silk scarf tied tightly round her neck, her face showing even to the inexperienced eye every symptom of strangulation.

"Then Tremlett, Lady Donaldson's confidential maid, was called. Closely examined by Crown Counsel, she gave an account of the ball at Charlotte Square on the 23rd, and the wearing of the jewels by Miss Crawford on that occasion.

"'I helped Miss Crawford on with the tiara over her hair,' she said; 'and my lady put the two necklaces round Miss Crawford's neck herself. There were also some beautiful brooches, bracelets, and earrings. At four o'clock in the morning when the ball was over, Miss Crawford brought the jewels back to my lady's room. My lady had already gone to bed, and I had put out the electric light, as I was going, too. There was only one candle left in the room, close to the bed.

"'Miss Crawford took all the jewels off, and asked Lady Donaldson for the key of the safe, so that she might put them away. My lady gave her the key and said to me, "You can go to bed, Tremlett, you must be dead tired." I was glad to go, for I could hardly stand up—I was so tired. I said "Good night!" to my lady and also to Miss Crawford, who was busy putting the jewels away. As I was going out of the room I heard Lady Donaldson saying: "Have you managed it, my dear?" Miss Crawford said: "I have put everything away very nicely."'

"In answer to Sir James Fenwick, Tremlett said that Lady Donaldson always carried the key of her jewel safe on a ribbon round her neck, and had done so the whole day preceding her death.

"'On the night of the 24th,' she continued, 'Lady Donaldson still seemed rather tired, and went up to her room directly after dinner, and while the family were still sitting in the dining-room. She made me dress her hair, then she slipped on her dressing-gown and sat in the arm-chair with a book. She told me that she then felt strangely uncomfortable and nervous, and could not account for it.

"'However, she did not want me to sit with her, so I thought that the best thing I could do was to tell Mr. David Graham that her ladyship did not seem very cheerful. Her ladyship was so fond of Mr. David; it always made her happy to have him with her. I then went to my room, and at half-past eight Mr. David called me. He said: "Your mistress does seem a little restless to-night. If I were you I would just go and listen at her door in about an hour's time, and if she has not gone to bed I would go in and stay with her until she has." At about ten o'clock I did as Mr. David suggested, and listened at her ladyship's door. However, all was quiet in the room, and, thinking her ladyship had gone to sleep, I went back to bed.

"'The next morning at eight o'clock, when I took in my mistress's cup of tea, I saw her lying on the floor, her poor dear face all purple and distorted. I screamed, and the other servants came rushing along. Then Mr. Graham had the door locked and sent for the doctor and the police.'

"The poor woman seemed to find it very difficult not to break down. She was closely questioned by Sir James Fenwick, but had nothing further to say. She had last seen her mistress alive at eight o'clock on the evening of the 24th.

"'And when you listened at her door at ten o'clock,' asked Sir James, 'did you try to open it?'

"'I did, but it was locked,' she replied.

"'Did Lady Donaldson usually lock her bedroom at night?'

"'Nearly always.'

"'And in the morning when you took in the tea?'

"'The door was open. I walked straight in.'

"'You are quite sure?' insisted Sir James.

"'I swear it,' solemnly asserted the woman.

"After that we were informed by several members of Mr. Graham's establishment that Miss Crawford had been in to tea at Charlotte Square in the afternoon of the 24th, that she told every one she was going to London by the night mail, as she had some special shopping she wished to do there. It appears that Mr. Graham and David both tried to persuade her to stay to dinner, and then to go by the 9.10 P.M. from the Caledonian Station. Miss Crawford however had refused, saying she always preferred to go from the Waverley Station. It was nearer to her own rooms, and she still had a good deal of writing to do.

"In spite of this, two witnesses saw the accused in Charlotte Square later on in the evening. She was carrying a bag which seemed heavy, and was walking towards the Caledonian Railway Station.

"But the most thrilling moment in that sensational trial was reached on the second day, when David Graham, looking wretchedly ill, unkempt, and haggard, stepped into the witness-box. A murmur of sympathy went round the audience at sight of him, who was the second, perhaps, most deeply stricken victim of the Charlotte Square tragedy.

"David Graham, in answer to Crown Counsel, gave an account of his last interview with Lady Donaldson.

"'Tremlett had told me that she seemed anxious and upset, and I went to have a chat with her; she soon cheered up and. . .'

"There the unfortunate young man hesitated visibly, but after a while resumed with an obvious effort.

"'She spoke of my marriage, and of the gift she was about to bestow upon me. She said the diamonds would be for my wife, and after that for my daughter, if I had one. She also complained that Mr. Macfinlay had been so punctilious about preparing the deed of gift, and that it was a great pity the £100,000 could not just pass from her hands to mine without so much fuss.

"'I stayed talking with her for about half an hour; then I left her, as she seemed ready to go to bed; but I told her maid to listen at the door in about an hour's time.'

"There was deep silence in the court for a few moments, a silence which to me seemed almost electrical. It was as if, some time before it was uttered, the next question put by Crown Counsel to the witness had hovered in the air.

"'You were engaged to Miss Edith Crawford at one time, were you not?'

"One felt, rather than heard, the almost inaudible 'Yes' which escaped from David Graham's compressed lips.

"'Under what circumstances was that engagement broken off?'

"Sir James Fenwick had already risen in protest, but David Graham had been the first to speak.

"'I do not think that I need answer that question.'

"'I will put it in a different form, then,' said Crown Counsel urbanely—'one to which my learned friend cannot possibly take exception. Did you or did you not on October 27th receive a letter from the accused, in which she desired to be released from her promise of marriage to you?'

"Again David Graham would have refused to answer, and he certainly gave no audible reply to the learned counsel's question; but every one in the audience there present—aye, every member of the jury and of the bar—read upon David Graham's pale countenance and large, sorrowful eyes that ominous 'Yes!' which had failed to reach his trembling lips."

XVI

"Non Proven"

"There is no doubt," continued the man in the corner, "that what little sympathy the young girl's terrible position had aroused in the public mind had died out the moment that David Graham left the witness-box on the second day of the trial. Whether Edith Crawford was guilty of murder or not, the callous way in which she had accepted a deformed lover, and then thrown him over, had set every one's mind against her.

"It was Mr. Graham himself who had been the first to put the Procurator Fiscal in possession of the fact that the accused had written to David from London, breaking off her engagement. This information had, no doubt, directed the attention of the Fiscal to Miss Crawford, and the police soon brought forward the evidence which had led to her arrest.

"We had a final sensation on the third day, when Mr. Campbell, jeweller, of High Street, gave his evidence. He said that on October 25th a lady came to his shop and offered to sell him a pair of diamond earrings. Trade had been very bad, and he had refused the bargain, although the lady seemed ready to part with the earrings for an extraordinarily low sum, considering the beauty of the stones.

"In fact it was because of this evident desire on the lady's part to sell at *any* cost that he had looked at her more keenly than he otherwise would have done. He was now ready to swear that the lady that offered him the diamond earrings was the prisoner in the dock.

"I can assure you that as we all listened to this apparently damnatory evidence, you might have heard a pin drop amongst the audience in that crowded court. The girl alone, there in the dock, remained calm and unmoved. Remember that for two days we had heard evidence to prove that old Dr. Crawford had died leaving his daughter penniless, that having no mother she had been brought up by a maiden aunt, who had trained her to be a governess, which occupation she had followed for years, and that certainly she had never been known by any of her friends to be in possession of solitaire diamond earrings.

"The prosecution had certainly secured an ace of trumps, but Sir James Fenwick, who during the whole of that day had seemed to take little interest in the proceedings, here rose from his seat, and I knew at once that he had got a tit-bit in the way of a 'point' up his sleeve. Gaunt, and unusually tall, and with his beak-like nose, he always looks strangely impressive when he seriously tackles a witness. He did it this time with a vengeance, I can tell you. He was all over the pompous little jeweller in a moment.

"'Had Mr. Campbell made a special entry in his book, as to the visit of the lady in question?'

"'No.'

"'Had he any special means of ascertaining when that visit did actually take place?'

"'No—but—'

"'What record had he of the visit?'

"Mr. Campbell had none. In fact, after about twenty minutes of cross-examination, he had to admit that he had given but little thought to the interview with the lady at the time, and certainly not in connection with the murder of Lady Donaldson, until he had read in the papers that a young lady had been arrested.

"Then he and his clerk talked the matter over, it appears, and together they had certainly recollected that a lady had brought some beautiful earrings for sale on a day which *must have been* the very morning after the murder. If Sir James Fenwick's object was to discredit this special witness, he certainly gained his point.

"All the pomposity went out of Mr. Campbell, he became flurried, then excited, then he lost his temper. After that he was allowed to leave the court, and Sir James Fenwick resumed his seat, and waited like a vulture for its prey.

"It presented itself in the person of Mr. Campbell's clerk, who, before the Procurator Fiscal, had corroborated his employer's evidence in every respect. In Scotland no witness in any one case is present in court during the examination of another, and Mr. Macfarlane, the clerk, was, therefore, quite unprepared for the pitfalls which Sir James Fenwick had prepared for him. He tumbled into them, head foremost, and the eminent advocate turned him inside out like a glove.

"Mr. Macfarlane did not lose his temper; he was of too humble a frame of mind to do that, but he got into a hopeless quagmire of mixed recollections, and he too left the witness-box quite unprepared to swear as to the day of the interview with the lady with the diamond earrings.

"I dare say, mind you," continued the man in the corner with a chuckle, "that to most people present, Sir James Fenwick's cross-questioning seemed completely irrelevant. Both Mr. Campbell and his clerk were quite ready to swear that they had had an interview concerning some diamond earrings with a lady, of whose identity with the accused they were perfectly convinced, and to the casual observer the question as to the time or even the day when that interview took place could make but little difference in the ultimate issue.

"Now I took in, in a moment, the entire drift of Sir James Fenwick's defence of Edith Crawford. When Mr. Macfarlane left the witness-box, the second victim of the eminent advocate's caustic tongue, I could read as in a book the whole history of that crime, its investigation, and the mistakes made by the police first and the Public Prosecutor afterwards.

"Sir James Fenwick knew them, too, of course, and he placed a finger upon each one, demolishing—like a child who blows upon a house of cards—the entire scaffolding erected by the prosecution.

"Mr. Campbell's and Mr. Macfarlane's identification of the accused with the lady who, on some date—admitted to be uncertain—had tried to sell a pair of diamond earrings, was the first point. Sir James had plenty of witnesses to prove that on the 25th, the day after the murder, the accused was in London, whilst, the day before, Mr. Campbell's shop had been closed long before the family circle had seen the last of Lady Donaldson. Clearly the jeweller and his clerk must have seen some other lady, whom their vivid imagination had pictured as being identical with the accused.

"Then came the great question of time. Mr. David Graham had been evidently the last to see Lady Donaldson alive. He had spoken to her as late as 8.30 P.M. Sir James Fenwick had called two porters at the Caledonian Railway Station who testified to Miss Crawford having taken her seat in a first-class carriage of the 9.10 train, some minutes before it started.

"'Was it conceivable, therefore,' argued Sir James, 'that in the space of half an hour the accused—a young girl—could have found her way surreptitiously into the house, at a time when the entire household was still astir, that she should have strangled Lady Donaldson, forced open the safe, and made away with the jewels? A man—an experienced burglar might have done it, but I contend that the accused is physically incapable of accomplishing such a feat.

"'With regard to the broken engagement,' continued the eminent counsel with a smile, 'it may have seemed a little heartless, certainly, but heartlessness is no crime in the eyes of the law. The accused has stated in her declaration that at the time she wrote to Mr. David Graham, breaking off her engagement, she had heard nothing of the Edinburgh tragedy.

"'The London papers had reported the crime very briefly. The accused was busy shopping; she knew nothing of Mr. David Graham's altered position. In no case was the breaking off of the engagement a proof that the accused had obtained possession of the jewels by so foul a deed.'

"It is, of course, impossible for me," continued the man in the corner apologetically, "to give you any idea of the eminent advocate's eloquence and masterful logic. It struck every one, I think, just as it did me, that he chiefly directed his attention to the fact that there was absolutely no *proof* against the accused.

"Be that as it may, the result of that remarkable trial was a verdict of 'Non Proven.' The jury was absent forty minutes, and it appears that in the mind of every one of them there remained, in spite of Sir James' arguments, a firmly rooted conviction—call it instinct, if you like—that Edith Crawford had done away with Lady Donaldson in order to become possessed of those jewels, and that in spite of the pompous jeweller's many contradictions, she had offered him some of those diamonds for sale. But there was not enough proof to convict, and she was given the benefit of the doubt.

"I have heard English people argue that in England she would have been hanged. Personally I doubt that. I think that an English jury, not having the judicial loophole of 'Non Proven,' would have been bound to acquit her. What do you think?"

XVII

Undeniable Facts

There was a moment's silence, for Polly did not reply immediately, and he went on making impossible knots in his bit of string. Then she said quietly—

"I think that I agree with those English people who say that an English jury would have condemned her. . . I have no doubt that she was guilty. She may not have committed that awful deed herself. Some one in the Charlotte Square house may have been her accomplice and killed and robbed Lady Donaldson while Edith Crawford waited outside for the jewels. David Graham left his godmother at 8.30 P.M. If the accomplice was one of the servants in the house, he or she would have had plenty of time for any amount of villainy, and Edith Crawford could have yet caught the 9.10 P.M. train from the Caledonian Station."

"Then who, in your opinion," he asked sarcastically, and cocking his funny birdlike head on one side, "tried to sell diamond earrings to Mr. Campbell, the jeweller?"

"Edith Crawford, of course," she retorted triumphantly; "he and his clerk both recognized her."

"When did she try to sell them the earrings?"

"Ah, that is what I cannot quite make out, and there to my mind lies the only mystery in this case. On the 25th she was certainly in London, and it is not very likely that she would go back to Edinburgh in order to dispose of the jewels there, where they could most easily be traced."

"Not very likely, certainly," he assented drily.

"And," added the young girl, "on the day before she left for London, Lady Donaldson was alive."

"And pray," he said suddenly, as with comic complacency he surveyed a beautiful knot he had just twisted up between his long fingers, "what has that fact got to do with it?"

"But it has everything to do with it!" she retorted.

"Ah, there you go," he sighed with comic emphasis. "My teachings don't seem to have improved your powers of reasoning. You are as bad as the police. Lady Donaldson has been robbed and murdered, and you immediately argue that she was robbed and murdered by the same person."

"But—" argued Polly.

"There is no but," he said, getting more and more excited. "See how simple it is. Edith Crawford wears the diamonds one night, then she brings them back to Lady Donaldson's room. Remember the maid's statement: 'My lady said: "Have you put them back, my dear?"—a simple statement, utterly ignored by the prosecution. But what did it mean? That Lady Donaldson could not see for herself whether Edith Crawford had put back the jewels or not, *since she asked the question*."

"Then you argue—"

"I never argue," he interrupted excitedly; "I state undeniable facts. Edith Crawford, who wanted to steal the jewels, took them then and there, when she had the opportunity. Why in the world should she have waited? Lady Donaldson was in bed, and Tremlett, the maid, had gone.

"The next day—namely, the 25th—she tries to dispose of a pair of earrings to Mr. Campbell; she fails, and decides to go to London, where she has a better chance. Sir James Fenwick did not think it desirable to bring forward witnesses to prove what I have since ascertained is a fact, namely, that on the 27th of October, three days before her arrest, Miss Crawford crossed over to Belgium, and came back to London the next day. In Belgium, no doubt, Lady Donaldson's diamonds, taken out of their settings, calmly repose at this moment, while the money derived from their sale is safely deposited in a Belgian bank."

"But then, who murdered Lady Donaldson, and why?" gasped Polly.

"Cannot you guess?" he queried blandly. "Have I not placed the case clearly enough before you? To me it seems so simple. It was a daring, brutal murder, remember. Think of one who, not being the thief himself, would, nevertheless, have the strongest of all motives to shield the thief from the consequences of her own misdeed: aye! and the power too— since it would be absolutely illogical, nay, impossible, that he should be an accomplice."

"Surely—"

"Think of a curious nature, warped morally, as well as physically—do you know how those natures feel? A thousand times more strongly than the even, straight natures in everyday life. Then think of such a nature brought face to face with this awful problem.

"Do you think that such a nature would hesitate a moment before committing a crime to save the loved one from the consequences of that deed? Mind you, I don't assert for a moment that David Graham had any *intention* of murdering Lady Donaldson. Tremlett tells him that she seems strangely upset; he goes to her room and finds that she has discovered that she has been robbed. She naturally suspects Edith Crawford, recollects the incidents of the other night, and probably expresses her feelings to David Graham, and threatens immediate prosecution, scandal, what you will.

"I repeat it again, I dare say he had no wish to kill her. Probably he merely threatened to. A medical gentleman who spoke of sudden heart failure was no doubt right. Then imagine David Graham's remorse, his horror and his fears. The empty safe probably is the first object that suggested to him the grim tableau of robbery and murder, which he arranges in order to ensure his own safety.

"But remember one thing: no miscreant was seen to enter or leave the house surreptitiously; the murderer left no signs of entrance, and none of exit. An armed burglar would have left some trace—*some one* would have heard *something*. Then who locked and unlocked Lady Donaldson's door that night while she herself lay dead?

"Some one in the house, I tell you—some one who left no trace—some one against whom there could be no suspicion—some one who killed without apparently the slightest premeditation, and without the slightest motive. Think of it—I know I am right—and then tell me if I have at all enlisted your sympathies in the author of the Edinburgh Mystery."

He was gone. Polly looked again at the photo of David Graham. Did a crooked mind really dwell in that crooked body, and were there in the world such crimes that were great enough to be deemed sublime?

XVIII

The Theft at the English Provident Bank

"That question of motive is a very difficult and complicated one at times," said the man in the corner, leisurely pulling off a huge pair of flaming dog-skin gloves from his meagre fingers. "I have known experienced criminal investigators declare, as an infallible axiom, that to find the person interested in the committal of the crime is to find the criminal.

"Well, that may be so in most cases, but my experience has proved to me that there is one factor in this world of ours which is the mainspring of human actions, and that factor is human passions. For good or evil passions rule this poor humanity of ours. Remember, there are the women! French detectives, who are acknowledged masters in their craft, never proceed till after they have discovered the feminine element in a crime; whether in theft, murder, or fraud, according to their theory, there is always a woman.

"Perhaps the reason why the Phillimore Terrace robbery was never brought home to its perpetrators is because there was no woman in any way connected with it, and I am quite sure, on the other hand, that the reason why the thief at the English Provident Bank is still unpunished is because a clever woman has escaped the eyes of our police force."

He had spoken at great length and very dictatorially. Miss Polly Burton did not venture to contradict him, knowing by now that whenever he was irritable he was invariably rude, and she then had the worst of it.

"When I am old," he resumed, "and have nothing more to do, I think I shall take professionally to the police force; they have much to learn."

Could anything be more ludicrous than the self-satisfaction, the abnormal conceit of this remark, made by that shrivelled piece of mankind, in a nervous, hesitating tone of voice? Polly made no comment, but drew from her pocket a beautiful piece of string, and knowing his custom of knotting such an article while unravelling his mysteries, she handed it across the table to him. She positively thought that he blushed.

"As an adjunct to thought," she said, moved by a conciliatory spirit.

He looked at the invaluable toy which the young girl had tantalisingly placed close to his hand: then he forced himself to look all round the coffee-room: at Polly, at the waitresses, at the piles of pallid buns upon the counter. But, involuntarily, his mild blue eyes wandered back lovingly to the long piece of string, on which his playful imagination no doubt already saw a series of knots which would be equally tantalising to tie and to untie.

"Tell me about the theft at the English Provident Bank," suggested Polly condescendingly.

He looked at her, as if she had proposed some mysterious complicity in an unheard-of crime. Finally his lean fingers sought the end of the piece of string, and drew it towards him. His face brightened up in a moment.

"There was an element of tragedy in that particular robbery," he began, after a few moments of beatified knotting, "altogether different to that connected with most crimes; a tragedy which, as far as I am concerned, would seal my lips for ever, and forbid them to utter a word, which might lead the police on the right track."

"Your lips," suggested Polly sarcastically, "are, as far as I can see, usually sealed before our long-suffering, incompetent police and—"

"And you should be the last to grumble at this," he quietly interrupted, "for you have spent some very pleasant half-hours already, listening to what you have termed my 'cock-and-bull' stories. You know the English Provident Bank, of course, in Oxford Street; there were plenty of sketches of it at the time in the illustrated papers. Here is a photo of the outside. I took it myself some time ago, and only wish I had been cheeky or lucky enough to get a snap-shot of the interior. But you see that the office has a separate entrance from the rest of the house, which was, and still is, as is usual in such cases, inhabited by the manager and his family.

"Mr. Ireland was the manager then; it was less than six months ago. He lived over the bank, with his wife and family, consisting of a son, who was clerk in the business, and two or three younger children. The house is really smaller than it looks on this photo, for it has no depth, and only one set of rooms on each floor looking out into the street, the back of the house being nothing but the staircase. Mr. Ireland and his family, therefore, occupied the whole of it.

"As for the business premises, they were, and, in fact, are, of the usual pattern; an office with its rows of desks, clerks, and cashiers, and beyond, through a glass door, the manager's private room, with the ponderous safe, and desk, and so on.

"The private room has a door into the hall of the house, so that the manager is not obliged to go out into the street in order to go to business. There are no living-rooms on the ground floor, and the house has no basement.

"I am obliged to put all these architectural details before you, though they may sound rather dry and uninteresting, but they are really necessary in order to make my argument clear.

"At night, of course, the bank premises are barred and bolted against the street, and as an additional precaution there is always a night watchman in the office. As I mentioned before, there is only a glass door between the office and the manager's private room. This, of course, accounted for the fact that the night watchman heard all that he did hear, on that memorable night, and so helped further to entangle the thread of that impenetrable mystery.

"Mr. Ireland as a rule went into his office every morning a little before ten o'clock, but on that particular morning, for some reason which he never could or would explain, he went down before having his breakfast at about nine o'clock. Mrs. Ireland stated subsequently that, not hearing him return, she sent the servant down to tell the master that breakfast was getting cold. The girl's shrieks were the first intimation that something alarming had occurred.

"Mrs. Ireland hastened downstairs. On reaching the hall she found the door of her husband's room open, and it was from there that the girl's shrieks proceeded.

"'The master, mum—the poor master—he is dead, mum—I am sure he is dead!'—accompanied by vigorous thumps against the glass partition, and not very measured language on the part of the watchman from the outer office, such as—'Why don't you open the door instead of making that row?'

"Mrs. Ireland is not the sort of woman who, under any circumstances, would lose her presence of mind. I think she proved that throughout the many trying circumstances connected with the investigation of the case. She gave only one glance at the room and realized the situation. On the arm-chair, with head thrown back and eyes closed, lay Mr. Ireland, apparently in a dead faint; some terrible shock must have very suddenly shattered his nervous system, and rendered him prostrate for the moment. What that shock had been it was pretty easy to guess.

"The door of the safe was wide open, and Mr. Ireland had evidently tottered and fainted before some awful fact which the open safe had revealed to him; he had caught himself against a chair which lay on the floor, and then finally sunk, unconscious, into the arm-chair.

"All this, which takes some time to describe," continued the man in the corner, "took, remember, only a second to pass like a flash through Mrs. Ireland's mind; she quickly turned the key of the glass door, which was on the inside, and with the help of James Fairbairn, the watchman, she carried her husband upstairs to his room, and immediately sent both for the police and for a doctor.

"As Mrs. Ireland had anticipated, her husband had received a severe mental shock which had completely prostrated him. The doctor prescribed absolute quiet, and forbade all worrying questions for the present. The patient was not a young man; the shock had been very severe—it was a case, a very slight one, of cerebral congestion—and Mr. Ireland's reason, if not his life, might be gravely jeopardised by any attempt to recall before his enfeebled mind the circumstances which had preceded his collapse.

"The police therefore could proceed but slowly in their investigations. The detective who had charge of the case was necessarily handicapped, whilst one of the chief actors concerned in the drama was unable to help him in his work.

"To begin with, the robber or robbers had obviously not found their way into the manager's inner room through the bank premises. James Fairbairn had been on the watch all night, with the electric light full on, and obviously no one could have crossed the outer office or forced the heavily barred doors without his knowledge.

"There remained the other access to the room, that is, the one through the hall of the house. The hall door, it appears, was always barred and bolted by Mr. Ireland himself when he came home, whether from the theatre or his club. It was a duty he never allowed any one to perform but himself. During his annual holiday, with his wife and family, his son, who usually had the sub-manager to stay with him on those occasions, did the bolting and barring—but with the distinct understanding that this should be done by ten o'clock at night.

"As I have already explained to you, there is only a glass partition between the general office and the manager's private room, and, according to James Fairbairn's account, this was naturally always left wide open so that he, during his night watch, would of necessity hear the faintest sound. As a rule there was no light left in the manager's room, and the other door—that leading into the hall—was bolted from the inside by James Fairbairn the moment he had satisfied himself that the premises were safe, and he had begun his night-watch. An electric bell in both the offices communicated with Mr. Ireland's bedroom and that of his son, Mr. Robert Ireland, and there was a telephone installed to the nearest district messengers' office, with an understood signal which meant 'Police.'

"At nine o'clock in the morning it was the night watchman's duty, as soon as the first cashier had arrived, to dust and tidy the manager's room, and to undo the bolts; after that he was free to go home to his breakfast and rest.

"You will see, of course, that James Fairbairn's position in the English Provident Bank is one of great responsibility and trust; but then in every bank and business house there are men who hold similar positions. They are always men of well-known and tried characters, often old soldiers with good-conduct records behind them. James Fairbairn is a fine, powerful Scotchman; he had been night watchman to the English Provident Bank for fifteen years, and was then not more than forty-three or forty-four years old. He is an ex-guardsman, and stands six feet three inches in his socks.

"It was his evidence, of course, which was of such paramount importance, and which somehow or other managed, in spite of the utmost care exercised by the police, to become public property, and to cause the wildest excitement in banking and business circles.

"James Fairbairn stated that at eight o'clock in the evening of March 25th, having bolted and barred all the shutters and the door of the back premises, he was about to lock the manager's door as usual, when Mr. Ireland called to him from the floor above, telling him to leave that door open, as he might want to go into the office again for a minute when he came home at eleven o'clock. James Fairbairn asked if he should leave the light on, but Mr. Ireland said: 'No, turn it out. I can switch it on if I want it.'

"The night watchman at the English Provident Bank has permission to smoke, he also is allowed a nice fire, and a tray consisting of a plate of substantial sandwiches and one glass of ale, which he can take when he likes. James Fairbairn settled himself in front of the fire, lit his pipe, took out his newspaper, and began to read. He thought he had heard the street door open and shut at about a quarter to ten; he supposed that it was Mr. Ireland going out to his club, but at ten minutes to ten o'clock the watchman heard the door of the manager's room open, and some one enter, immediately closing the glass partition door and turning the key.

"He naturally concluded it was Mr. Ireland himself.

"From where he sat he could not see into the room, but he noticed that the electric light had not been switched on, and that the manager seemingly had no light but an occasional match.

"'For the minute,' continued James Fairbairn, 'a thought did just cross my mind that something might perhaps be wrong, and I put my newspaper aside and went to the other end of the room towards the glass partition. The manager's room was still quite dark, and I could not clearly see into it, but the door into the hall was open, and there was, of course, a light through there. I had got quite close to the partition, when I saw Mrs. Ireland standing in the doorway, and heard her saying in a very astonished tone of voice: 'Why, Lewis, I thought you had gone to your club ages ago. What in the world are you doing here in the dark?'

"'Lewis is Mr. Ireland's Christian name,' was James Fairbairn's further statement. 'I did not hear the manager's reply, but quite satisfied now that nothing was wrong, I went back to my pipe and my newspaper. Almost directly afterwards I heard the manager leave his room, cross the hall and go out by the street door. It was only after he had gone that I recollected that he must have forgotten to unlock the glass partition and that I could not therefore bolt the door into the hall the same as usual, and I suppose that is how those confounded thieves got the better of me.'"

XIX

Conflicting Evidence

By the time the public had been able to think over James Fairbairn's evidence, a certain disquietude and unrest had begun to make itself felt both in the bank itself and among those of our detective force who had charge of the case. The newspapers spoke of the matter with very obvious caution, and warned all their readers to await the further development of this sad case.

"While the manager of the English Provident Bank lay in such a precarious condition of health, it was impossible to arrive at any definite knowledge as to what the thief had actually made away with. The chief cashier, however, estimated the loss at about £5000 in gold and notes of the bank money—that was, of course, on the assumption that Mr. Ireland had no private money or valuables of his own in the safe.

"Mind you, at this point public sympathy was much stirred in favour of the poor man who lay ill, perhaps dying, and yet whom, strangely enough, suspicion had already slightly touched with its poisoned wing.

"Suspicion is a strong word, perhaps, to use at this point in the story. No one suspected anybody at present. James Fairbairn had told his story, and had vowed that some thief with false keys must have sneaked through the house into the inner office.

"Public excitement, you will remember, lost nothing by waiting. Hardly had we all had time to wonder over the night watchman's singular evidence, and, pending further and fuller detail, to check our growing sympathy for the man who was ill, than the sensational side of this mysterious case culminated in one extraordinary, absolutely unexpected fact. Mrs. Ireland, after a twenty-four hours' untiring watch beside her husband's sick bed, had at last been approached by the detective, and been asked to reply to a few simple questions, and thus help to throw some light on the mystery which had caused Mr. Ireland's illness and her own consequent anxiety.

"She professed herself quite ready to reply to any questions put to her, and she literally astounded both inspector and detective when she firmly and emphatically declared that James Fairbairn must have been dreaming or asleep when he thought he saw her in the doorway at ten o'clock that night, and fancied he heard her voice.

"She may or may not have been down in the hall at that particular hour, for she usually ran down herself to see if the last post had brought any letters, but most certainly she had neither seen nor spoken to Mr. Ireland at that hour, for Mr. Ireland had gone out an hour before, she herself having seen him to the front door. Never for a moment did she swerve from this extraordinary statement. She spoke to James Fairbairn in the presence of the detective, and told him he *must* absolutely have been mistaken, that she had *not* seen Mr. Ireland, and that she had *not* spoken to him.

"One other person was questioned by the police, and that was Mr. Robert Ireland, the manager's eldest son. It was presumed that he would know something of his father's affairs; the idea having now taken firm hold of the detective's mind that perhaps grave financial difficulties had tempted the unfortunate manager to appropriate some of the firm's money.

"Mr. Robert Ireland, however, could not say very much. His father did not confide in him to the extent of telling him all his private affairs, but money never seemed scarce at home certainly, and Mr. Ireland had, to his son's knowledge, not a single extravagant habit. He himself had been dining out with a friend on that memorable evening, and had gone on with him to the Oxford Music Hall. He met his father on the doorstep of the bank at about 11.30 P.M. and they went in together. There certainly was nothing remarkable about Mr. Ireland then, his son averred; he appeared in no way excited, and bade his son good night quite cheerfully.

"There was the extraordinary, the remarkable hitch," continued the man in the corner, waxing more and more excited every moment. "The public—who is at times very dense—saw it clearly nevertheless: of course, every one at once jumped to the natural conclusion that Mrs. Ireland was telling a lie—a noble lie, a self-sacrificing lie, a lie endowed with all the virtues if you like, but still a lie.

"She was trying to save her husband, and was going the wrong way to work. James Fairbairn, after all, could not have dreamt quite all that he declared he had seen and heard. No one suspected James Fairbairn; there was no occasion to do that; to begin with he was a great heavy Scotchman with obviously no powers of invention, such as Mrs. Ireland's strange assertion credited him with; moreover, the theft of the bank-notes could not have been of the slightest use to him.

"But, remember, there was the hitch; without it the public mind would already have condemned the sick man upstairs, without hope of rehabilitation. This fact struck every one.

"Granting that Mr. Ireland had gone into his office at ten minutes to ten o'clock at night for the purpose of extracting £5000 worth of notes and gold from the bank safe, whilst giving the theft the appearance of a night burglary; granting that he was disturbed in his nefarious project by his wife, who, failing to persuade him to make restitution, took his side boldly, and very clumsily attempted to rescue him out of his difficult position—why should he, at nine o'clock the following morning, fall in a dead faint and get cerebral congestion at sight of a defalcation he knew had occurred? One might simulate a fainting fit, but no one can assume a high temperature and a congestion, which the most ordinary practitioner who happened to be called in would soon see were non-existent.

"Mr. Ireland, according to James Fairbairn's evidence, must have gone out soon after the theft, come in again with his son an hour and a half later, talked to him, gone quietly to bed, and waited for nine hours before he fell ill at sight of his own crime. It was not logical, you will admit. Unfortunately, the poor man himself was unable to give any explanation of the night's tragic adventures.

"He was still very weak, and though under strong suspicion, he was left, by the doctor's orders, in absolute ignorance of the heavy charges which were gradually accumulating against him. He had made many anxious inquiries from all those who had access to his bedside as to the result of the investigation, and the probable speedy capture of the burglars, but every one had strict orders to inform him merely that the police so far had no clue of any kind.

"You will admit, as every one did, that there was something very pathetic about the unfortunate man's position, so helpless to defend himself, if defence there was, against so much overwhelming evidence. That is why I think public sympathy remained with him. Still, it was terrible to think of his wife presumably knowing him to be guilty, and anxiously waiting whilst dreading the moment when, restored to health, he would have to face the doubts, the suspicions, probably the open accusations, which were fast rising up around him."

XX

An *Alibi*

I t was close on six weeks before the doctor at last allowed his patient to attend to the grave business which had prostrated him for so long.

"In the meantime, among the many people who directly or indirectly were made to suffer in this mysterious affair, no one, I think, was more pitied, and more genuinely sympathised with, than Robert Ireland, the manager's eldest son.

"You remember that he had been clerk in the bank? Well, naturally, the moment suspicion began to fasten on his father his position in the business became untenable. I think every one was very kind to him. Mr. Sutherland French, who was made acting manager 'during Mr. Lewis Ireland's regrettable absence,' did everything in his power to show his goodwill and sympathy to the young man, but I don't think that he or any one else was much astonished when, after Mrs. Ireland's extraordinary attitude in the case had become public property, he quietly intimated to the acting manager that he had determined to sever his connection with the bank.

"The best of recommendations was, of course, placed at his disposal, and it was finally understood that, as soon as his father was completely restored to health and would no longer require his presence in London, he would try to obtain employment somewhere abroad. He spoke of the new volunteer corps organized for the military policing of the new colonies, and, truth to tell, no one could blame him that he should wish to leave far behind him all London banking connections. The son's attitude certainly did not tend to ameliorate the father's position. It was pretty evident that his own family had ceased to hope in the poor manager's innocence.

"And yet he was absolutely innocent. You must remember how that fact was clearly demonstrated as soon as the poor man was able to say a word for himself. And he said it to some purpose, too.

"Mr. Ireland was, and is, very fond of music. On the evening in question, while sitting in his club, he saw in one of the daily papers the announcement of a peculiarly attractive programme at the Queen's Hall concert. He was not dressed, but nevertheless felt an irresistible desire to hear one or two of these attractive musical items, and he strolled down to the Hall. Now, this sort of alibi is usually very difficult to prove, but Dame Fortune, oddly enough, favoured Mr. Ireland on this occasion, probably to compensate him for the hard knocks she had been dealing him pretty freely of late.

"It appears that there was some difficulty about his seat, which was sold to him at the box office, and which he, nevertheless, found wrongfully occupied by a determined lady, who refused to move. The management had to be appealed to; the attendants also remembered not only the incident, but also the face and appearance of the gentleman who was the innocent cause of the altercation.

"As soon as Mr. Ireland could speak for himself he mentioned the incident and the persons who had been witness to it. He was identified by them, to the amazement, it must be confessed, of police and public alike, who had comfortably decided that no one *could* be guilty save the manager of the Provident Bank himself. Moreover, Mr. Ireland was a fairly wealthy man, with a good balance at the Union Bank, and plenty of private means, the result of years of provident living.

"He had but to prove that if he really had been in need of an immediate £5000—which was all the amount extracted from the bank safe that night—he had plenty of securities on which he could, at an hour's notice, have raised twice that sum. His life insurances had been fully paid up; he had not a debt which a £5 note could not easily have covered.

"On the fatal night he certainly did remember asking the watchman not to bolt the door to his office, as he thought he might have one or two letters to write when he came home, but later on he had forgotten all about this. After the concert he met his son in Oxford Street, just outside the house, and thought no more about the office, the door of which was shut, and presented no unusual appearance.

"Mr. Ireland absolutely denied having been in his office at the hour when James Fairbairn positively asserted he heard Mrs. Ireland say in an astonished tone of voice: 'Why, Lewis, what in the world are you doing here?' It became pretty clear therefore that James Fairbairn's view of the manager's wife had been a mere vision.

"Mr. Ireland gave up his position as manager of the English Provident: both he and his wife felt no doubt that on the whole, perhaps, there had been too much talk, too much scandal connected with their name, to be altogether advantageous to the bank. Moreover, Mr. Ireland's health was not so good as it had been. He has a pretty house now at Sittingbourne, and amuses himself during his leisure hours with amateur horticulture, and I, who alone in London besides the persons directly connected with this mysterious affair, know the true solution of the enigma, often wonder how much of it is known to the ex-manager of the English Provident Bank."

The man in the corner had been silent for some time. Miss Polly Burton, in her presumption, had made up her mind, at the commencement of his tale, to listen attentively to every point of the evidence in connection with the case which he recapitulated before her, and to follow the point, in order to try and arrive at a conclusion of her own, and overwhelm the antediluvian scarecrow with her sagacity.

She said nothing, for she had arrived at no conclusion; the case puzzled every one, and had amazed the public in its various stages, from the moment when opinion began to cast doubt on Mr. Ireland's honesty to that when his integrity was proved beyond a doubt. One or two people had suspected Mrs. Ireland to have been the actual thief, but that idea had soon to be abandoned.

Mrs. Ireland had all the money she wanted; the theft occurred six months ago, and not a single bank-note was ever traced to her pocket; moreover, she must have had an accomplice, since some one else was in the manager's room that night; and if that some one else was her accomplice, why did she risk betraying him by speaking loudly in the presence of James Fairbairn, when it would have been so much simpler to turn out the light and plunge the hall into darkness?

"You are altogether on the wrong track," sounded a sharp voice in direct answer to Polly's thoughts—"altogether wrong. If you want to acquire my method of induction, and improve your reasoning power, you must follow my system. First think of the one absolutely undisputed, positive fact. You must have a starting-point, and not go wandering about in the realms of suppositions."

"But there are no positive facts," she said irritably.

"You don't say so?" he said quietly. "Do you not call it a positive fact that the bank safe was robbed of £5000 on the evening of March 25th before 11.30 P.M."

"Yes, that is all which is positive and—"

"Do you not call it a positive fact," he interrupted quietly, "that the lock of the safe not being picked, it must have been opened by its own key?"

"I know that," she rejoined crossly, "and that is why every one agreed that James Fairbairn could not possibly—"

"And do you not call it a positive fact, then, that James Fairbairn could not possibly, etc., etc., seeing that the glass partition door was locked from the inside; Mrs. Ireland herself let James Fairbairn into her husband's office when she saw him lying fainting before the open safe. Of course that was a positive fact, and so was the one that proved to any thinking mind that if that safe was opened with a key, it could only have been done by a person having access to that key."

"But the man in the private office—"

"Exactly! the man in the private office. Enumerate his points, if you please," said the funny creature, marking each point with one of his favourite knots. "He was a man who might that night have had access to the key of the safe, unsuspected by the manager or even his wife, and a man for whom Mrs. Ireland was willing to tell a downright lie. Are there many men for whom a woman of the better middle class, and an Englishwoman, would be ready to perjure herself? Surely not! She might do it for her husband. The public thought she had. It never struck them that she might have done it for her son!"

"Her son!" exclaimed Polly.

"Ah! she was a clever woman," he exclaimed enthusiastically, "one with courage and presence of mind, which I don't think I have ever seen equalled. She runs downstairs before going to bed in order to see whether the last post has brought any letters. She sees the door of her husband's office ajar, she pushes it open, and there, by the sudden flash of a hastily struck match she realizes in a moment that a thief stands before the open safe, and in that thief she has already recognized her son. At that very moment she hears the watchman's step approaching the partition. There is no time to warn her son; she does not know the glass door is locked; James Fairbairn may switch on the electric light and see the young man in the very act of robbing his employers' safe.

"One thing alone can reassure the watchman. One person alone had the right to be there at that hour of the night, and without hesitation she pronounces her husband's name.

"Mind you, I firmly believe that at the time the poor woman only wished to gain time, that she had every hope that her son had not yet had the opportunity to lay so heavy a guilt upon his conscience.

"What passed between mother and son we shall never know, but this much we do know, that the young villain made off with his booty, and trusted that his mother would never betray him. Poor woman! what a night of it she must have spent; but she was clever and far-seeing. She knew that her husband's character could not suffer through her action. Accordingly, she took the only course open to her to save her son even from his father's wrath, and boldly denied James Fairbairn's statement.

"Of course, she was fully aware that her husband could easily clear himself, and the worst that could be said of her was that she had thought him guilty and had tried to save him. She trusted to the future to clear her of any charge of complicity in the theft.

"By now every one has forgotten most of the circumstances; the police are still watching the career of James Fairbairn and Mrs. Ireland's expenditure. As you know, not a single note, so far, has been traced to her. Against that, one or two of the notes have found their way back to England. No one realizes how easy it is to cash English bank-notes at the smaller *agents de change* abroad. The *changeurs* are only too glad to get them; what do they care where they come from as long as they are genuine? And a week or two later *M. le Changeur* could not swear who tendered him any one particular note.

"You see, young Robert Ireland went abroad, he will come back some day having made a fortune. There's his photo. And this is his mother—a clever woman, wasn't she?"

And before Polly had time to reply he was gone. She really had never seen any one move across a room so quickly. But he always left an interesting trail behind: a piece of string knotted from end to end and a few photos.

XXI

THE DUBLIN MYSTERY

I always thought that the history of that forged will was about as interesting as any I had read," said the man in the corner that day. He had been silent for some time, and was meditatively sorting and looking through a packet of small photographs in his pocket-book. Polly guessed that some of these would presently be placed before her for inspection—and she had not long to wait.

"That is old Brooks," he said, pointing to one of the photographs, "Millionaire Brooks, as he was called, and these are his two sons, Percival and Murray. It was a curious case, wasn't it? Personally I don't wonder that the police were completely at sea. If a member of that highly estimable force happened to be as clever as the clever author of that forged will, we should have very few undetected crimes in this country."

"That is why I always try to persuade you to give our poor ignorant police the benefit of your great insight and wisdom," said Polly, with a smile.

"I know," he said blandly, "you have been most kind in that way, but I am only an amateur. Crime interests me only when it resembles a clever game of chess, with many intricate moves which all tend to one solution, the checkmating of the antagonist—the detective force of the country. Now, confess that, in the Dublin mystery, the clever police there were absolutely checkmated."

"Absolutely."

"Just as the public was. There were actually two crimes committed in one city which have completely baffled detection: the murder of Patrick Wethered the lawyer, and the forged will of Millionaire Brooks. There are not many millionaires in Ireland; no wonder old Brooks was a notability in his way, since his business—bacon curing, I believe it is—is said to be worth over £2,000,000 of solid money.

"His younger son Murray was a refined, highly educated man, and was, moreover, the apple of his father's eye, as he was the spoilt darling of Dublin society; good-looking, a splendid dancer, and a perfect rider, he was the acknowledged 'catch' of the matrimonial market of

Ireland, and many a very aristocratic house was opened hospitably to the favourite son of the millionaire.

"Of course, Percival Brooks, the eldest son, would inherit the bulk of the old man's property and also probably the larger share in the business; he, too, was good-looking, more so than his brother; he, too, rode, danced, and talked well, but it was many years ago that mammas with marriageable daughters had given up all hopes of Percival Brooks as a probable son-in-law. That young man's infatuation for Maisie Fortescue, a lady of undoubted charm but very doubtful antecedents, who had astonished the London and Dublin music-halls with her extravagant dances, was too well known and too old-established to encourage any hopes in other quarters.

"Whether Percival Brooks would ever marry Maisie Fortescue was thought to be very doubtful. Old Brooks had the full disposal of all his wealth, and it would have fared ill with Percival if he introduced an undesirable wife into the magnificent Fitzwilliam Place establishment.

"That is how matters stood," continued the man in the corner, "when Dublin society one morning learnt, with deep regret and dismay, that old Brooks had died very suddenly at his residence after only a few hours' illness. At first it was generally understood that he had had an apoplectic stroke; anyway, he had been at business hale and hearty as ever the day before his death, which occurred late on the evening of February 1st.

"It was the morning papers of February 2nd which told the sad news to their readers, and it was those selfsame papers which on that eventful morning contained another even more startling piece of news, that proved the prelude to a series of sensations such as tranquil, placid Dublin had not experienced for many years. This was, that on that very afternoon which saw the death of Dublin's greatest millionaire, Mr. Patrick Wethered, his solicitor, was murdered in Phoenix Park at five o'clock in the afternoon while actually walking to his own house from his visit to his client in Fitzwilliam Place.

"Patrick Wethered was as well known as the proverbial town pump; his mysterious and tragic death filled all Dublin with dismay. The lawyer, who was a man sixty years of age, had been struck on the back of the head by a heavy stick, garrotted, and subsequently robbed, for neither money, watch, or pocket-book were found upon his person, whilst the police soon gathered from Patrick Wethered's household that he had left home at two o'clock that afternoon, carrying both watch and pocket-book, and undoubtedly money as well.

"An inquest was held, and a verdict of wilful murder was found against some person or persons unknown.

"But Dublin had not exhausted its stock of sensations yet. Millionaire Brooks had been buried with due pomp and magnificence, and his will had been proved (his business and personalty being estimated at £2,500,000) by Percival Gordon Brooks, his eldest son and sole executor. The younger son, Murray, who had devoted the best years of his life to being a friend and companion to his father, while Percival ran after ballet-dancers and music-hall stars—Murray, who had avowedly been the apple of his father's eye in consequence—was left with a miserly pittance of £300 a year, and no share whatever in the gigantic business of Brooks & Sons, bacon curers, of Dublin.

"Something had evidently happened within the precincts of the Brooks' town mansion, which the public and Dublin society tried in vain to fathom. Elderly mammas and blushing *débutantes* were already thinking of the best means whereby next season they might more easily show the cold shoulder to young Murray Brooks, who had so suddenly become a hopeless 'detrimental' in the marriage market, when all these sensations terminated in one gigantic, overwhelming bit of scandal, which for the next three months furnished food for gossip in every drawing-room in Dublin.

"Mr. Murray Brooks, namely, had entered a claim for probate of a will, made by his father in 1891, declaring that the later will made the very day of his father's death and proved by his brother as sole executor, was null and void, that will being a forgery."

XXII

Forgery

The facts that transpired in connection with this extraordinary case were sufficiently mysterious to puzzle everybody. As I told you before, all Mr. Brooks' friends never quite grasped the idea that the old man should so completely have cut off his favourite son with the proverbial shilling.

"You see, Percival had always been a thorn in the old man's flesh. Horse-racing, gambling, theatres, and music-halls were, in the old pork-butcher's eyes, so many deadly sins which his son committed every day of his life, and all the Fitzwilliam Place household could testify to the many and bitter quarrels which had arisen between father and son over the latter's gambling or racing debts. Many people asserted that Brooks would sooner have left his money to charitable institutions than seen it squandered upon the brightest stars that adorned the music-hall stage.

"The case came up for hearing early in the autumn. In the meanwhile Percival Brooks had given up his racecourse associates, settled down in the Fitzwilliam Place mansion, and conducted his father's business, without a manager, but with all the energy and forethought which he had previously devoted to more unworthy causes.

"Murray had elected not to stay on in the old house; no doubt associations were of too painful and recent a nature; he was boarding with the family of a Mr. Wilson Hibbert, who was the late Patrick Wethered's, the murdered lawyer's, partner. They were quiet, homely people, who lived in a very pokey little house in Kilkenny Street, and poor Murray must, in spite of his grief, have felt very bitterly the change from his luxurious quarters in his father's mansion to his present tiny room and homely meals.

"Percival Brooks, who was now drawing an income of over a hundred thousand a year, was very severely criticised for adhering so strictly to the letter of his father's will, and only paying his brother that paltry £300 a year, which was very literally but the crumbs off his own magnificent dinner table.

"The issue of that contested will case was therefore awaited with eager interest. In the meanwhile the police, who had at first seemed fairly loquacious on the subject of the murder of Mr. Patrick Wethered, suddenly became strangely reticent, and by their very reticence aroused a certain amount of uneasiness in the public mind, until one day the *Irish Times* published the following extraordinary, enigmatic paragraph:

"'We hear on authority which cannot be questioned, that certain extraordinary developments are expected in connection with the brutal murder of our distinguished townsman Mr. Wethered; the police, in fact, are vainly trying to keep it secret that they hold a clue which is as important as it is sensational, and that they only await the impending issue of a well-known litigation in the probate court to effect an arrest.'

"The Dublin public flocked to the court to hear the arguments in the great will case. I myself journeyed down to Dublin. As soon as I succeeded in fighting my way to the densely crowded court, I took stock of the various actors in the drama, which I as a spectator was prepared to enjoy. There were Percival Brooks and Murray his brother, the two litigants, both good-looking and well dressed, and both striving, by keeping up a running conversation with their lawyer, to appear unconcerned and confident of the issue. With Percival Brooks was Henry Oranmore, the eminent Irish K.C., whilst Walter Hibbert, a rising young barrister, the son of Wilson Hibbert, appeared for Murray.

"The will of which the latter claimed probate was one dated 1891, and had been made by Mr. Brooks during a severe illness which threatened to end his days. This will had been deposited in the hands of Messrs. Wethered and Hibbert, solicitors to the deceased, and by it Mr. Brooks left his personalty equally divided between his two sons, but had left his business entirely to his youngest son, with a charge of £2000 a year upon it, payable to Percival. You see that Murray Brooks therefore had a very deep interest in that second will being found null and void.

"Old Mr. Hibbert had very ably instructed his son, and Walter Hibbert's opening speech was exceedingly clever. He would show, he said, on behalf of his client, that the will dated February 1st, 1908, could never have been made by the late Mr. Brooks, as it was absolutely contrary to his avowed intentions, and that if the late Mr. Brooks did on the day in question make any fresh will at all, it certainly was *not* the one proved by Mr. Percival Brooks, for that was absolutely a forgery from beginning to end. Mr. Walter Hibbert proposed to call several witnesses in support of both these points.

"On the other hand, Mr. Henry Oranmore, K.C., very ably and courteously replied that he too had several witnesses to prove that

Mr. Brooks certainly did make a will on the day in question, and that, whatever his intentions may have been in the past, he must have modified them on the day of his death, for the will proved by Mr. Percival Brooks was found after his death under his pillow, duly signed and witnessed and in every way legal.

"Then the battle began in sober earnest. There were a great many witnesses to be called on both sides, their evidence being of more or less importance—chiefly less. But the interest centred round the prosaic figure of John O'Neill, the butler at Fitzwilliam Place, who had been in Mr. Brooks' family for thirty years.

"'I was clearing away my breakfast things,' said John, 'when I heard the master's voice in the study close by. Oh my, he was that angry! I could hear the words "disgrace," and "villain," and "liar," and "ballet-dancer," and one or two other ugly words as applied to some female lady, which I would not like to repeat. At first I did not take much notice, as I was quite used to hearing my poor dear master having words with Mr. Percival. So I went downstairs carrying my breakfast things; but I had just started cleaning my silver when the study bell goes ringing violently, and I hear Mr. Percival's voice shouting in the hall: "John! quick! Send for Dr. Mulligan at once. Your master is not well! Send one of the men, and you come up and help me to get Mr. Brooks to bed."

"'I sent one of the grooms for the doctor,' continued John, who seemed still affected at the recollection of his poor master, to whom he had evidently been very much attached, 'and I went up to see Mr. Brooks. I found him lying on the study floor, his head supported in Mr. Percival's arms. "My father has fallen in a faint," said the young master; "help me to get him up to his room before Dr. Mulligan comes."

"'Mr. Percival looked very white and upset, which was only natural; and when we had got my poor master to bed, I asked if I should not go and break the news to Mr. Murray, who had gone to business an hour ago. However, before Mr. Percival had time to give me an order the doctor came. I thought I had seen death plainly writ in my master's face, and when I showed the doctor out an hour later, and he told me that he would be back directly, I knew that the end was near.

"'Mr. Brooks rang for me a minute or two later. He told me to send at once for Mr. Wethered, or else for Mr. Hibbert, if Mr. Wethered could not come. "I haven't many hours to live, John," he says to me—"my heart is broke, the doctor says my heart is broke. A man shouldn't marry and have children, John, for they will sooner or later break his heart." I was so upset I couldn't speak; but I sent round at once for Mr. Wethered, who came himself just about three o'clock that afternoon.

"'After he had been with my master about an hour I was called in, and Mr. Wethered said to me that Mr. Brooks wished me and one other of us servants to witness that he had signed a paper which was on a table by his bedside. I called Pat Mooney, the head footman, and before us both Mr. Brooks put his name at the bottom of that paper. Then Mr. Wethered give me the pen and told me to write my name as a witness, and that Pat Mooney was to do the same. After that we were both told that we could go.'

"The old butler went on to explain that he was present in his late master's room on the following day when the undertakers, who had come to lay the dead man out, found a paper underneath his pillow. John O'Neill, who recognized the paper as the one to which he had appended his signature the day before, took it to Mr. Percival, and gave it into his hands.

"In answer to Mr. Walter Hibbert, John asserted positively that he took the paper from the undertaker's hand and went straight with it to Mr. Percival's room.

"'He was alone,' said John; 'I gave him the paper. He just glanced at it, and I thought he looked rather astonished, but he said nothing, and I at once left the room.'

"'When you say that you recognized the paper as the one which you had seen your master sign the day before, how did you actually recognize that it was the same paper?' asked Mr. Hibbert amidst breathless interest on the part of the spectators. I narrowly observed the witness's face.

"'It looked exactly the same paper to me, sir,' replied John, somewhat vaguely.

"'Did you look at the contents, then?'

"'No, sir; certainly not.'

"'Had you done so the day before?'

"'No, sir, only at my master's signature.'

"'Then you only thought by the *outside* look of the paper that it was the same?'

"'It looked the same thing, sir,' persisted John obstinately.

"You see," continued the man in the corner, leaning eagerly forward across the narrow marble table, "the contention of Murray Brooks' adviser was that Mr. Brooks, having made a will and hidden it—for some reason or other under his pillow—that will had fallen, through the means related by John O'Neill, into the hands of Mr. Percival Brooks, who had destroyed it and substituted a forged one in its place, which adjudged the whole of Mr. Brooks' millions to himself. It was a terrible and very daring accusation directed against a gentleman who, in spite of his many wild oats sowed in early youth, was a prominent and important figure in Irish high life.

"All those present were aghast at what they heard, and the whispered comments I could hear around me showed me that public opinion, at least, did not uphold Mr. Murray Brooks' daring accusation against his brother.

"But John O'Neill had not finished his evidence, and Mr. Walter Hibbert had a bit of sensation still up his sleeve. He had, namely, produced a paper, the will proved by Mr. Percival Brooks, and had asked John O'Neill if once again he recognized the paper.

"'Certainly, sir,' said John unhesitatingly, 'that is the one the undertaker found under my poor dead master's pillow, and which I took to Mr. Percival's room immediately.'

"Then the paper was unfolded and placed before the witness.

"'Now, Mr. O'Neill, will you tell me if that is your signature?'

"John looked at it for a moment; then he said: 'Excuse me, sir,' and produced a pair of spectacles which he carefully adjusted before he again examined the paper. Then he thoughtfully shook his head.

"'It don't look much like my writing, sir,' he said at last. 'That is to say,' he added, by way of elucidating the matter, 'it does look like my writing, but then I don't think it is.'

"There was at that moment a look in Mr. Percival Brooks' face," continued the man in the corner quietly, "which then and there gave me the whole history of that quarrel, that illness of Mr. Brooks, of the will, aye! and of the murder of Patrick Wethered too.

"All I wondered at was how every one of those learned counsel on both sides did not get the clue just the same as I did, but went on arguing, speechifying, cross-examining for nearly a week, until they arrived at the one conclusion which was inevitable from the very first, namely, that the will *was* a forgery—a gross, clumsy, idiotic forgery, since both John O'Neill and Pat Mooney, the two witnesses, absolutely repudiated the signatures as their own. The only successful bit of caligraphy the forger had done was the signature of old Mr. Brooks.

"It was a very curious fact, and one which had undoubtedly aided the forger in accomplishing his work quickly, that Mr. Wethered the lawyer having, no doubt, realized that Mr. Brooks had not many moments in life to spare, had not drawn up the usual engrossed, magnificent document dear to the lawyer heart, but had used for his client's will one of those regular printed forms which can be purchased at any stationer's.

"Mr. Percival Brooks, of course, flatly denied the serious allegation brought against him. He admitted that the butler had brought him the document the morning after his father's death, and that he certainly, on glancing at it, had been very much astonished to see that that document was his father's will. Against that he declared that its contents did not astonish him in the slightest degree, that he himself knew of the testator's intentions, but that he certainly thought his father had entrusted the will to the care of Mr. Wethered, who did all his business for him.

"'I only very cursorily glanced at the signature,' he concluded, speaking in a perfectly calm, clear voice; 'you must understand that the thought of forgery was very far from my mind, and that my father's signature is exceedingly well imitated, if, indeed, it is not his own, which I am not at all prepared to believe. As for the two witnesses' signatures, I don't think I had ever seen them before. I took the document to Messrs. Barkston and Maud, who had often done business for me before, and they assured me that the will was in perfect form and order.'

"Asked why he had not entrusted the will to his father's solicitors, he replied:

"'For the very simple reason that exactly half an hour before the will was placed in my hands, I had read that Mr. Patrick Wethered had been murdered the night before. Mr. Hibbert, the junior partner, was not personally known to me.'

"After that, for form's sake, a good deal of expert evidence was heard on the subject of the dead man's signature. But that was quite unanimous, and merely went to corroborate what had already been established beyond a doubt, namely, that the will dated February 1st, 1908, was a forgery, and probate of the will dated 1891 was therefore granted to Mr. Murray Brooks, the sole executor mentioned therein."

XXIII

A Memorable Day

Two days later the police applied for a warrant for the arrest of Mr. Percival Brooks on a charge of forgery.

"The Crown prosecuted, and Mr. Brooks had again the support of Mr. Oranmore, the eminent K.C. Perfectly calm, like a man conscious of his own innocence and unable to grasp the idea that justice does sometimes miscarry, Mr. Brooks, the son of the millionaire, himself still the possessor of a very large fortune under the former will, stood up in the dock on that memorable day in October, 1908, which still no doubt lives in the memory of his many friends.

"All the evidence with regard to Mr. Brooks' last moments and the forged will was gone through over again. That will, it was the contention of the Crown, had been forged so entirely in favour of the accused, cutting out every one else, that obviously no one but the beneficiary under that false will would have had any motive in forging it.

"Very pale, and with a frown between his deep-set, handsome Irish eyes, Percival Brooks listened to this large volume of evidence piled up against him by the Crown.

"At times he held brief consultations with Mr. Oranmore, who seemed as cool as a cucumber. Have you ever seen Oranmore in court? He is a character worthy of Dickens. His pronounced brogue, his fat, podgy, clean-shaven face, his not always immaculately clean large hands, have often delighted the caricaturist. As it very soon transpired during that memorable magisterial inquiry, he relied for a verdict in favour of his client upon two main points, and he had concentrated all his skill upon making these two points as telling as he possibly could.

"The first point was the question of time, John O'Neill, cross-examined by Oranmore, stated without hesitation that he had given the will to Mr. Percival at eleven o'clock in the morning. And now the eminent K.C. brought forward and placed in the witness-box the very lawyers into whose hands the accused had then immediately placed the will. Now, Mr. Barkston, a very well-known solicitor of King Street, declared positively that Mr. Percival Brooks was in his office at a quarter before twelve; two of his clerks testified to the same time exactly, and it was *impossible*, contended Mr. Oranmore, that within three-quarters of an hour Mr. Brooks could have gone to a stationer's, bought a will form, copied Mr. Wethered's writing, his father's signature, and that of John O'Neill and Pat Mooney.

"Such a thing might have been planned, arranged, practised, and ultimately, after a great deal of trouble, successfully carried out, but human intelligence could not grasp the other as a possibility.

"Still the judge wavered. The eminent K.C. had shaken but not shattered his belief in the prisoner's guilt. But there was one point more, and this Oranmore, with the skill of a dramatist, had reserved for the fall of the curtain.

"He noted every sign in the judge's face, he guessed that his client was not yet absolutely safe, then only did he produce his last two witnesses.

"One of them was Mary Sullivan, one of the housemaids in the Fitzwilliam mansion. She had been sent up by the cook at a quarter past four o'clock on the afternoon of February 1st with some hot water, which the nurse had ordered, for the master's room. Just as she was about to knock at the door Mr. Wethered was coming out of the room. Mary stopped with the tray in her hand, and at the door Mr. Wethered turned and said quite loudly: 'Now, don't fret, don't be anxious; do try and be calm. Your will is safe in my pocket, nothing can change it or alter one word of it but yourself.'

"It was, of course, a very ticklish point in law whether the housemaid's evidence could be accepted. You see, she was quoting the words of a man since dead, spoken to another man also dead. There is no doubt that had there been very strong evidence on the other side against Percival Brooks, Mary Sullivan's would have counted for nothing; but, as I told you before, the judge's belief in the prisoner's guilt was already very seriously shaken, and now the final blow aimed at it by Mr. Oranmore shattered his last lingering doubts.

"Dr. Mulligan, namely, had been placed by Mr. Oranmore into the witness-box. He was a medical man of unimpeachable authority, in fact, absolutely at the head of his profession in Dublin. What he said practically corroborated Mary Sullivan's testimony. He had gone in to see Mr. Brooks at half-past four, and understood from him that his lawyer had just left him.

"Mr. Brooks certainly, though terribly weak, was calm and more composed. He was dying from a sudden heart attack, and Dr. Mulligan foresaw the almost immediate end. But he was still conscious and managed to murmur feebly: 'I feel much easier in my mind now, doctor—have made my will—Wethered has been—he's got it in his pocket—it is safe there—safe from that—' But the words died on his lips, and after that he spoke but little. He saw his two sons before he died, but hardly knew them or even looked at them.

"You see," concluded the man in the corner, "you see that the prosecution was bound to collapse. Oranmore did not give it a leg to stand on. The will was forged, it is true, forged in the favour of Percival Brooks and of no one else, forged for him and for his benefit. Whether he knew and connived at the forgery was never proved or, as far as I know, even hinted, but it was impossible to go against all the evidence, which pointed that, as far as the act itself was concerned, he at least was innocent. You see, Dr. Mulligan's evidence was not to be shaken. Mary Sullivan's was equally strong.

"There were two witnesses swearing positively that old Brooks' will was in Mr. Wethered's keeping when that gentleman left the Fitzwilliam mansion at a quarter past four. At five o'clock in the afternoon the lawyer was found dead in Phoenix Park. Between a quarter past four and eight o'clock in the evening Percival Brooks never left the house— that was subsequently proved by Oranmore up to the hilt and beyond a doubt. Since the will found under old Brooks' pillow was a forged will, where then was the will he did make, and which Wethered carried away with him in his pocket?"

"Stolen, of course," said Polly, "by those who murdered and robbed him; it may have been of no value to them, but they naturally would destroy it, lest it might prove a clue against them."

"Then you think it was mere coincidence?" he asked excitedly.

"What?"

"That Wethered was murdered and robbed at the very moment that he carried the will in his pocket, whilst another was being forged in its place?"

"It certainly would be very curious, if it *were* a coincidence," she said musingly.

"Very," he repeated with biting sarcasm, whilst nervously his bony fingers played with the inevitable bit of string. "Very curious indeed. Just think of the whole thing. There was the old man with all his wealth, and two sons, one to whom he is devoted, and the other with whom he does nothing but quarrel. One day there is another of these quarrels, but more violent, more terrible than any that have previously occurred, with the result that the father, heartbroken by it all, has an attack of apoplexy and practically dies of a broken heart. After that he alters his will, and subsequently a will is proved which turns out to be a forgery.

"Now everybody—police, press, and public alike—at once jump to the conclusion that, as Percival Brooks benefits by that forged will, Percival Brooks must be the forger."

"Seek for him whom the crime benefits, is your own axiom," argued the girl.

"I beg your pardon?"

"Percival Brooks benefited to the tune of £2,000,000."

"I beg your pardon. He did nothing of the sort. He was left with less than half the share that his younger brother inherited."

"Now, yes; but that was a former will and—"

"And that forged will was so clumsily executed, the signature so carelessly imitated, that the forgery was bound to come to light. Did *that* never strike you?"

"Yes, but—"

"There is no but," he interrupted. "It was all as clear as daylight to me from the very first. The quarrel with the old man, which broke his heart, was not with his eldest son, with whom he was used to quarrelling, but with the second son whom he idolised, in whom he believed. Don't you remember how John O'Neill heard the words 'liar' and 'deceit'? Percival Brooks had never deceived his father. His sins were all on the surface. Murray had led a quiet life, had pandered to his father, and fawned upon him, until, like most hypocrites, he at last got found out. Who knows what ugly gambling debt or debt of honour, suddenly revealed to old Brooks, was the cause of that last and deadly quarrel?

"You remember that it was Percival who remained beside his father and carried him up to his room. Where was Murray throughout that long and painful day, when his father lay dying—he, the idolised son, the apple of the old man's eye? You never hear his name mentioned as being present there all that day. But he knew that he had offended his father mortally, and that his father meant to cut him off with a shilling. He knew that Mr. Wethered had been sent for, that Wethered left the house soon after four o'clock.

"And here the cleverness of the man comes in. Having lain in wait for Wethered and knocked him on the back of the head with a stick, he could not very well make that will disappear altogether. There remained the faint chance of some other witnesses knowing that Mr. Brooks had made a fresh will, Mr. Wethered's partner, his clerk, or one of the confidential servants in the house. Therefore *a* will must be discovered after the old man's death.

"Now, Murray Brooks was not an expert forger, it takes years of training to become that. A forged will executed by himself would be sure to be found out—yes, that's it, sure to be found out. The forgery will be palpable—let it be palpable, and then it will be found out, branded as such, and the original will of 1891, so favourable to the young blackguard's interests, would be held as valid. Was it devilry or merely additional caution which prompted Murray to pen that forged will so glaringly in Percival's favour? It is impossible to say.

"Anyhow, it was the cleverest touch in that marvellously devised crime. To plan that evil deed was great, to execute it was easy enough. He had several hours' leisure in which to do it. Then at night it was simplicity itself to slip the document under the dead man's pillow. Sacrilege causes no shudder to such natures as Murray Brooks. The rest of the drama you know already—"

"But Percival Brooks?"

"The jury returned a verdict of 'Not guilty.' There was no evidence against him."

"But the money? Surely the scoundrel does not have the enjoyment of it still?"

"No; he enjoyed it for a time, but he died, about three months ago, and forgot to take the precaution of making a will, so his brother Percival has got the business after all. If you ever go to Dublin, I should order some of Brooks' bacon if I were you. It is very good."

XXIV

An Unparalleled Outrage

D o you care for the seaside?" asked the man in the corner when he had finished his lunch. "I don't mean the seaside at Ostend or Trouville, but honest English seaside with nigger minstrels, three-shilling excursionists, and dirty, expensive furnished apartments, where they charge you a shilling for lighting the hall gas on Sundays and sixpence on other evenings. Do you care for that?"

"I prefer the country."

"Ah! perhaps it is preferable. Personally I only liked one of our English seaside resorts once, and that was for a week, when Edward Skinner was up before the magistrate, charged with what was known as the 'Brighton Outrage.' I don't know if you remember the memorable day in Brighton, memorable for that elegant town, which deals more in amusements than mysteries, when Mr. Francis Morton, one of its most noted residents, disappeared. Yes! disappeared as completely as any vanishing lady in a music-hall. He was wealthy, had a fine house, servants, a wife and children, and he disappeared. There was no getting away from that.

"Mr. Francis Morton lived with his wife in one of the large houses in Sussex Square at the Kemp Town end of Brighton. Mrs. Morton was well known for her Americanisms, her swagger dinner parties, and beautiful Paris gowns. She was the daughter of one of the many American millionaires (I think her father was a Chicago pork-butcher), who conveniently provide wealthy wives for English gentlemen; and she had married Mr. Francis Morton a few years ago and brought him her quarter of a million, for no other reason but that she fell in love with him. He was neither good-looking nor distinguished, in fact, he was one of those men who seem to have City stamped all over their person.

"He was a gentleman of very regular habits, going up to London every morning on business and returning every afternoon by the 'husband's train.' So regular was he in these habits that all the servants at the Sussex Square house were betrayed into actual gossip over the fact that on Wednesday, March 17th, the master was not home for dinner. Hales, the butler, remarked that the mistress seemed a bit anxious and didn't eat much food. The evening wore on and Mr. Morton did not appear. At nine o'clock the young footman was dispatched to the station to make inquiries whether his master had been seen there in the afternoon, or whether—which Heaven forbid—there had been an accident on the line. The young man interviewed two or three porters, the bookstall boy, and ticket clerk; all were agreed that Mr. Morton did not go up to London during the day; no one had seen him within the precincts of the station. There certainly had been no accident reported either on the up or down line.

"But the morning of the 18th came, with its initial postman's knock, but neither Mr. Morton nor any sign or news from him. Mrs. Morton, who evidently had spent a sleepless night, for she looked sadly changed and haggard, sent a wire to the hall porter at the large building in Cannon Street, where her husband had his office. An hour later she had the reply: 'Not seen Mr. Morton all day yesterday, not here to-day.' By the afternoon every one in Brighton knew that a fellow-resident had mysteriously disappeared from or in the city.

"A couple of days, then another, elapsed, and still no sign of Mr. Morton. The police were doing their best. The gentleman was so well known in Brighton—as he had been a resident two years—that it was not difficult to firmly establish the one fact that he had not left the city, since no one saw him in the station on the morning of the 17th, nor at any time since then. Mild excitement prevailed throughout the town. At first the newspapers took the matter somewhat jocosely. 'Where is Mr. Morton?' was the usual placard on the evening's contents bills, but after three days had gone by and the worthy Brighton resident was still missing, while Mrs. Morton was seen to look more haggard and careworn every day, mild excitement gave place to anxiety.

"There were vague hints now as to foul play. The news had leaked out that the missing gentleman was carrying a large sum of money on the day of his disappearance. There were also vague rumours of a scandal not unconnected with Mrs. Morton herself and her own past history, which in her anxiety for her husband she had been forced to reveal to the detective-inspector in charge of the case.

"Then on Saturday the news which the late evening papers contained was this:

"'Acting on certain information received, the police to-day forced an entrance into one of the rooms of Russell House, a high-class furnished apartment on the King's Parade, and there they discovered our missing distinguished townsman, Mr. Francis Morton, who had been robbed and subsequently locked up in that room since Wednesday, the 17th. When discovered he was in the last stages of inanition; he was tied into an arm-chair with ropes, a thick wool shawl had been wound round his mouth, and it is a positive marvel that, left thus without food and very little air, the unfortunate gentleman survived the horrors of these four days of incarceration.

"'He has been conveyed to his residence in Sussex Square, and we are pleased to say that Doctor Mellish, who is in attendance, has declared his patient to be out of serious danger, and that with care and rest he will be soon quite himself again.

"'At the same time our readers will learn with unmixed satisfaction that the police of our city, with their usual acuteness and activity, have already discovered the identity and whereabouts of the cowardly ruffian who committed this unparalleled outrage.'"

XXV

THE PRISONER

I really don't know," continued the man in the corner blandly, "what it was that interested me in the case from the very first. Certainly it had nothing very out of the way or mysterious about it, but I journeyed down to Brighton nevertheless, as I felt that something deeper and more subtle lay behind that extraordinary assault, following a robbery, no doubt.

"I must tell you that the police had allowed it to be freely circulated abroad that they held a clue. It had been easy enough to ascertain who the lodger was who had rented the furnished room in Russell House. His name was supposed to be Edward Skinner, and he had taken the room about a fortnight ago, but had gone away ostensibly for two or three days on the very day of Mr. Morton's mysterious disappearance. It was on the 20th that Mr. Morton was found, and thirty-six hours later the public were gratified to hear that Mr. Edward Skinner had been traced to London and arrested on the charge of assault upon the person of Mr. Francis Morton and of robbing him of the sum of £10,000.

"Then a further sensation was added to the already bewildering case by the startling announcement that Mr. Francis Morton refused to prosecute.

"Of course, the Treasury took up the case and subpoenaed Mr. Morton as a witness, so that gentleman—if he wished to hush the matter up, or had been in any way terrorised into a promise of doing so—gained nothing by his refusal, except an additional amount of curiosity in the public mind and further sensation around the mysterious case.

"It was all this, you see, which had interested me and brought me down to Brighton on March 23rd to see the prisoner Edward Skinner arraigned before the beak. I must say that he was a very ordinary-looking individual. Fair, of ruddy complexion, with snub nose and the beginning of a bald place on the top of his head, he, too, looked the embodiment of a prosperous, stodgy 'City gent.'

"I took a quick survey of the witnesses present, and guessed that the handsome, stylish woman sitting next to Mr. Reginald Pepys, the noted lawyer for the Crown, was Mrs. Morton.

"There was a large crowd in court, and I heard whispered comments among the feminine portion thereof as to the beauty of Mrs. Morton's gown, the value of her large picture hat, and the magnificence of her diamond rings.

"The police gave all the evidence required with regard to the finding of Mr. Morton in the room at Russell House and also to the arrest of Skinner at the Langham Hotel in London. It appears that the prisoner seemed completely taken aback at the charge preferred against him, and declared that though he knew Mr. Francis Morton slightly in business he knew nothing as to his private life.

"'Prisoner stated,' continued Inspector Buckle, 'that he was not even aware Mr. Morton lived in Brighton, but I have evidence here, which I will place before your Honour, to prove that the prisoner was seen in the company of Mr. Morton at 9.30 o'clock on the morning of the assault.'

"Cross-examined by Mr. Matthew Quiller, the detective-inspector admitted that prisoner merely said that he did not know that Mr. Morton was a *resident* of Brighton—he never denied having met him there.

"The witness, or rather witnesses, referred to by the police were two Brighton tradesmen who knew Mr. Morton by sight and had seen him on the morning of the 17th walking with the accused.

"In this instance Mr. Quiller had no question to ask of the witnesses, and it was generally understood that the prisoner did not wish to contradict their statement.

"Constable Hartrick told the story of the finding of the unfortunate Mr. Morton after his four days' incarceration. The constable had been sent round by the chief inspector, after certain information given by Mrs. Chapman, the landlady of Russell House. He had found the door locked and forced it open. Mr. Morton was in an arm-chair, with several yards of rope wound loosely round him; he was almost unconscious, and there was a thick wool shawl tied round his mouth which must have deadened any cry or groan the poor gentleman might have uttered. But, as a matter of fact, the constable was under the impression that Mr. Morton had been either drugged or stunned in some way at first, which had left him weak and faint and prevented him from making himself heard or extricating himself from his bonds, which were very clumsily, evidently very hastily, wound round his body.

"The medical officer who was called in, and also Dr. Mellish who attended Mr. Morton, both said that he seemed dazed by some stupefying drug, and also, of course, terribly weak and faint with the want of food.

"The first witness of real importance was Mrs. Chapman, the proprietress of Russell House, whose original information to the police led to the discovery of Mr. Morton. In answer to Mr. Pepys, she said that on March 1st the accused called at her house and gave his name as Mr. Edward Skinner.

"'He required, he said, a furnished room at a moderate rental for a permanency, with full attendance when he was in, but he added that he would often be away for two or three days, or even longer, at a time.

"'He told me that he was a traveller for a tea-house,' continued Mrs. Chapman, 'and I showed him the front room on the third floor, as he did not want to pay more than twelve shillings a week. I asked him for a reference, but he put three sovereigns in my hand, and said with a laugh that he supposed paying for his room a month in advance was sufficient reference; if I didn't like him after that, I could give him a week's notice to quit.'

"'You did not think of asking him the name of the firm for which he travelled?' asked Mr. Pepys.

"'No, I was quite satisfied as he paid me for the room. The next day he sent in his luggage and took possession of the room. He went out most mornings on business, but was always in Brighton for Saturday and Sunday. On the 16th he told me that he was going to Liverpool for a couple of days; he slept in the house that night, and went off early on the 17th, taking his portmanteau with him.'

"'At what time did he leave?' asked Mr. Pepys.

"'I couldn't say exactly,' replied Mrs. Chapman with some hesitation. 'You see this is the off season here. None of my rooms are let, except the one to Mr. Skinner, and I only have one servant. I keep four during the summer, autumn, and winter season,' she added with conscious pride, fearing that her former statement might prejudice the reputation of Russell House. 'I thought I had heard Mr. Skinner go out about nine o'clock, but about an hour later the girl and I were both in the basement, and we heard the front door open and shut with a bang, and then a step in the hall.

"'"That's Mr. Skinner," said Mary. "So it is," I said, "why, I thought he had gone an hour ago." "He did go out then," said Mary, "for he left his bedroom door open and I went in to do his bed and tidy his room."

"Just go and see if that's him, Mary," I said, and Mary ran up to the hall and up the stairs, and came back to tell me that that was Mr. Skinner all right enough; he had gone straight up to his room. Mary didn't see him, but he had another gentleman with him, as she could hear them talking in Mr. Skinner's room.'

"'Then you can't tell us at what time the prisoner left the house finally?'

"'No, that I can't. I went out shopping soon after that. When I came in it was twelve o'clock. I went up to the third floor and found that Mr. Skinner had locked his door and taken the key with him. As I knew Mary had already done, the room I did not trouble more about it, though I did think it strange for a gentleman to look up his room and not leave the key with me.'

"'And, of course, you heard no noise of any kind in the room then?'

"'No. Not that day or the next, but on the third day Mary and I both thought we heard a funny sound. I said that Mr. Skinner had left his window open, and it was the blind flapping against the window-pane; but when we heard that funny noise again I put my ear to the keyhole and I thought I could hear a groan. I was very frightened, and sent Mary for the police.'

"Mrs. Chapman had nothing more of interest to say. The prisoner certainly was her lodger. She had last seen him on the evening of the 16th going up to his room with his candle. Mary the servant had much the same story to relate as her mistress.

"'I think it was 'im, right enough,' said Mary guardedly. 'I didn't see 'im, but I went up to 'is landing and stopped a moment outside 'is door. I could 'ear loud voices in the room—gentlemen talking.'

"'I suppose you would not do such a thing as to listen, Mary?' queried Mr. Pepys with a smile.

"'No, sir,' said Mary with a bland smile, 'I didn't catch what the gentlemen said, but one of them spoke so loud I thought they must be quarrelling.'

"'Mr. Skinner was the only person in possession of a latch-key, I presume. No one else could have come in without ringing at the door?'

"'Oh no, sir.'

"That was all. So far, you see, the case was progressing splendidly for the Crown against the prisoner. The contention, of course, was that Skinner had met Mr. Morton, brought him home with him, assaulted, drugged, then gagged and bound him, and finally robbed him of whatever money he had in his possession, which, according to certain affidavits which presently would be placed before the magistrate, amounted to £10,000 in notes.

"But in all this there still remained the great element of mystery for which the public and the magistrate would demand an explanation: namely, what were the relationships between Mr. Morton and Skinner, which had induced the former to refuse the prosecution of the man who had not only robbed him, but had so nearly succeeded in leaving him to die a terrible and lingering death?

"Mr. Morton was too ill as yet to appear in person. Dr. Mellish had absolutely forbidden his patient to undergo the fatigue and excitement of giving evidence himself in court that day. But his depositions had been taken at his bedside, were sworn to by him, and were now placed before the magistrate by the prosecuting counsel, and the facts they revealed were certainly as remarkable as they were brief and enigmatical.

"As they were read by Mr. Pepys, an awed and expectant hush seemed to descend over the large crowd gathered there, and all necks were strained eagerly forward to catch a glimpse of a tall, elegant woman, faultlessly dressed and wearing exquisite jewellery, but whose handsome face wore, as the prosecuting counsel read her husband's deposition, a more and more ashen hue.

"'This, your Honour, is the statement made upon oath by Mr. Francis Morton,' commenced Mr. Pepys in that loud, sonorous voice of his which sounds so impressive in a crowded and hushed court. "'I was obliged, for certain reasons which I refuse to disclose, to make a payment of a large sum of money to a man whom I did not know and have never seen. It was in a matter of which my wife was cognisant and which had entirely to do with her own affairs. I was merely the go-between, as I thought it was not fit that she should see to this matter herself. The individual in question had made certain demands, of which she kept me in ignorance as long as she could, not wishing to unnecessarily worry me. At last she decided to place the whole matter before me, and I agreed with her that it would be best to satisfy the man's demands.

"'I then wrote to that individual whose name I do not wish to disclose, addressing the letter, as my wife directed me to do, to the Brighton post office, saying that I was ready to pay the £10,000 to him, at any place or time and in what manner he might appoint. I received a reply which bore the Brighton postmark, and which desired me to be outside Furnival's, the drapers, in West Street, at 9.30 on the morning of March 17th, and to bring the money (£10,000) in Bank of England notes.

"'On the 16th my wife gave me a cheque for the amount and I cashed it at her bank—Bird's in Fleet Street. At half-past nine the following morning I was at the appointed place. An individual wearing a grey overcoat, bowler hat, and red tie accosted me by name and requested me to walk as far as his lodgings in the King's Parade. I followed him. Neither of us spoke. He stopped at a house which bore the name 'Russell House,' and which I shall be able to swear to as soon as I am able to go out. He let himself in with a latch-key, and asked me to follow him up to his room on the third floor. I thought I noticed when we were in the room that he locked the door; however, I had nothing of any value about me except the £10,000, which I was ready to give him. We had not exchanged the slightest word.

"'I gave him the notes, and he folded them and put them in his pocket-book. Then I turned towards the door, and, without the slightest warning, I felt myself suddenly gripped by the shoulder, while a handkerchief was pressed to my nose and mouth. I struggled as best I could, but the handkerchief was saturated with chloroform, and I soon lost consciousness. I hazily remember the man saying to me in short, jerky sentences, spoken at intervals while I was still weakly struggling:

"'What a fool you must think me, my dear sir! Did you really think that I was going to let you quietly walk out of here, straight to the police-station, eh? Such dodges have been done before, I know, when a man's silence has to be bought for money. Find out who he is, see where he lives, give him the money, then inform against him. No you don't! not this time. I am off to the continent with this £10,000, and I can get to Newhaven in time for the midday boat, so you'll have to keep quiet until I am the other side of the Channel, my friend. You won't be much inconvenienced; my landlady will hear your groans presently and release you, so you'll be all right. There, now, drink this—that's better.' He forced something bitter down my throat, then I remember nothing more.

"'When I regained consciousness I was sitting in an arm-chair with some rope tied round me and a wool shawl round my mouth. I hadn't the strength to make the slightest effort to disentangle myself or to utter a scream. I felt terribly sick and faint.'"

"Mr. Reginald Pepys had finished reading, and no one in that crowded court had thought of uttering a sound; the magistrate's eyes were fixed upon the handsome lady in the magnificent gown, who was mopping her eyes with a dainty lace handkerchief.

"The extraordinary narrative of the victim of so daring an outrage had kept every one in suspense; one thing was still expected to make the measure of sensation as full as it had ever been over any criminal case, and that was Mrs. Morton's evidence. She was called by the prosecuting counsel, and slowly, gracefully, she entered the witness-box. There was no doubt that she had felt keenly the tortures which her husband had undergone, and also the humiliation of seeing her name dragged forcibly into this ugly, blackmailing scandal.

"Closely questioned by Mr. Reginald Pepys, she was forced to admit that the man who blackmailed her was connected with her early life in a way which would have brought terrible disgrace upon her and upon her children. The story she told, amidst many tears and sobs, and much use of her beautiful lace handkerchief and beringed hands, was exceedingly pathetic.

"It appears that when she was barely seventeen she was inveigled into a secret marriage with one of those foreign adventurers who swarm in every country, and who styled himself Comte Armand de la Tremouille. He seems to have been a blackguard of unusually low pattern, for, after he had extracted from her some £200 of her pin money and a few diamond brooches, he left her one fine day with a laconic word to say that he was sailing for Europe by the *Argentina*, and would not be back for some time. She was in love with the brute, poor young soul, for when, a week later, she read that the *Argentina* was wrecked, and presumably every soul on board had perished, she wept very many bitter tears over her early widowhood.

"Fortunately her father, a very wealthy pork-butcher of Chicago, had known nothing of his daughter's culpable foolishness. Four years later he took her to London, where she met Mr. Francis Morton and married him. She led six or seven years of very happy married life when one day, like a thunderbolt from a clear, blue sky, she received a typewritten letter, signed 'Armand de la Tremouille,' full of protestations of undying love, telling a long and pathetic tale of years of suffering in a foreign land, whither he had drifted after having been rescued almost miraculously from the wreck of the *Argentina*, and where he never had been able to scrape a sufficient amount of money to pay for his passage home. At last fate had favoured him. He had, after many vicissitudes, found the whereabouts of his dear wife, and was now ready to forgive all that was past and take her to his loving arms once again.

"What followed was the usual course of events when there is a blackguard and a fool of a woman. She was terrorised and did not dare to tell her husband for some time; she corresponded with the Comte de la Tremouille, begging him for her sake and in memory of the past not to attempt to see her. She found him amenable to reason in the shape of several hundred pounds which passed through the Brighton post office into his hands. At last one day, by accident, Mr. Morton came across one of the Comte de la Tremouille's interesting letters. She confessed everything, throwing herself upon her husband's mercy.

"Now, Mr. Francis Morton was a business man, who viewed life practically and soberly. He liked his wife, who kept him in luxury, and wished to keep her, whereas the Comte de la Tremouille seemed willing enough to give her up for a consideration. Mrs. Morton, who had the sole and absolute control of her fortune, on the other hand, was willing enough to pay the price and hush up the scandal, which she believed— since she was a bit of a fool—would land her in prison for bigamy. Mr. Francis Morton wrote to the Comte de la Tremouille that his wife was ready to pay him the sum of £10,000 which he demanded in payment for her absolute liberty and his own complete disappearance out of her life now and for ever. The appointment was made, and Mr. Morton left his house at 9 a.m. on March 17th with the £10,000 in his pocket.

"The public and the magistrate had hung breathless upon her words. There was nothing but sympathy felt for this handsome woman, who throughout had been more sinned against than sinning, and whose gravest fault seems to have been a total lack of intelligence in dealing with her own life. But I can assure you of one thing, that in no case within my recollection was there ever such a sensation in a court as when the magistrate, after a few minutes' silence, said gently to Mrs. Morton:

"'And now, Mrs. Morton, will you kindly look at the prisoner, and tell me if in him you recognize your former husband?'

"And she, without even turning to look at the accused, said quietly:

"'Oh no! your Honour! of course that man is *not* the Comte de la Tremouille.'"

XXVI

A Sensation

"I can assure you that the situation was quite dramatic," continued the man in the corner, whilst his funny, claw-like hands took up a bit of string with renewed feverishness.

"In answer to further questions from the magistrate, she declared that she had never seen the accused; he might have been the go-between, however, that she could not say. The letters she received were all typewritten, but signed 'Armand de la Tremouille,' and certainly the signature was identical with that on the letters she used to receive from him years ago, all of which she had kept.

"'And did it *never* strike you,' asked the magistrate with a smile, 'that the letters you received might be forgeries?'

"'How could they be?' she replied decisively; no one knew of my marriage to the Comte de la Tremouille, no one in England certainly. And, besides, if some one did know the Comte intimately enough to forge his handwriting and to blackmail me, why should that some one have waited all these years? I have been married seven years, your Honour.'

"That was true enough, and there the matter rested as far as she was concerned. But the identity of Mr. Francis Morton's assailant had to be finally established, of course, before the prisoner was committed for trial. Dr. Mellish promised that Mr. Morton would be allowed to come to court for half an hour and identify the accused on the following day, and the case was adjourned until then. The accused was led away between two constables, bail being refused, and Brighton had perforce to moderate its impatience until the Wednesday.

"On that day the court was crowded to overflowing; actors, playwrights, literary men of all sorts had fought for admission to study for themselves the various phases and faces in connection with the case. Mrs. Morton was not present when the prisoner, quiet and self-possessed, was brought in and placed in the dock. His solicitor was with him, and a sensational defence was expected.

"Presently there was a stir in the court, and that certain sound, half rustle, half sigh, which preludes an expected palpitating event.

Mr. Morton, pale, thin, wearing yet in his hollow eyes the stamp of those five days of suffering, walked into court leaning on the arm of his doctor—Mrs. Morton was not with him.

"He was at once accommodated with a chair in the witness-box, and the magistrate, after a few words of kindly sympathy, asked him if he had anything to add to his written statement. On Mr. Morton replying in the negative, the magistrate added:

"'And now, Mr. Morton, will you kindly look at the accused in the dock and tell me whether you recognize the person who took you to the room in Russell House and then assaulted you?'

"Slowly the sick man turned towards the prisoner and looked at him; then he shook his head and replied quietly:

"'No, sir, that certainly was not the man.'

"'You are quite sure?' asked the magistrate in amazement, while the crowd literally gasped with wonder.

"'I swear it,' asserted Mr. Morton.

"'Can you describe the man who assaulted you?'

"'Certainly. He was dark, of swarthy complexion, tall, thin, with bushy eyebrows and thick black hair and short beard. He spoke English with just the faintest suspicion of a foreign accent.'

"The prisoner, as I told you before, was English in every feature. English in his ruddy complexion, and absolutely English in his speech.

"After that the case for the prosecution began to collapse. Every one had expected a sensational defence, and Mr. Matthew Quiller, counsel for Skinner, fully justified all these expectations. He had no fewer than four witnesses present who swore positively that at 9.45 A.M. on the morning of Wednesday, March 17th, the prisoner was in the express train leaving Brighton for Victoria.

"Not being endowed with the gift of being in two places at once, and Mr. Morton having added the whole weight of his own evidence in Mr. Edward Skinner's favour, that gentleman was once more remanded by the magistrate, pending further investigation by the police, bail being allowed this time in two sureties of £50 each."

XXVII

Two Blackguards

"Tell me what you think of it," said the man in the corner, seeing that Polly remained silent and puzzled.

"Well," she replied dubiously, "I suppose that the so-called Armand de la Tremouille's story was true in substance. That he did not perish on the *Argentina*, but drifted home, and blackmailed his former wife."

"Doesn't it strike you that there are at least two very strong points against that theory?" he asked, making two gigantic knots in his piece of string.

"Two?"

"Yes. In the first place, if the blackmailer was the 'Comte de la Tremouille' returned to life, why should he have been content to take £10,000 from a lady who was his lawful wife, and who could keep him in luxury for the rest of his natural life upon her large fortune, which was close upon a quarter of a million? The real Comte de la Tremouille, remember, had never found it difficult to get money out of his wife during their brief married life, whatever Mr. Morton's subsequent experience in the same direction might have been. And, secondly, why should he have typewritten his letters to his wife?"

"Because—"

"That was a point which, to my mind, the police never made the most of. Now, my experience in criminal cases has invariably been that when a typewritten letter figures in one, that letter is a forgery. It is not very difficult to imitate a signature, but it is a jolly sight more difficult to imitate a handwriting throughout an entire letter."

"Then, do you think—"

"I think, if you will allow me," he interrupted excitedly, "that we will go through the points—the sensible, tangible points of the case. Firstly: Mr. Morton disappears with £10,000 in his pocket for four entire days; at the end of that time he is discovered loosely tied to an arm-chair, and a wool shawl round his mouth. Secondly: A man named Skinner is accused of the outrage. Mr. Morton, although he himself is able, mind you, to furnish the best defence possible for Skinner, by denying his identity with the man who assaulted him, refuses to prosecute. Why?"

"He did not wish to drag his wife's name into the case."

"He must have known that the Crown would take up the case. Then, again, how is it no one saw him in the company of the swarthy foreigner he described?"

"Two witnesses did see Mr. Morton in company with Skinner," argued Polly.

"Yes, at 9.20 in West Street; that would give Edward Skinner time to catch the 9.45 at the station, and to entrust Mr. Morton with the latchkey of Russell House," remarked the man in the corner dryly.

"What nonsense!" Polly exclaimed.

"Nonsense, is it?" he said, tugging wildly at his bit of string; "is it nonsense to affirm that if a man wants to make sure that his victim shall not escape, he does not usually wind rope 'loosely' round his figure, nor does he throw a wool shawl lightly round his mouth. The police were idiotic beyond words; they themselves discovered that Morton was so 'loosely' fastened to his chair that very little movement would have disentangled him, and yet it never struck them that nothing was easier for that particular type of scoundrel to sit down in an arm-chair and wind a few yards of rope round himself, then, having wrapped a wool shawl round his throat, to slip his two arms inside the ropes."

"But what object would a man in Mr. Morton's position have for playing such extraordinary pranks?"

"Ah, the motive! There you are! What do I always tell you? Seek the motive! Now, what was Mr. Morton's position? He was the husband of a lady who owned a quarter of a million of money, not one penny of which he could touch without her consent, as it was settled on herself, and who, after the terrible way in which she had been plundered and then abandoned in her early youth, no doubt kept a very tight hold upon the purse-strings. Mr. Morton's subsequent life has proved that he had certain expensive, not altogether avowable, tastes. One day he discovers the old love letters of the 'Comte Armand de la Tremouille.'

"Then he lays his plans. He typewrites a letter, forges the signature of the erstwhile Count, and awaits events. The fish does rise to the bait. He gets sundry bits of money, and his success makes him daring. He looks round him for an accomplice—clever, unscrupulous, greedy—and selects Mr. Edward Skinner, probably some former pal of his wild oats days.

"The plan was very neat, you must confess. Mr. Skinner takes the room in Russell House, and studies all the manners and customs of his landlady and her servant. He then draws the full attention of the police upon himself. He meets Morton in West Street, then disappears ostensibly after the 'assault.' In the meanwhile Morton goes to Russell House. He walks upstairs, talks loudly in the room, then makes elaborate preparations for his comedy."

"Why! he nearly died of starvation!"

"That, I dare say, was not a part of his reckoning. He thought, no doubt, that Mrs. Chapman or the servant would discover and rescue him pretty soon. He meant to appear just a little faint, and endured quietly the first twenty-four hours of inanition. But the excitement and want of food told on him more than he expected. After twenty-four hours he turned very giddy and sick, and, falling from one fainting fit into another, was unable to give the alarm.

"However, he is all right again now, and concludes his part of a downright blackguard to perfection. Under the plea that his conscience does not allow him to live with a lady whose first husband is still alive, he has taken a bachelor flat in London, and only pays afternoon calls on his wife in Brighton. But presently he will tire of his bachelor life, and will return to his wife. And I'll guarantee that the Comte de la Tremouille will never be heard of again."

And that afternoon the man in the corner left Miss Polly Burton alone with a couple of photos of two uninteresting, stodgy, quiet-looking men—Morton and Skinner—who, if the old scarecrow was right in his theories, were a pair of the finest blackguards unhung.

XXVIII

The Regent's Park Murder

B y this time Miss Polly Burton had become quite accustomed to her extraordinary *vis-à-vis* in the corner.

He was always there, when she arrived, in the selfsame corner, dressed in one of his remarkable check tweed suits; he seldom said good morning, and invariably when she appeared he began to fidget with increased nervousness, with some tattered and knotty piece of string.

"Were you ever interested in the Regent's Park murder?" he asked her one day.

Polly replied that she had forgotten most of the particulars connected with that curious murder, but that she fully remembered the stir and flutter it had caused in a certain section of London Society.

"The racing and gambling set, particularly, you mean," he said. "All the persons implicated in the murder, directly or indirectly, were of the type commonly called 'Society men,' or 'men about town,' whilst the Harewood Club in Hanover Square, round which centred all the scandal in connection with the murder, was one of the smartest clubs in London.

"Probably the doings of the Harewood Club, which was essentially a gambling club, would for ever have remained 'officially' absent from the knowledge of the police authorities but for the murder in the Regent's Park and the revelations which came to light in connection with it.

"I dare say you know the quiet square which lies between Portland Place and the Regent's Park and is called Park Crescent at its south end, and subsequently Park Square East and West. The Marylebone Road, with all its heavy traffic, cuts straight across the large square and its pretty gardens, but the latter are connected together by a tunnel under the road; and of course you must remember that the new tube station in the south portion of the Square had not yet been planned.

"February 6th, 1907, was a very foggy night, nevertheless Mr. Aaron Cohen, of 30, Park Square West, at two o'clock in the morning, having finally pocketed the heavy winnings which he had just swept off the green table of the Harewood Club, started to walk home alone. An hour later most of the inhabitants of Park Square West were aroused from their peaceful slumbers by the sounds of a violent altercation in the road. A man's angry voice was heard shouting violently for a minute or two, and was followed immediately by frantic screams of 'Police' and 'Murder.' Then there was the double sharp report of firearms, and nothing more.

"The fog was very dense, and, as you no doubt have experienced yourself, it is very difficult to locate sound in a fog. Nevertheless, not more than a minute or two had elapsed before Constable F 18, the point policeman at the corner of Marylebone Road, arrived on the scene, and, having first of all whistled for any of his comrades on the beat, began to grope his way about in the fog, more confused than effectually assisted by contradictory directions from the inhabitants of the houses close by, who were nearly falling out of the upper windows as they shouted out to the constable.

"'By the railings, policeman.'

"'Higher up the road.'

"'No, lower down.'

"'It was on this side of the pavement I am sure.'

"'No, the other.'

"At last it was another policeman, F 22, who, turning into Park Square West from the north side, almost stumbled upon the body of a man lying on the pavement with his head against the railings of the Square. By this time quite a little crowd of people from the different houses in the road had come down, curious to know what had actually happened.

"The policeman turned the strong light of his bull's-eye lantern on the unfortunate man's face.

"'It looks as if he had been strangled, don't it?' he murmured to his comrade.

"And he pointed to the swollen tongue, the eyes half out of their sockets, bloodshot and congested, the purple, almost black, hue of the face.

"At this point one of the spectators, more callous to horrors, peered curiously into the dead man's face. He uttered an exclamation of astonishment.

"'Why, surely, it's Mr. Cohen from No. 30!'

"The mention of a name familiar down the length of the street had caused two or three other men to come forward and to look more closely into the horribly distorted mask of the murdered man.

"'Our next-door neighbour, undoubtedly,' asserted Mr. Ellison, a young barrister, residing at No. 31.

"'What in the world was he doing this foggy night all alone, and on foot?' asked somebody else.

"'He usually came home very late. I fancy he belonged to some gambling club in town. I dare say he couldn't get a cab to bring him out here. Mind you, I don't know much about him. We only knew him to nod to.'

"'Poor beggar! it looks almost like an old-fashioned case of garroting.'

"'Anyway, the blackguardly murderer, whoever he was, wanted to make sure he had killed his man!' added Constable F 18, as he picked up an object from the pavement. 'Here's the revolver, with two cartridges missing. You gentlemen heard the report just now?'

"'He don't seem to have hit him though. The poor bloke was strangled, no doubt.'

"'And tried to shoot at his assailant, obviously,' asserted the young barrister with authority.

"'If he succeeded in hitting the brute, there might be a chance of tracing the way he went.'

"'But not in the fog.'

"Soon, however, the appearance of the inspector, detective, and medical officer, who had quickly been informed of the tragedy, put an end to further discussion.

"The bell at No. 30 was rung, and the servants—all four of them women—were asked to look at the body.

"Amidst tears of horror and screams of fright, they all recognized in the murdered man their master, Mr. Aaron Cohen. He was therefore conveyed to his own room pending the coroner's inquest.

"The police had a pretty difficult task, you will admit; there were so very few indications to go by, and at first literally no clue.

"The inquest revealed practically nothing. Very little was known in the neighbourhood about Mr. Aaron Cohen and his affairs. His female servants did not even know the name or whereabouts of the various clubs he frequented.

"He had an office in Throgmorton Street and went to business every day. He dined at home, and sometimes had friends to dinner. When he was alone he invariably went to the club, where he stayed until the small hours of the morning.

"The night of the murder he had gone out at about nine o'clock. That was the last his servants had seen of him. With regard to the revolver, all four servants swore positively that they had never seen it before, and that, unless Mr. Cohen had bought it that very day, it did not belong to their master.

"Beyond that, no trace whatever of the murderer had been found, but on the morning after the crime a couple of keys linked together by a short metal chain were found close to a gate at the opposite end of the Square, that which immediately faced Portland Place. These were proved to be, firstly, Mr. Cohen's latch-key, and, secondly, his gate-key of the Square.

"It was therefore presumed that the murderer, having accomplished his fell design and ransacked his victim's pockets, had found the keys and made good his escape by slipping into the Square, cutting under the tunnel, and out again by the further gate. He then took the precaution not to carry the keys with him any further, but threw them away and disappeared in the fog.

"The jury returned a verdict of wilful murder against some person or persons unknown, and the police were put on their mettle to discover the unknown and daring murderer. The result of their investigations, conducted with marvellous skill by Mr. William Fisher, led, about a week after the crime, to the sensational arrest of one of London's smartest young bucks.

"The case Mr. Fisher had got up against the accused briefly amounted to this:

"On the night of February 6th, soon after midnight, play began to run very high at the Harewood Club, in Hanover Square. Mr. Aaron Cohen held the bank at roulette against some twenty or thirty of his friends, mostly young fellows with no wits and plenty of money. 'The Bank' was winning heavily, and it appears that this was the third consecutive night on which Mr. Aaron Cohen had gone home richer by several hundreds than he had been at the start of play.

"Young John Ashley, who is the son of a very worthy county gentleman who is M.F.H. somewhere in the Midlands, was losing heavily, and in his case also it appears that it was the third consecutive night that Fortune had turned her face against him.

"Remember," continued the man in the corner, "that when I tell you all these details and facts, I am giving you the combined evidence of several witnesses, which it took many days to collect and to classify.

"It appears that young Mr. Ashley, though very popular in society, was generally believed to be in what is vulgarly termed 'low water'; up to his eyes in debt, and mortally afraid of his dad, whose younger son he was, and who had on one occasion threatened to ship him off to Australia with a £5 note in his pocket if he made any further extravagant calls upon his paternal indulgence.

"It was also evident to all John Ashley's many companions that the worthy M.F.H. held the purse-strings in a very tight grip. The young man, bitten with the desire to cut a smart figure in the circles in which he moved, had often recourse to the varying fortunes which now and again smiled upon him across the green tables in the Harewood Club.

"Be that as it may, the general consensus of opinion at the Club was that young Ashley had changed his last 'pony' before he sat down to a turn of roulette with Aaron Cohen on that particular night of February 6th.

"It appears that all his friends, conspicuous among whom was Mr. Walter Hatherell, tried their very best to dissuade him from pitting his luck against that of Cohen, who had been having a most unprecedented run of good fortune. But young Ashley, heated with wine, exasperated at his own bad luck, would listen to no one; he tossed one £5 note after another on the board, he borrowed from those who would lend, then played on parole for a while. Finally, at half-past one in the morning, after a run of nineteen on the red, the young man found himself without a penny in his pockets, and owing a debt—gambling debt—a debt of honour of £1500 to Mr. Aaron Cohen.

"Now we must render this much maligned gentleman that justice which was persistently denied to him by press and public alike; it was positively asserted by all those present that Mr. Cohen himself repeatedly tried to induce young Mr. Ashley to give up playing. He himself was in a delicate position in the matter, as he was the winner, and once or twice the taunt had risen to the young man's lips, accusing the holder of the bank of the wish to retire on a competence before the break in his luck.

"Mr. Aaron Cohen, smoking the best of Havanas, had finally shrugged his shoulders and said: 'As you please!'

"But at half-past one he had had enough of the player, who always lost and never paid—never could pay, so Mr. Cohen probably believed. He therefore at that hour refused to accept Mr. John Ashley's 'promissory' stakes any longer. A very few heated words ensued, quickly checked by the management, who are ever on the alert to avoid the least suspicion of scandal.

"In the meanwhile Mr. Hatherell, with great good sense, persuaded young Ashley to leave the Club and all its temptations and go home; if possible to bed.

"The friendship of the two young men, which was very well known in society, consisted chiefly, it appears, in Walter Hatherell being the willing companion and helpmeet of John Ashley in his mad and extravagant pranks. But to-night the latter, apparently tardily sobered by his terrible and heavy losses, allowed himself to be led away by his friend from the scene of his disasters. It was then about twenty minutes to two.

"Here the situation becomes interesting," continued the man in the corner in his nervous way. "No wonder that the police interrogated at least a dozen witnesses before they were quite satisfied that every statement was conclusively proved.

"Walter Hatherell, after about ten minutes' absence, that is to say at ten minutes to two, returned to the club room. In reply to several inquiries, he said that he had parted with his friend at the corner of New Bond Street, since he seemed anxious to be alone, and that Ashley said he would take a turn down Piccadilly before going home—he thought a walk would do him good.

"At two o'clock or thereabouts Mr. Aaron Cohen, satisfied with his evening's work, gave up his position at the bank and, pocketing his heavy winnings, started on his homeward walk, while Mr. Walter Hatherell left the club half an hour later.

"At three o'clock precisely the cries of 'Murder' and the report of fire-arms were heard in Park Square West, and Mr. Aaron Cohen was found strangled outside the garden railings."

XXIX

The Motive

Now at first sight the murder in the Regent's Park appeared both to police and public as one of those silly, clumsy crimes, obviously the work of a novice, and absolutely purposeless, seeing that it could but inevitably lead its perpetrators, without any difficulty, to the gallows.

"You see, a motive had been established. 'Seek him whom the crime benefits,' say our French *confrères*. But there was something more than that.

"Constable James Funnell, on his beat, turned from Portland Place into Park Crescent a few minutes after he had heard the clock at Holy Trinity Church, Marylebone, strike half-past two. The fog at that moment was perhaps not quite so dense as it was later on in the morning, and the policeman saw two gentlemen in overcoats and top-hats leaning arm in arm against the railings of the Square, close to the gate. He could not, of course, distinguish their faces because of the fog, but he heard one of them saying to the other:

"'It is but a question of time, Mr. Cohen. I know my father will pay the money for me, and you will lose nothing by waiting.'

"To this the other apparently made no reply, and the constable passed on; when he returned to the same spot, after having walked over his beat, the two gentlemen had gone, but later on it was near this very gate that the two keys referred to at the inquest had been found.

"Another interesting fact," added the man in the corner, with one of those sarcastic smiles of his which Polly could not quite explain, "was the finding of the revolver upon the scene of the crime. That revolver, shown to Mr. Ashley's valet, was sworn to by him as being the property of his master.

"All these facts made, of course, a very remarkable, so far quite unbroken, chain of circumstantial evidence against Mr. John Ashley. No wonder, therefore, that the police, thoroughly satisfied with Mr. Fisher's work and their own, applied for a warrant against the young man, and arrested him in his rooms in Clarges Street exactly a week after the committal of the crime.

"As a matter of fact, you know, experience has invariably taught me that when a murderer seems particularly foolish and clumsy, and proofs against him seem particularly damning, that is the time when the police should be most guarded against pitfalls.

"Now in this case, if John Ashley had indeed committed the murder in Regent's Park in the manner suggested by the police, he would have been a criminal in more senses than one, for idiocy of that kind is to my mind worse than many crimes.

"The prosecution brought its witnesses up in triumphal array one after another. There were the members of the Harewood Club—who had seen the prisoner's excited condition after his heavy gambling losses to Mr. Aaron Cohen; there was Mr. Hatherell, who, in spite of his friendship for Ashley, was bound to admit that he had parted from him at the corner of Bond Street at twenty minutes to two, and had not seen him again till his return home at five A.M.

"Then came the evidence of Arthur Chipps, John Ashley's valet. It proved of a very sensational character.

"He deposed that on the night in question his master came home at about ten minutes to two. Chipps had then not yet gone to bed. Five minutes later Mr. Ashley went out again, telling the valet not to sit up for him. Chipps could not say at what time either of the young gentlemen had come home.

"That short visit home—presumably to fetch the revolver—was thought to be very important, and Mr. John Ashley's friends felt that his case was practically hopeless.

"The valet's evidence and that of James Funnell, the constable, who had overheard the conversation near the park railings, were certainly the two most damning proofs against the accused. I assure you I was having a rare old time that day. There were two faces in court to watch which was the greatest treat I had had for many a day. One of these was Mr. John Ashley's.

"Here's his photo—short, dark, dapper, a little 'racy' in style, but otherwise he looks a son of a well-to-do farmer. He was very quiet and placid in court, and addressed a few words now and again to his solicitor. He listened gravely, and with an occasional shrug of the shoulders, to the recital of the crime, such as the police had reconstructed it, before an excited and horrified audience.

"Mr. John Ashley, driven to madness and frenzy by terrible financial difficulties, had first of all gone home in search of a weapon, then waylaid Mr. Aaron Cohen somewhere on that gentleman's way home. The young man had begged for delay. Mr. Cohen perhaps was obdurate; but Ashley followed him with his importunities almost to his door.

"There, seeing his creditor determined at last to cut short the painful interview, he had seized the unfortunate man at an unguarded moment from behind, and strangled him; then, fearing that his dastardly work was not fully accomplished, he had shot twice at the already dead body, missing it both times from sheer nervous excitement. The murderer then must have emptied his victim's pockets, and, finding the key of the garden, thought that it would be a safe way of evading capture by cutting across the squares, under the tunnel, and so through the more distant gate which faced Portland Place.

"The loss of the revolver was one of those unforeseen accidents which a retributive Providence places in the path of the miscreant, delivering him by his own act of folly into the hands of human justice.

"Mr. John Ashley, however, did not appear the least bit impressed by the recital of his crime. He had not engaged the services of one of the most eminent lawyers, expert at extracting contradictions from witnesses by skilful cross-examinations—oh, dear me, no! he had been contented with those of a dull, prosy, very second-rate limb of the law, who, as he called his witnesses, was completely innocent of any desire to create a sensation.

"He rose quietly from his seat, and, amidst breathless silence, called the first of three witnesses on behalf of his client. He called three—but he could have produced twelve—gentlemen, members of the Ashton Club in Great Portland Street, all of whom swore that at three o'clock on the morning of February 6th, that is to say, at the very moment when the cries of 'Murder' roused the inhabitants of Park Square West, and the crime was being committed, Mr. John Ashley was sitting quietly in the club-rooms of the Ashton playing bridge with the three witnesses. He had come in a few minutes before three—as the hall porter of the Club testified—and stayed for about an hour and a half.

"I need not tell you that this undoubted, this fully proved, *alibi* was a positive bombshell in the stronghold of the prosecution. The most accomplished criminal could not possibly be in two places at once, and though the Ashton Club transgresses in many ways against the gambling laws of our very moral country, yet its members belong to the best, most unimpeachable classes of society. Mr. Ashley had been seen and spoken to at the very moment of the crime by at least a dozen gentlemen whose testimony was absolutely above suspicion.

"Mr. John Ashley's conduct throughout this astonishing phase of the inquiry remained perfectly calm and correct. It was no doubt the consciousness of being able to prove his innocence with such absolute conclusion that had steadied his nerves throughout the proceedings.

"His answers to the magistrate were clear and simple, even on the ticklish subject of the revolver.

"'I left the club, sir,' he explained, 'fully determined to speak with Mr. Cohen alone in order to ask him for a delay in the settlement of my debt to him. You will understand that I should not care to do this in the presence of other gentlemen. I went home for a minute or two—not in order to fetch a revolver, as the police assert, for I always carry a revolver about with me in foggy weather—but in order to see if a very important business letter had come for me in my absence.

"'Then I went out again, and met Mr. Aaron Cohen not far from the Harewood Club. I walked the greater part of the way with him, and our conversation was of the most amicable character. We parted at the top of Portland Place, near the gate of the Square, where the policeman saw us. Mr. Cohen then had the intention of cutting across the Square, as being a shorter way to his own house. I thought the Square looked dark and dangerous in the fog, especially as Mr. Cohen was carrying a large sum of money.

"'We had a short discussion on the subject, and finally I persuaded him to take my revolver, as I was going home only through very frequented streets, and moreover carried nothing that was worth stealing. After a little demur Mr. Cohen accepted the loan of my revolver, and that is how it came to be found on the actual scene of the crime; finally I parted from Mr. Cohen a very few minutes after I had heard the church clock striking a quarter before three. I was at the Oxford Street end of Great Portland Street at five minutes to three, and it takes at least ten minutes to walk from where I was to the Ashton Club.'

"This explanation was all the more credible, mind you, because the question of the revolver had never been very satisfactorily explained by the prosecution. A man who has effectually strangled his victim would not discharge two shots of his revolver for, apparently, no other purpose than that of rousing the attention of the nearest passer-by. It was far more likely that it was Mr. Cohen who shot—perhaps wildly into the air, when suddenly attacked from behind. Mr. Ashley's explanation therefore was not only plausible, it was the only possible one.

"You will understand therefore how it was that, after nearly half an hour's examination, the magistrate, the police, and the public were alike pleased to proclaim that the accused left the court without a stain upon his character."

XXX

FRIENDS

"Yes," interrupted Polly eagerly, since, for once, her acumen had been at least as sharp as his, "but suspicion of that horrible crime only shifted its taint from one friend to another, and, of course, I know—"

"But that's just it," he quietly interrupted, "you don't know—Mr. Walter Hatherell, of course, you mean. So did every one else at once. The friend, weak and willing, committing a crime on behalf of his cowardly, yet more assertive friend who had tempted him to evil. It was a good theory; and was held pretty generally, I fancy, even by the police.

"I say 'even' because they worked really hard in order to build up a case against young Hatherell, but the great difficulty was that of time. At the hour when the policeman had seen the two men outside Park Square together, Walter Hatherell was still sitting in the Harewood Club, which he never left until twenty minutes to two. Had he wished to waylay and rob Aaron Cohen he would not have waited surely till the time when presumably the latter would already have reached home.

"Moreover, twenty minutes was an incredibly short time in which to walk from Hanover Square to Regent's Park without the chance of cutting across the squares, to look for a man, whose whereabouts you could not determine to within twenty yards or so, to have an argument with him, murder him, and ransack his pockets. And then there was the total absence of motive."

"But—" said Polly meditatively, for she remembered now that the Regent's Park murder, as it had been popularly called, was one of those which had remained as impenetrable a mystery as any other crime had ever been in the annals of the police.

The man in the corner cocked his funny birdlike head well on one side and looked at her, highly amused evidently at her perplexity.

"You do not see how that murder was committed?" he asked with a grin.

Polly was bound to admit that she did not.

"If you had happened to have been in Mr. John Ashley's predicament," he persisted, "you do not see how you could conveniently have done away with Mr. Aaron Cohen, pocketed his winnings, and then led the police of your country entirely by the nose, by proving an indisputable *alibi*?"

"I could not arrange conveniently," she retorted, "to be in two different places half a mile apart at one and the same time."

"No! I quite admit that you could not do this unless you also had a friend—"

"A friend? But you say—"

"I say that I admired Mr. John Ashley, for his was the head which planned the whole thing, but he could not have accomplished the fascinating and terrible drama without the help of willing and able hands."

"Even then—" she protested.

"Point number one," he began excitedly, fidgeting with his inevitable piece of string. "John Ashley and his friend Walter Hatherell leave the club together, and together decide on the plan of campaign. Hatherell returns to the club, and Ashley goes to fetch the revolver—the revolver which played such an important part in the drama, but not the part assigned to it by the police. Now try to follow Ashley closely, as he dogs Aaron Cohen's footsteps. Do you believe that he entered into conversation with him? That he walked by his side? That he asked for delay? No! He sneaked behind him and caught him by the throat, as the garroters used to do in the fog. Cohen was apoplectic, and Ashley is young and powerful. Moreover, he meant to kill—"

"But the two men talked together outside the Square gates," protested Polly, "one of whom was Cohen, and the other Ashley."

"Pardon me," he said, jumping up in his seat like a monkey on a stick, "there were not two men talking outside the Square gates. According to the testimony of James Funnell, the constable, two men were leaning arm in arm against the railings and *one* man was talking."

"Then you think that—"

"At the hour when James Funnell heard Holy Trinity clock striking half-past two Aaron Cohen was already dead. Look how simple the whole thing is," he added eagerly, "and how easy after that—easy, but oh, dear me! how wonderfully, how stupendously clever. As soon as James Funnell has passed on, John Ashley, having opened the gate, lifts the body of Aaron Cohen in his arms and carries him across the Square. The Square is deserted, of course, but the way is easy enough, and we must presume that Ashley had been in it before. Anyway, there was no fear of meeting any one.

"In the meantime Hatherell has left the club: as fast as his athletic legs can carry him he rushes along Oxford Street and Portland Place. It had been arranged between the two miscreants that the Square gate should be left on the latch.

"Close on Ashley's heels now, Hatherell too cuts across the Square, and reaches the further gate in good time to give his confederate a hand in disposing the body against the railings. Then, without another instant's delay, Ashley runs back across the gardens, straight to the Ashton Club, throwing away the keys of the dead man, on the very spot where he had made it a point of being seen and heard by a passer-by.

"Hatherell gives his friend six or seven minutes' start, then he begins the altercation which lasts two or three minutes, and finally rouses the neighbourhood with cries of 'Murder' and report of pistol in order to establish that the crime was committed at the hour when its perpetrator has already made out an indisputable *alibi*."

"I don't know what you think of it all, of course," added the funny creature as he fumbled for his coat and his gloves, "but I call the planning of that murder—on the part of novices, mind you—one of the cleverest pieces of strategy I have ever come across. It is one of those cases where there is no possibility whatever now of bringing the crime home to its perpetrator or his abettor. They have not left a single proof behind them; they foresaw everything, and each acted his part with a coolness and courage which, applied to a great and good cause, would have made fine statesmen of them both.

"As it is, I fear, they are just a pair of young blackguards, who have escaped human justice, and have only deserved the full and ungrudging admiration of yours very sincerely."

He had gone. Polly wanted to call him back, but his meagre person was no longer visible through the glass door. There were many things she would have wished to ask of him—what were his proofs, his facts? His were theories, after all, and yet, somehow, she felt that he had solved once again one of the darkest mysteries of great criminal London.

XXXI

The De Genneville Peerage

The man in the corner rubbed his chin thoughtfully, and looked out upon the busy street below.

"I suppose," he said, "there is some truth in the saying that Providence watches over bankrupts, kittens, and lawyers."

"I didn't know there was such a saying," replied Polly, with guarded dignity.

"Isn't there? Perhaps I am misquoting; anyway, there should be. Kittens, it seems, live and thrive through social and domestic upheavals which would annihilate a self-supporting tom-cat, and to-day I read in the morning papers the account of a noble lord's bankruptcy, and in the society ones that of his visit at the house of a Cabinet minister, where he is the most honoured guest. As for lawyers, when Providence had exhausted all other means of securing their welfare, it brought forth the peerage cases."

"I believe, as a matter of fact, that this special dispensation of Providence, as you call it, requires more technical knowledge than any other legal complication that comes before the law courts," she said.

"And also a great deal more money in the client's pocket than any other complication. Now, take the Brockelsby peerage case. Have you any idea how much money was spent over that soap bubble, which only burst after many hundreds, if not thousands, of pounds went in lawyers' and counsels' fees?"

"I suppose a great deal of money was spent on both sides," she replied, "until that sudden, awful issue—"

"Which settled the dispute effectually," he interrupted with a dry chuckle. "Of course, it is very doubtful if any reputable solicitor would have taken up the case. Timothy Beddingfield, the Birmingham lawyer, is a gentleman who—well—has had some misfortunes, shall we say? He is still on the rolls, mind you, but I doubt if any case would have its chances improved by his conducting it. Against that there is just this to be said, that some of these old peerages have such peculiar histories, and own such wonderful archives, that a claim is always worth investigating—you never know what may be the rights of it.

"I believe that, at first, every one laughed over the pretensions of the Hon. Robert Ingram de Genneville to the joint title and part revenues of the old barony of Genneville, but, obviously, he *might* have got his case. It certainly sounded almost like a fairy-tale, this claim based upon the supposed validity of an ancient document over 400 years old. It was *then* that a mediaeval Lord de Genneville, more endowed with muscle than common sense, became during his turbulent existence much embarrassed and hopelessly puzzled through the presentation made to him by his lady of twin-born sons.

"His embarrassment chiefly arose from the fact that my lady's attendants, while ministering to the comfort of the mother, had, in a moment of absent-mindedness, so placed the two infants in their cot that subsequently no one, not even—perhaps least of all—the mother, could tell which was the one who had been the first to make his appearance into this troublesome and puzzling world.

"After many years of cogitation, during which the Lord de Genneville approached nearer to the grave and his sons to man's estate, he gave up trying to solve the riddle as to which of the twins should succeed to his title and revenues; he appealed to his Liege Lord and King—Edward, fourth of that name—and with the latter's august sanction he drew up a certain document, wherein he enacted that both his sons should, after his death, share his titles and goodly revenues, and that the first son born in wedlock of *either* father should subsequently be the sole heir.

"In this document was also added that if in future times should any Lords de Genneville be similarly afflicted with twin sons, who had equal rights to be considered the eldest born, the same rule should apply as to the succession.

"Subsequently a Lord de Genneville was created Earl of Brockelsby by one of the Stuart kings, but for four hundred years after its enactment the extraordinary deed of succession remained a mere tradition, the Countesses of Brockelsby having, seemingly, no predilection for twins. But in 1878 the mistress of Brockelsby Castle presented her lord with twin-born sons.

"Fortunately, in modern times, science is more wide-awake, and attendants more careful. The twin brothers did not get mixed up, and one of them was styled Viscount Tirlemont, and was heir to the earldom, whilst the other, born two hours later, was that fascinating, dashing young Guardsman, well known at Hurlingham, Goodwood, London, and in his own county—the Hon. Robert Ingram de Genneville.

"It certainly was an evil day for this brilliant young scion of the ancient race when he lent an ear to Timothy Beddingfield. This man, and his family before him, had been solicitors to the Earls of Brockelsby for many generations, but Timothy, owing to certain 'irregularities,' had forfeited the confidence of his client, the late earl.

"He was still in practice in Birmingham, however, and, of course, knew the ancient family tradition anent the twin succession. Whether he was prompted by revenge or merely self-advertisement no one knows.

"Certain it is that he did advise the Hon. Robert de Genneville—who apparently had more debts than he conveniently could pay, and more extravagant tastes than he could gratify on a younger son's portion—to lay a claim, on his father's death, to the joint title and a moiety of the revenues of the ancient barony of Genneville, that claim being based upon the validity of the fifteenth-century document.

"You may gather how extensive were the pretensions of the Hon. Robert from the fact that the greater part of Edgbaston is now built upon land belonging to the old barony. Anyway, it was the last straw in an ocean of debt and difficulties, and I have no doubt that Beddingfield had not much trouble in persuading the Hon. Robert to commence litigation at once.

"The young Earl of Brockelsby's attitude, however, remained one of absolute quietude in his nine points of the law. He was in possession both of the title and of the document. It was for the other side to force him to produce the one or to share the other.

"It was at this stage of the proceedings that the Hon. Robert was advised to marry, in order to secure, if possible, the first male heir of the next generation, since the young earl himself was still a bachelor. A suitable *fiancée* was found for him by his friends in the person of Miss Mabel Brandon, the daughter of a rich Birmingham manufacturer, and the marriage was fixed to take place at Birmingham on Thursday, September 15th, 1907.

"On the 13th the Hon. Robert Ingram de Genneville arrived at the Castle Hotel in New Street for his wedding, and on the 14th, at eight o'clock in the morning, he was discovered lying on the floor of his bedroom—murdered.

"The sensation which the awful and unexpected sequel to the De Genneville peerage case caused in the minds of the friends of both litigants was quite unparalleled. I don't think any crime of modern times created quite so much stir in all classes of society. Birmingham was wild with excitement, and the employés of the Castle Hotel had real difficulty in keeping off the eager and inquisitive crowd who thronged daily to the hall, vainly hoping to gather details of news relating to the terrible tragedy.

"At present there was but little to tell. The shrieks of the chambermaid, who had gone into the Hon. Robert's room with his shaving water at eight o'clock, had attracted some of the waiters. Soon the manager and his secretary came up, and immediately sent for the police.

"It seemed at first sight as if the young man had been the victim of a homicidal maniac, so brutal had been the way in which he had been assassinated. The head and body were battered and bruised by some heavy stick or poker, almost past human shape, as if the murderer had wished to wreak some awful vengeance upon the body of his victim. In fact, it would be impossible to recount the gruesome aspect of that room and of the murdered man's body such as the police and the medical officer took note of that day.

"It was supposed that the murder had been committed the evening before, as the victim was dressed in his evening clothes, and all the lights in the room had been left fully turned on. Robbery, also, must have had a large share in the miscreant's motives, for the drawers and cupboards, the portmanteau and dressing-bag had been ransacked as if in search of valuables. On the floor there lay a pocket-book torn in half and only containing a few letters addressed to the Hon. Robert de Genneville.

"The Earl of Brockelsby, next-of-kin to the deceased, was also telegraphed for. He drove over from Brockelsby Castle, which is about seven miles from Birmingham. He was terribly affected by the awfulness of the tragedy, and offered a liberal reward to stimulate the activity of the police in search of the miscreant.

"The inquest was fixed for the 17th, three days later, and the public was left wondering where the solution lay of the terrible and gruesome murder at the Castle Hotel."

XXXII

A High-Bred Gentleman

The central figure in the coroner's court that day was undoubtedly the Earl of Brockelsby in deep black, which contrasted strongly with his florid complexion and fair hair. Sir Marmaduke Ingersoll, his solicitor, was with him, and he had already performed the painful duty of identifying the deceased as his brother. This had been an exceedingly painful duty owing to the terribly mutilated state of the body and face; but the clothes and various trinkets he wore, including a signet ring, had fortunately not tempted the brutal assassin, and it was through them chiefly that Lord Brockelsby was able to swear to the identity of his brother.

"The various employés at the hotel gave evidence as to the discovery of the body, and the medical officer gave his opinion as to the immediate cause of death. Deceased had evidently been struck at the back of the head with a poker or heavy stick, the murderer then venting his blind fury upon the body by battering in the face and bruising it in a way that certainly suggested the work of a maniac.

"Then the Earl of Brockelsby was called, and was requested by the coroner to state when he had last seen his brother alive.

"'The morning before his death,' replied his lordship, 'he came up to Birmingham by an early train, and I drove up from Brockelsby to see him. I got to the hotel at eleven o'clock and stayed with him for about an hour.'

"'And that is the last you saw of the deceased?'

"'That is the last I saw of him,' replied Lord Brockelsby.

"He seemed to hesitate for a moment or two as if in thought whether he should speak or not, and then to suddenly make up his mind to speak, for he added: 'I stayed in town the whole of that day, and only drove back to Brockelsby late in the evening. I had some business to transact, and put up at the Grand, as I usually do, and dined with some friends.'

"'Would you tell us at what time you returned to Brockelsby Castle?'

"'I think it must have been about eleven o'clock. It is a seven-mile drive from here.'

"'I believe,' said the coroner after a slight pause, during which the attention of all the spectators was riveted upon the handsome figure of the young man as he stood in the witness-box, the very personification of a high-bred gentleman, 'I believe that I am right in stating that there was an unfortunate legal dispute between your lordship and your brother?'

"'That is so.'

"The coroner stroked his chin thoughtfully for a moment or two, then he added:

"'In the event of the deceased's claim to the joint title and revenues of De Genneville being held good in the courts of law, there would be a great importance, would there not, attached to his marriage, which was to have taken place on the 15th?'

"'In that event, there certainly would be.'

"'Is the jury to understand, then, that you and the deceased parted on amicable terms after your interview with him in the morning?'

"The Earl of Brockelsby hesitated again for a minute or two, while the crowd and the jury hung breathless on his lips.

"'There was no enmity between us,' he replied at last.

"'From which we may gather that there may have been—shall I say—a slight disagreement at that interview?'

"'My brother had unfortunately been misled by the misrepresentations or perhaps the too optimistic views of his lawyer. He had been dragged into litigation on the strength of an old family document which he had never seen, which, moreover, is antiquated, and, owing to certain wording in it, invalid. I thought that it would be kinder and more considerate if I were to let my brother judge of the document for himself. I knew that when he had seen it he would be convinced of the absolutely futile basis of his claim, and that it would be a terrible disappointment to him. That is the reason why I wished to see him myself about it, rather than to do it through the more formal—perhaps more correct—medium of our respective lawyers. I placed the facts before him with, on my part, a perfectly amicable spirit.'

"The young Earl of Brockelsby had made this somewhat lengthy, perfectly voluntary explanation of the state of affairs in a calm, quiet voice, with much dignity and perfect simplicity, but the coroner did not seem impressed by it, for he asked very drily:

"'Did you part good friends?'

"'On my side absolutely so.'

"'But not on his?' insisted the coroner.

"'I think he felt naturally annoyed that he had been so ill-advised by his solicitors.'

"'And you made no attempt later on in the day to adjust any ill-feeling that may have existed between you and him?' asked the coroner, marking with strange, earnest emphasis every word he uttered.

"'If you mean did I go and see my brother again that day—no, I did not.'

"'And your lordship can give us no further information which might throw some light upon the mystery which surrounds the Hon. Robert de Genneville's death?' still persisted the coroner.

"'I am sorry to say I cannot,' replied the Earl of Brockelsby with firm decision.

"The coroner still looked puzzled and thoughtful. It seemed at first as if he wished to press his point further; every one felt that some deep import had lain behind his examination of the witness, and all were on tenter-hooks as to what the next evidence might bring forth. The Earl of Brockelsby had waited a minute or two, then, at a sign from the coroner, had left the witness-box in order to have a talk with his solicitor.

"At first he paid no attention to the depositions of the cashier and hall porter of the Castle Hotel, but gradually it seemed to strike him that curious statements were being made by these witnesses, and a frown of anxious wonder settled between his brows, whilst his young face lost some of its florid hue.

"Mr. Tremlett, the cashier at the hotel, had been holding the attention of the court. He stated that the Hon. Robert Ingram de Genneville had arrived at the hotel at eight o'clock on the morning of the 13th; he had the room which he usually occupied when he came to the 'Castle,' namely, No. 21, and he went up to it immediately on his arrival, ordering some breakfast to be brought up to him.

"At eleven o'clock the Earl of Brockelsby called to see his brother and remained with him until about twelve. In the afternoon the deceased went out, and returned for his dinner at seven o'clock in company with a gentleman whom the cashier knew well by sight, Mr. Timothy Beddingfield, the lawyer, of Paradise Street. The gentlemen had their dinner downstairs, and after that they went up to the Hon. Mr. de Genneville's room for coffee and cigars.

"'I could not say at what time Mr. Beddingfield left,' continued the cashier, 'but I rather fancy I saw him in the hall at about 9.15 P.M. He was wearing an Inverness cape over his dress clothes and a Glengarry cap. It was just at the hour when the visitors who had come down for the night from London were arriving thick and fast; the hall was very full, and there was a large party of Americans monopolising most of our *personnel*, so I could not swear positively whether I did see Mr. Beddingfield or not then, though I am quite sure that it was Mr. Timothy Beddingfield who dined and spent the evening with the Hon. Mr. de Genneville, as I know him quite well by sight. At ten o'clock I am off duty, and the night porter remains alone in the hall.'

"Mr. Tremlett's evidence was corroborated in most respects by a waiter and by the hall porter. They had both seen the deceased come in at seven o'clock in company with a gentleman, and their description of the latter coincided with that of the appearance of Mr. Timothy Beddingfield, whom, however, they did not actually know.

"At this point of the proceedings the foreman of the jury wished to know why Mr. Timothy Beddingfield's evidence had not been obtained, and was informed by the detective-inspector in charge of the case that that gentleman had seemingly left Birmingham, but was expected home shortly. The coroner suggested an adjournment pending Mr. Beddingfield's appearance, but at the earnest request of the detective he consented to hear the evidence of Peter Tyrrell, the night porter at the Castle Hotel, who, if you remember the case at all, succeeded in creating the biggest sensation of any which had been made through this extraordinary and weirdly gruesome case.

"'It was the first time I had been on duty at "The Castle," he said, 'for I used to be night porter at "Bright's," in Wolverhampton, but just after I had come on duty at ten o'clock a gentleman came and asked if he could see the Hon. Robert de Genneville. I said that I thought he was in, but would send up and see. The gentleman said: "It doesn't matter. Don't trouble; I know his room. Twenty-one, isn't it?" And up he went before I could say another word.'

"'Did he give you any name?' asked the coroner.

"'No, sir.'

"'What was he like?'

"'A young gentleman, sir, as far as I can remember, in an Inverness cape and Glengarry cap, but I could not see his face very well as he stood with his back to the light, and the cap shaded his eyes, and he only spoke to me for a minute.'

"'Look all round you,' said the coroner quietly. 'Is there any one in this court at all like the gentleman you speak of?'

"An awed hush fell over the many spectators there present as Peter Tyrrell, the night porter of the Castle Hotel, turned his head towards the body of the court and slowly scanned the many faces there present; for a moment he seemed to hesitate—only for a moment though, then, as if vaguely conscious of the terrible importance his next words might have, he shook his head gravely and said:

"'I wouldn't like to swear.'

"The coroner tried to press him, but with true British stolidity he repeated: 'I wouldn't like to say.'

"'Well, then, what happened?' asked the coroner, who had perforce to abandon his point.

"'The gentleman went upstairs, sir, and about a quarter of an hour later he come down again, and I let him out. He was in a great hurry then, he threw me a half-crown and said: "Good night."'

"'And though you saw him again then, you cannot tell us if you would know him again?'

"Once more the hall porter's eyes wandered as if instinctively to a certain face in the court; once more he hesitated for many seconds which seemed like so many hours, during which a man's honour, a man's life, hung perhaps in the balance.

"Then Peter Tyrrell repeated slowly: 'I wouldn't swear.'

"But coroner and jury alike, aye, and every spectator in that crowded court, had seen that the man's eyes had rested during that one moment of hesitation upon the face of the Earl of Brockelsby."

XXXIII

The Living and the Dead

The man in the corner blinked across at Polly with his funny mild blue eyes.

"No wonder you are puzzled," he continued, "so was everybody in the court that day, every one save myself. I alone could see in my mind's eye that gruesome murder such as it had been committed, with all its details, and, above all, its motive, and such as you will see it presently, when I place it all clearly before you.

"But before you see daylight in this strange case, I must plunge you into further darkness, in the same manner as the coroner and jury were plunged on the following day, the second day of that remarkable inquest. It had to be adjourned, since the appearance of Mr. Timothy Beddingfield had now become of vital importance. The public had come to regard his absence from Birmingham at this critical moment as decidedly remarkable, to say the least of it, and all those who did not know the lawyer by sight wished to see him in his Inverness cape and Glengarry cap such as he had appeared before the several witnesses on the night of the awful murder.

"When the coroner and jury were seated, the first piece of information which the police placed before them was the astounding statement that Mr. Timothy Beddingfield's whereabouts had not been ascertained, though it was confidently expected that he had not gone far and could easily be traced. There was a witness present who, the police thought, might throw some light as to the lawyer's probable destination, for obviously he had left Birmingham directly after his interview with the deceased.

"This witness was Mrs. Higgins, who was Mr. Beddingfield's housekeeper. She stated that her master was in the constant habit—especially latterly—of going up to London on business. He usually left by a late evening train on those occasions, and mostly was only absent thirty-six hours. He kept a portmanteau always ready packed for the purpose, for he often left at a few moments' notice. Mrs. Higgins added that her master stayed at the Great Western Hotel in London, for it was there that she was instructed to wire if anything urgent required his presence back in Birmingham.

"'On the night of the 14th,' she continued, 'at nine o'clock or thereabouts, a messenger came to the door with the master's card, and said that he was instructed to fetch Mr. Beddingfield's portmanteau, and then to meet him at the station in time to catch the 9.35 P.M. up train. I gave him the portmanteau, of course, as he had brought the card, and I had no idea there could be anything wrong; but since then I have heard nothing of my master, and I don't know when he will return.'

"Questioned by the coroner, she added that Mr. Beddingfield had never stayed away quite so long without having his letters forwarded to him. There was a large pile waiting for him now; she had written to the Great Western Hotel, London, asking what she should do about the letters, but had received no reply. She did not know the messenger by sight who had called for the portmanteau. Once or twice before Mr. Beddingfield had sent for his things in that manner when he had been dining out.

"Mr. Beddingfield certainly wore his Inverness cape over his dress clothes when he went out at about six o'clock in the afternoon. He also wore a Glengarry cap.

"The messenger had so far not yet been found, and from this point—namely, the sending for the portmanteau—all traces of Mr. Timothy Beddingfield seem to have been lost. Whether he went up to London by that 9.35 train or not could not be definitely ascertained. The police had questioned at least a dozen porters at the railway, as well as ticket collectors; but no one had any special recollection of a gentleman in an Inverness cape and Glengarry cap, a costume worn by more than one first-class passenger on a cold night in September.

"There was the hitch, you see; it all lay in this. Mr. Timothy Beddingfield, the lawyer, had undoubtedly made himself scarce. He was last seen in company with the deceased, and wearing an Inverness cape and Glengarry cap; two or three witnesses saw him leaving the hotel at about 9.15. Then the messenger calls at the lawyer's house for the portmanteau, after which Mr. Timothy Beddingfield seems to vanish into thin air; but—and that is a great 'but'—the night porter at the 'Castle' seems to have seen some one wearing the momentous Inverness and Glengarry half an hour or so later on, and going up to deceased's room, where he stayed about a quarter of an hour.

"Undoubtedly you will say, as every one said to themselves that day after the night porter and Mrs. Higgins had been heard, that there was a very ugly and very black finger which pointed unpleasantly at Mr. Timothy Beddingfield, especially as that gentleman, for some reason which still required an explanation, was not there to put matters right for himself. But there was just one little thing—a mere trifle, perhaps—which neither the coroner nor the jury dared to overlook, though, strictly speaking, it was not evidence.

"You will remember that when the night porter was asked if he could, among the persons present in court, recognize the Hon. Robert de Genneville's belated visitor, every one had noticed his hesitation, and marked that the man's eyes had rested doubtingly upon the face and figure of the young Earl of Brockelsby.

"Now, if that belated visitor had been Mr. Timothy Beddingfield—tall, lean, dry as dust, with a bird-like beak and clean-shaven chin—no one could for a moment have mistaken his face—even if they only saw it very casually and recollected it but very dimly—with that of young Lord Brockelsby, who was florid and rather short—the only point in common between them was their Saxon hair.

"You see that it was a curious point, don't you?" added the man in the corner, who now had become so excited that his fingers worked like long thin tentacles round and round his bit of string. "It weighed very heavily in favour of Timothy Beddingfield. Added to which you must also remember that, as far as he was concerned, the Hon. Robert de Genneville was to him the goose with the golden eggs.

"The 'De Genneville peerage case' had brought Beddingfield's name in great prominence. With the death of the claimant all hopes of prolonging the litigation came to an end. There was a total lack of motive as far as Beddingfield was concerned."

"Not so with the Earl of Brockelsby," said Polly, "and I've often maintained—"

"What?" he interrupted. "That the Earl of Brockelsby changed clothes with Beddingfield in order more conveniently to murder his own brother? Where and when could the exchange of costume have been effected, considering that the Inverness cape and Glengarry cap were in the hall of the Castle Hotel at 9.15, and at that hour and until ten o'clock Lord Brockelsby was at the Grand Hotel finishing dinner with some friends? That was subsequently proved, remember, and also that he was back at Brockelsby Castle, which is seven miles from Birmingham, at eleven o'clock sharp. Now, the visit of the individual in the Glengarry occurred some time after 10 P.M."

"Then there was the disappearance of Beddingfield," said the girl musingly. "That certainly points very strongly to him. He was a man in good practice, I believe, and fairly well known."

"And has never been heard of from that day to this," concluded the old scarecrow with a chuckle. "No wonder you are puzzled. The police were quite baffled, and still are, for a matter of that. And yet see how simple it is! Only the police would not look further than these two men—Lord Brockelsby with a strong motive and the night porter's hesitation against him, and Beddingfield without a motive, but with strong circumstantial evidence and his own disappearance as condemnatory signs.

"If only they would look at the case as I did, and think a little about the dead as well as about the living. If they had remembered that peerage case, the Hon. Robert's debts, his last straw which proved a futile claim.

"Only that very day the Earl of Brockelsby had, by quietly showing the original ancient document to his brother, persuaded him how futile were all his hopes. Who knows how many were the debts contracted, the promises made, the money borrowed and obtained on the strength of that claim which was mere romance? Ahead nothing but ruin, enmity with his brother, his marriage probably broken off, a wasted life, in fact.

"Is it small wonder that, though ill-feeling against the Earl of Brockelsby may have been deep, there was hatred, bitter, deadly hatred against the man who with false promises had led him into so hopeless a quagmire? Probably the Hon. Robert owed a great deal of money to Beddingfield, which the latter hoped to recoup at usurious interest, with threats of scandal and what not.

"Think of all that," he added, "and then tell me if you believe that a stronger motive for the murder of such an enemy could well be found."

"But what you suggest is impossible," said Polly, aghast.

"Allow me," he said, "it is more than possible—it is very easy and simple. The two men were alone together in the Hon. Robert de Genneville's room after dinner. You, as representing the public, and the police say that Beddingfield went away and returned half an hour later in order to kill his client. I say that it was the lawyer who was murdered at nine o'clock that evening, and that Robert de Genneville, the ruined man, the hopeless bankrupt, was the assassin."

"Then—"

"Yes, of course, now you remember, for I have put you on the track. The face and the body were so battered and bruised that they were past recognition. Both men were of equal height. The hair, which alone could not be disfigured or obliterated, was in both men similar in colour.

"Then the murderer proceeds to dress his victim in his own clothes. With the utmost care he places his own rings on the fingers of the dead man, his own watch in the pocket; a gruesome task, but an important one, and it is thoroughly well done. Then he himself puts on the clothes of his victim, with finally the Inverness cape and Glengarry, and when the hall is full of visitors he slips out unperceived. He sends the messenger for Beddingfield's portmanteau and starts off by the night express."

"But then his visit at the Castle Hotel at ten o'clock—" she urged. "How dangerous!"

"Dangerous? Yes! but oh, how clever. You see, he was the Earl of Brockelsby's twin brother, and twin brothers are always somewhat alike. He wished to appear dead, murdered by some one, he cared not whom, but what he did care about was to throw clouds of dust in the eyes of the police, and he succeeded with a vengeance. Perhaps—who knows?— he wished to assure himself that he had forgotten nothing in the *mise en scène*, that the body, battered and bruised past all semblance of any human shape save for its clothes, really would appear to every one as that of the Hon. Robert de Genneville, while the latter disappeared for ever from the old world and started life again in the new.

"Then you must always reckon with the practically invariable rule that a murderer always revisits, if only once, the scene of his crime.

"Two years have elapsed since the crime; no trace of Timothy Beddingfield, the lawyer, has ever been found, and I can assure you that it will never be, for his plebeian body lies buried in the aristocratic family vault of the Earl of Brockelsby."

He was gone before Polly could say another word. The faces of Timothy Beddingfield, of the Earl of Brockelsby, of the Hon. Robert de Genneville seemed to dance before her eyes and to mock her for the hopeless bewilderment in which she found herself plunged because of them; then all the faces vanished, or, rather, were merged in one long, thin, bird-like one, with bone-rimmed spectacles on the top of its beak, and a wide, rude grin beneath it, and, still puzzled, still doubtful, the young girl too paid for her scanty luncheon and went her way.

XXXIV

The Mysterious Death in Percy Street

Miss Polly Burton had had many an argument with Mr. Richard Frobisher about that old man in the corner, who seemed far more interesting and deucedly more mysterious than any of the crimes over which he philosophised.

Dick thought, moreover, that Miss Polly spent more of her leisure time now in that A.B.C. shop than she had done in his own company before, and told her so, with that delightful air of sheepish sulkiness which the male creature invariably wears when he feels jealous and won't admit it.

Polly liked Dick to be jealous, but she liked that old scarecrow in the A.B.C. shop very much too, and though she made sundry vague promises from time to time to Mr. Richard Frobisher, she nevertheless drifted back instinctively day after day to the tea-shop in Norfolk Street, Strand, and stayed there sipping coffee for as long as the man in the corner chose to talk.

On this particular afternoon she went to the A.B.C. shop with a fixed purpose, that of making him give her his views of Mrs. Owen's mysterious death in Percy Street.

The facts had interested and puzzled her. She had had countless arguments with Mr. Richard Frobisher as to the three great possible solutions of the puzzle—"Accident, Suicide, Murder?"

"Undoubtedly neither accident nor suicide," he said dryly.

Polly was not aware that she had spoken. What an uncanny habit that creature had of reading her thoughts!

"You incline to the idea, then, that Mrs. Owen was murdered. Do you know by whom?"

He laughed, and drew forth the piece of string he always fidgeted with when unravelling some mystery.

"You would like to know who murdered that old woman?" he asked at last.

"I would like to hear your views on the subject," Polly replied.

"I have no views," he said dryly. "No one can know who murdered the woman, since no one ever saw the person who did it. No one can give the faintest description of the mysterious man who alone could have committed that clever deed, and the police are playing a game of blind man's buff."

"But you must have formed some theory of your own," she persisted.

It annoyed her that the funny creature was obstinate about this point, and she tried to nettle his vanity.

"I suppose that as a matter of fact your original remark that 'there are no such things as mysteries' does not apply universally. There is a mystery—that of the death in Percy Street, and you, like the police, are unable to fathom it."

He pulled up his eyebrows and looked at her for a minute or two.

"Confess that that murder was one of the cleverest bits of work accomplished outside Russian diplomacy," he said with a nervous laugh. "I must say that were I the judge, called upon to pronounce sentence of death on the man who conceived that murder, I could not bring myself to do it. I would politely request the gentleman to enter our Foreign Office—we have need of such men. The whole *mise en scène* was truly artistic, worthy of its *milieu*—the Rubens Studios in Percy Street, Tottenham Court Road.

"Have you ever noticed them? They are only studios by name, and are merely a set of rooms in a corner house, with the windows slightly enlarged, and the rents charged accordingly in consideration of that additional five inches of smoky daylight, filtering through dusty windows. On the ground floor there is the order office of some stained glass works, with a workshop in the rear, and on the first floor landing a small room allotted to the caretaker, with gas, coal, and fifteen shillings a week, for which princely income she is deputed to keep tidy and clean the general aspect of the house.

"Mrs. Owen, who was the caretaker there, was a quiet, respectable woman, who eked out her scanty wages by sundry—mostly very meagre—tips doled out to her by impecunious artists in exchange for promiscuous domestic services in and about the respective studios.

"But if Mrs. Owen's earnings were not large, they were very regular, and she had no fastidious tastes. She and her cockatoo lived on her wages; and all the tips added up, and never spent, year after year, went to swell a very comfortable little account at interest in the Birkbeck Bank. This little account had mounted up to a very tidy sum, and the thrifty widow—or old maid—no one ever knew which she was—was generally referred to by the young artists of the Rubens Studios as a 'lady of means.' But this is a digression.

"No one slept on the premises except Mrs. Owen and her cockatoo. The rule was that one by one as the tenants left their rooms in the evening they took their respective keys to the caretaker's room. She would then, in the early morning, tidy and dust the studios and the office downstairs, lay the fire and carry up coals.

"The foreman of the glass works was the first to arrive in the morning. He had a latch-key, and let himself in, after which it was the custom of the house that he should leave the street door open for the benefit of the other tenants and their visitors.

"Usually, when he came at about nine o'clock, he found Mrs. Owen busy about the house doing her work, and he had often a brief chat with her about the weather, but on this particular morning of February 2nd he neither saw nor heard her. However, as the shop had been tidied and the fire laid, he surmised that Mrs. Owen had finished her work earlier than usual, and thought no more about it. One by one the tenants of the studios turned up, and the day sped on without any one's attention being drawn noticeably to the fact that the caretaker had not appeared upon the scene.

"It had been a bitterly cold night, and the day was even worse; a cutting north-easterly gale was blowing, there had been a great deal of snow during the night which lay quite thick on the ground, and at five o'clock in the afternoon, when the last glimmer of the pale winter daylight had disappeared, the confraternity of the brush put palette and easel aside and prepared to go home. The first to leave was Mr. Charles Pitt; he locked up his studio and, as usual, took his key into the caretaker's room.

"He had just opened the door when an icy blast literally struck him in the face; both the windows were wide open, and the snow and sleet were beating thickly into the room, forming already a white carpet upon the floor.

"The room was in semi-obscurity, and at first Mr. Pitt saw nothing, but instinctively realizing that something was wrong, he lit a match, and saw before him the spectacle of that awful and mysterious tragedy which has ever since puzzled both police and public. On the floor, already half covered by the drifting snow, lay the body of Mrs. Owen face downwards, in a nightgown, with feet and ankles bare, and these and her hands were of a deep purple colour; whilst in a corner of the room, huddled up with the cold, the body of the cockatoo lay stark and stiff."

XXXV

SUICIDE OR MURDER?

At first there was only talk of a terrible accident, the result of some inexplicable carelessness which perhaps the evidence at the inquest would help to elucidate.

"Medical assistance came too late; the unfortunate woman was indeed dead, frozen to death, inside her own room. Further examination showed that she had received a severe blow at the back of the head, which must have stunned her and caused her to fall, helpless, beside the open window. Temperature at five degrees below zero had done the rest. Detective Inspector Howell discovered close to the window a wrought-iron gas bracket, the height of which corresponded exactly with the bruise at the back of Mrs. Owen's head.

"Hardly however had a couple of days elapsed when public curiosity was whetted by a few startling headlines, such as the halfpenny evening papers alone know how to concoct.

"'The mysterious death in Percy Street.' 'Is it Suicide or Murder?' 'Thrilling details—Strange developments.' 'Sensational Arrest.'

"What had happened was simply this:

"At the inquest a few certainly very curious facts connected with Mrs. Owen's life had come to light, and this had led to the apprehension of a young man of very respectable parentage on a charge of being concerned in the tragic death of the unfortunate caretaker.

"To begin with, it happened that her life, which in an ordinary way should have been very monotonous and regular, seemed, at any rate latterly, to have been more than usually chequered and excited. Every witness who had known her in the past concurred in the statement that since October last a great change had come over the worthy and honest woman.

"I happen to have a photo of Mrs. Owen as she was before this great change occurred in her quiet and uneventful life, and which led, as far as the poor soul was concerned, to such disastrous results.

"Here she is to the life," added the funny creature, placing the photo before Polly—"as respectable, as stodgy, as uninteresting as it is well possible for a member of your charming sex to be; not a face, you will admit, to lead any youngster to temptation or to induce him to commit a crime.

"Nevertheless one day all the tenants of the Rubens Studios were surprised and shocked to see Mrs. Owen, quiet, respectable Mrs. Owen, sallying forth at six o'clock in the afternoon, attired in an extravagant bonnet and a cloak trimmed with imitation astrakhan which—slightly open in front—displayed a gold locket and chain of astonishing proportions.

"Many were the comments, the hints, the bits of sarcasm levelled at the worthy woman by the frivolous confraternity of the brush.

"The plot thickened when from that day forth a complete change came over the worthy caretaker of the Rubens Studios. While she appeared day after day before the astonished gaze of the tenants and the scandalized looks of the neighbours, attired in new and extravagant dresses, her work was hopelessly neglected, and she was always 'out' when wanted.

"There was, of course, much talk and comment in various parts of the Rubens Studios on the subject of Mrs. Owen's 'dissipations.' The tenants began to put two and two together, and after a very little while the general consensus of opinion became firmly established that the honest caretaker's demoralisation coincided week for week, almost day for day, with young Greenhill's establishment in No. 8 Studio.

"Every one had remarked that he stayed much later in the evening than any one else, and yet no one presumed that he stayed for purposes of work. Suspicions soon rose to certainty when Mrs. Owen and Arthur Greenhill were seen by one of the glass workmen dining together at Gambia's Restaurant in Tottenham Court Road.

"The workman, who was having a cup of tea at the counter, noticed particularly that when the bill was paid the money came out of Mrs. Owen's purse. The dinner had been sumptuous—veal cutlets, a cut from the joint, dessert, coffee and liqueurs. Finally the pair left the restaurant apparently very gay, young Greenhill smoking a choice cigar.

"Irregularities such as these were bound sooner or later to come to the ears and eyes of Mr. Allman, the landlord of the Rubens Studios; and a month after the New Year, without further warning, he gave her a week's notice to quit his house.

"'Mrs. Owen did not seem the least bit upset when I gave her notice,' Mr. Allman declared in his evidence at the inquest; 'on the contrary, she told me that she had ample means, and had only worked latterly for the sake of something to do. She added that she had plenty of friends who would look after her, for she had a nice little pile to leave to any one who would know how "to get the right side of her."'

"Nevertheless, in spite of this cheerful interview, Miss Bedford, the tenant of No. 6 Studio, had stated that when she took her key to the caretaker's room at 6.30 that afternoon she found Mrs. Owen in tears. The caretaker refused to be comforted, nor would she speak of her trouble to Miss Bedford.

"Twenty-four hours later she was found dead.

"The coroner's jury returned an open verdict, and Detective-Inspector Jones was charged by the police to make some inquiries about young Mr. Greenhill, whose intimacy with the unfortunate woman had been universally commented upon.

"The detective, however, pushed his investigations as far as the Birkbeck Bank. There he discovered that after her interview with Mr. Allman, Mrs. Owen had withdrawn what money she had on deposit, some £800, the result of twenty-five years' saving and thrift.

"But the immediate result of Detective-Inspector Jones's labours was that Mr. Arthur Greenhill, lithographer, was brought before the magistrate at Bow Street on the charge of being concerned in the death of Mrs. Owen, caretaker of the Rubens Studios, Percy Street.

"Now that magisterial inquiry is one of the few interesting ones which I had the misfortune to miss," continued the man in the corner, with a nervous shake of the shoulders. "But you know as well as I do how the attitude of the young prisoner impressed the magistrate and police so unfavourably that, with every new witness brought forward, his position became more and more unfortunate.

"Yet he was a good-looking, rather coarsely built young fellow, with one of those awful Cockney accents which literally make one jump. But he looked painfully nervous, stammered at every word spoken, and repeatedly gave answers entirely at random.

"His father acted as lawyer for him, a rough-looking elderly man, who had the appearance of a common country attorney rather than of a London solicitor.

"The police had built up a fairly strong case against the lithographer. Medical evidence revealed nothing new: Mrs. Owen had died from exposure, the blow at the back of the head not being sufficiently serious to cause anything but temporary disablement. When the medical officer had been called in, death had intervened for some time; it was quite impossible to say how long, whether one hour or five or twelve.

"The appearance and state of the room, when the unfortunate woman was found by Mr. Charles Pitt, were again gone over in minute detail. Mrs. Owen's clothes, which she had worn during the day, were folded neatly on a chair. The key of her cupboard was in the pocket of her dress. The door had been slightly ajar, but both the windows were wide open; one of them, which had the sash-line broken, had been fastened up most scientifically with a piece of rope.

"Mrs. Owen had obviously undressed preparatory to going to bed, and the magistrate very naturally soon made the remark how untenable the theory of an accident must be. No one in their five senses would undress with a temperature at below zero, and the windows wide open.

"After these preliminary statements the cashier of the Birkbeck was called and he related the caretaker's visit at the bank.

"'It was then about one o'clock,' he stated. 'Mrs. Owen called and presented a cheque to self for £827, the amount of her balance. She seemed exceedingly happy and cheerful, and talked about needing plenty of cash, as she was going abroad to join her nephew, for whom she would in future keep house. I warned her about being sufficiently careful with so large a sum, and parting from it injudiciously, as women of her class are very apt to do. She laughingly declared that not only was she careful of it in the present, but meant to be so for the far-off future, for she intended to go that very day to a lawyer's office and to make a will.'

"The cashier's evidence was certainly startling in the extreme, since in the widow's room no trace of any kind was found of any money; against that, two of the notes handed over by the bank to Mrs. Owen on that day were cashed by young Greenhill on the very morning of her mysterious death. One was handed in by him to the West End Clothiers Company, in payment for a suit of clothes, and the other he changed at the Post Office in Oxford Street.

"After that all the evidence had of necessity to be gone through again on the subject of young Greenhill's intimacy with Mrs. Owen. He listened to it all with an air of the most painful nervousness, his cheeks were positively green, his lips seemed dry and parched, for he repeatedly passed his tongue over them, and when Constable E 18 deposed that at 2 A.M. on the morning of February 2nd he had seen the accused and spoken to him at the corner of Percy Street and Tottenham Court Road, young Greenhill all but fainted.

"The contention of the police was that the caretaker had been murdered and robbed during that night before she went to bed, that young Greenhill had done the murder, seeing that he was the only person known to have been intimate with the woman, and that it was, moreover, proved unquestionably that he was in the immediate neighbourhood of the Rubens Studios at an extraordinarily late hour of the night.

"His own account of himself, and of that same night, could certainly not be called very satisfactory. Mrs. Owen was a relative of his late mother's, he declared. He himself was a lithographer by trade, with a good deal of time and leisure on his hands. He certainly had employed some of that time in taking the old woman to various places of amusement. He had on more than one occasion suggested that she should give up menial work, and come and live with him, but, unfortunately, she was a great deal imposed upon by her nephew, a man of the name of Owen, who exploited the good-natured woman in every possible way, and who had on more than one occasion made severe attacks upon her savings at the Birkbeck Bank.

"Severely cross-examined by the prosecuting counsel about this supposed relative of Mrs. Owen, Greenhill admitted that he did not know him—had, in fact, never seen him. He knew that his name was Owen and that was all. His chief occupation consisted in sponging on the kind-hearted old woman, but he only went to see her in the evenings, when he presumably knew that she would be alone, and invariably after all the tenants of the Rubens Studios had left for the day.

"I don't know whether at this point it strikes you at all, as it did both magistrate and counsel, that there was a direct contradiction in this statement and the one made by the cashier of the Birkbeck on the subject of his last conversation with Mrs. Owen. 'I am going abroad to join my nephew, for whom I am going to keep house,' was what the unfortunate woman had said.

"Now Greenhill, in spite of his nervousness and at times contradictory answers, strictly adhered to his point, that there was a nephew in London, who came frequently to see his aunt.

"Anyway, the sayings of the murdered woman could not be taken as evidence in law. Mr. Greenhill senior put the objection, adding: 'There may have been two nephews,' which the magistrate and the prosecution were bound to admit.

"With regard to the night immediately preceding Mrs. Owen's death, Greenhill stated that he had been with her to the theatre, had seen her home, and had had some supper with her in her room. Before he left her, at 2 A.M., she had of her own accord made him a present of £10, saying: 'I am a sort of aunt to you, Arthur, and if you don't have it, Bill is sure to get it.'

"She had seemed rather worried in the early part of the evening, but later on she cheered up.

"'Did she speak at all about this nephew of hers or about her money affairs?' asked the magistrate.

"Again the young man hesitated, but said, 'No! she did not mention either Owen or her money affairs.'

"If I remember rightly," added the man in the corner, "for recollect I was not present, the case was here adjourned. But the magistrate would not grant bail. Greenhill was removed looking more dead than alive—though every one remarked that Mr. Greenhill senior looked determined and not the least worried. In the course of his examination on behalf of his son, of the medical officer and one or two other witnesses, he had very ably tried to confuse them on the subject of the hour at which Mrs. Owen was last known to be alive.

"He made a very great point of the fact that the usual morning's work was done throughout the house when the inmates arrived. Was it conceivable, he argued, that a woman would do that kind of work overnight, especially as she was going to the theatre, and therefore would wish to dress in her smarter clothes? It certainly was a very nice point levelled against the prosecution, who promptly retorted: Just as conceivable as that a woman in those circumstances of life should, having done her work, undress beside an open window at nine o'clock in the morning with the snow beating into the room.

"Now it seems that Mr. Greenhill senior could produce any amount of witnesses who could help to prove a conclusive *alibi* on behalf of his son, if only some time subsequent to that fatal 2 A.M. the murdered woman had been seen alive by some chance passer-by.

"However, he was an able man and an earnest one, and I fancy the magistrate felt some sympathy for his strenuous endeavours on his son's behalf. He granted a week's adjournment, which seemed to satisfy Mr. Greenhill completely.

"In the meanwhile the papers had talked of and almost exhausted the subject of the mystery in Percy Street. There had been, as you no doubt know from personal experience, innumerable arguments on the puzzling alternatives:—

"Accident?

"Suicide?

"Murder?

"A week went by, and then the case against young Greenhill was resumed. Of course the court was crowded. It needed no great penetration to remark at once that the prisoner looked more hopeful, and his father quite elated.

"Again a great deal of minor evidence was taken, and then came the turn of the defence. Mr. Greenhill called Mrs. Hall, confectioner, of Percy Street, opposite the Rubens Studios. She deposed that at 8 o'clock in the morning of February 2nd, while she was tidying her shop window, she saw the caretaker of the Studios opposite, as usual, on her knees, her head and body wrapped in a shawl, cleaning her front steps. Her husband also saw Mrs. Owen, and Mrs. Hall remarked to her husband how thankful she was that her own shop had tiled steps, which did not need scrubbing on so cold a morning.

"Mr. Hall, confectioner, of the same address, corroborated this statement, and Mr. Greenhill, with absolute triumph, produced a third witness, Mrs. Martin, of Percy Street, who from her window on the second floor had, at 7.30 a.m., seen the caretaker shaking mats outside her front door. The description this witness gave of Mrs. Owen's get-up, with the shawl round her head, coincided point by point with that given by Mr. and Mrs. Hall.

"After that Mr. Greenhill's task became an easy one; his son was at home having his breakfast at 8 o'clock that morning—not only himself, but his servants would testify to that.

"The weather had been so bitter that the whole of that day Arthur had not stirred from his own fireside. Mrs. Owen was murdered after 8 a.m. on that day, since she was seen alive by three people at that hour, therefore his son could not have murdered Mrs. Owen. The police must find the criminal elsewhere, or else bow to the opinion originally expressed by the public that Mrs. Owen had met with a terrible untoward accident, or that perhaps she may have wilfully sought her own death in that extraordinary and tragic fashion.

"Before young Greenhill was finally discharged one or two witnesses were again examined, chief among these being the foreman of the glassworks. He had turned up at the Rubens Studios at 9 o'clock, and been in business all day. He averred positively that he did not specially notice any suspicious-looking individual crossing the hall that day. 'But,' he remarked with a smile, 'I don't sit and watch every one who goes up and downstairs. I am too busy for that. The street door is always left open; any one can walk in, up or down, who knows the way.'

"That there was a mystery in connection with Mrs. Owen's death—of that the police have remained perfectly convinced; whether young Greenhill held the key of that mystery or not they have never found out to this day.

"I could enlighten them as to the cause of the young lithographer's anxiety at the magisterial inquiry, but, I assure you, I do not care to do the work of the police for them. Why should I? Greenhill will never suffer from unjust suspicions. He and his father alone—besides myself—know in what a terribly tight corner he all but found himself.

"The young man did not reach home till nearly *five* o'clock that morning. His last train had gone; he had to walk, lost his way, and wandered about Hampstead for hours. Think what his position would have been if the worthy confectioners of Percy Street had not seen Mrs. Owen 'wrapped up in a shawl, on her knees, doing the front steps.'

"Moreover, Mr. Greenhill senior is a solicitor, who has a small office in John Street, Bedford Row. The afternoon before her death Mrs. Owen had been to that office and had there made a will by which she left all her savings to young Arthur Greenhill, lithographer. Had that will been in other than paternal hands, it would have been proved, in the natural course of such things, and one other link would have been added to the chain which nearly dragged Arthur Greenhill to the gallows—'the link of a very strong motive.'

"Can you wonder that the young man turned livid, until such time as it was proved beyond a doubt that the murdered woman was alive hours after he had reached the safe shelter of his home?

"I saw you smile when I used the word 'murdered,'" continued the man in the corner, growing quite excited now that he was approaching the *dénouement* of his story. "I know that the public, after the magistrate had discharged Arthur Greenhill, were quite satisfied to think that the mystery in Percy Street was a case of accident—or suicide."

"No," replied Polly, "there could be no question of suicide, for two very distinct reasons."

He looked at her with some degree of astonishment. She supposed that he was amazed at her venturing to form an opinion of her own.

"And may I ask what, in your opinion, these reasons are?" he asked very sarcastically.

"To begin with, the question of money," she said—"has any more of it been traced so far?"

"Not another £5 note," he said with a chuckle; "they were all cashed in Paris during the Exhibition, and you have no conception how easy a thing that is to do, at any of the hotels or smaller *agents de change*."

"That nephew was a clever blackguard," she commented.

"You believe, then, in the existence of that nephew?"

"Why should I doubt it? Some one must have existed who was sufficiently familiar with the house to go about in it in the middle of the day without attracting any one's attention."

"In the middle of the day?" he said with a chuckle.

"Any time after 8.30 in the morning."

"So you, too, believe in the 'caretaker, wrapped up in a shawl,' cleaning her front steps?" he queried.

"But—"

"It never struck you, in spite of the training your intercourse with me must have given you, that the person who carefully did all the work in the Rubens Studios, laid the fires and carried up the coals, merely did it in order to gain time; in order that the bitter frost might really and effectually do its work, and Mrs. Owen be not missed until she was truly dead."

"But—" suggested Polly again.

"It never struck you that one of the greatest secrets of successful crime is to lead the police astray with regard to the time when the crime was committed. That was, if you remember, the great point in the Regent's Park murder.

"In this case the 'nephew,' since we admit his existence, would—even if he were ever found, which is doubtful—be able to prove as good an *alibi* as young Greenhill."

"But I don't understand—"

"How the murder was committed?" he said eagerly. "Surely you can see it all for yourself, since you admit the 'nephew'—a scamp, perhaps— who sponges on the good-natured woman. He terrorises and threatens her, so much so that she fancies her money is no longer safe even in the Birkbeck Bank. Women of that class are apt at times to mistrust the Bank of England. Anyway, she withdraws her money. Who knows what she meant to do with it in the immediate future?

"In any case, she wishes to secure it after her death to a young man whom she likes, and who has known how to win her good graces. That afternoon the nephew begs, entreats for more money; they have a row; the poor woman is in tears, and is only temporarily consoled by a pleasant visit at the theatre.

"At 2 o'clock in the morning young Greenhill parts from her. Two minutes later the nephew knocks at the door. He comes with a plausible tale of having missed his last train, and asks for a 'shake down' somewhere in the house. The good-natured woman suggests a sofa in one of the studios, and then quietly prepares to go to bed. The rest is very simple and elementary. The nephew sneaks into his aunt's room, finds her standing in her nightgown; he demands money with threats of violence; terrified, she staggers, knocks her head against the gas bracket, and falls on the floor stunned, while the nephew seeks for her keys and takes possession of the £800. You will admit that the subsequent *mise en scène*—is worthy of a genius.

"No struggle, not the usual hideous accessories round a crime. Only the open windows, the bitter north-easterly gale, and the heavily falling snow—two silent accomplices, as silent as the dead.

"After that the murderer, with perfect presence of mind, busies himself in the house, doing the work which will ensure that Mrs. Owen shall not be missed, at any rate, for some time. He dusts and tidies; some few hours later he even slips on his aunt's skirt and bodice, wraps his head in a shawl, and boldly allows those neighbours who are astir to see what they believe to be Mrs. Owen. Then he goes back to her room, resumes his normal appearance and quietly leaves the house."

"He may have been seen."

"He undoubtedly *was* seen by two or three people, but no one thought anything of seeing a man leave the house at that hour. It was very cold, the snow was falling thickly, and as he wore a muffler round the lower part of his face, those who saw him would not undertake to know him again."

"That man was never seen nor heard of again?" Polly asked.

"He has disappeared off the face of the earth. The police are searching for him, and perhaps some day they will find him—then society will be rid of one of the most ingenious men of the age."

XXXVI

The End

He had paused, absorbed in meditation. The young girl also was silent. Some memory too vague as yet to take a definite form was persistently haunting her—one thought was hammering away in her brain, and playing havoc with her nerves. That thought was the inexplicable feeling within her that there was something in connection with that hideous crime which she ought to recollect, something which—if she could only remember what it was—would give her the clue to the tragic mystery, and for once ensure her triumph over this self-conceited and sarcastic scarecrow in the corner.

He was watching her through his great bone-rimmed spectacles, and she could see the knuckles of his bony hands, just above the top of the table, fidgeting, fidgeting, fidgeting, till she wondered if there existed another set of fingers in the world which could undo the knots his lean ones made in that tiresome piece of string.

Then suddenly—*à propos* of nothing, Polly *remembered*—the whole thing stood before her, short and clear like a vivid flash of lightning:—Mrs. Owen lying dead in the snow beside her open window; one of them with a broken sash-line, tied up most scientifically with a piece of string. She remembered the talk there had been at the time about this improvised sash-line.

That was after young Greenhill had been discharged, and the question of suicide had been voted an impossibility.

Polly remembered that in the illustrated papers photographs appeared of this wonderfully knotted piece of string, so contrived that the weight of the frame could but tighten the knots, and thus keep the window open. She remembered that people deduced many things from that improvised sash-line, chief among these deductions being that the murderer was a sailor—so wonderful, so complicated, so numerous were the knots which secured that window-frame.

But Polly knew better. In her mind's eye she saw those fingers, rendered doubly nervous by the fearful cerebral excitement, grasping at first mechanically, even thoughtlessly, a bit of twine with which to secure the window; then the ruling habit strongest through all, the girl could see it; the lean and ingenious fingers fidgeting, fidgeting with that piece of string, tying knot after knot, more wonderful, more complicated, than any she had yet witnessed.

"If I were you," she said, without daring to look into that corner where he sat, "I would break myself of the habit of perpetually making knots in a piece of string."

He did not reply, and at last Polly ventured to look up—the corner was empty, and through the glass door beyond the desk, where he had just deposited his few coppers, she saw the tails of his tweed coat, his extraordinary hat, his meagre, shrivelled-up personality, fast disappearing down the street.

Miss Polly Burton (of the *Evening Observer*) was married the other day to Mr. Richard Frobisher (of the *London Mail*). She has never set eyes on the man in the corner from that day to this.

FINIS

A Note About the Author

Baroness Emmuska Orczy (1865–1947) was initially born in Hungary but raised throughout Europe. She was educated in Brussels, London, Paris and Budapest where she studied creative arts. In 1899, Orczy would publish her first novel entitled, *The Emperor's Candlesticks*. It wasn't a massive success but led to more writing opportunities including a series of detective stories. A few years later, she wrote and produced a stage play called *The Scarlet Pimpernel*, which she'd later adapt into a novel. It went on to become her most famous work and is considered a literary masterpiece of the twentieth century.

A Note from the Publisher

Spanning many genres, from non-fiction essays to literature classics to children's books and lyric poetry, Mint Edition books showcase the master works of our time in a modern new package. The text is freshly typeset, is clean and easy to read, and features a new note about the author in each volume. Many books also include exclusive new introductory material. Every book boasts a striking new cover, which makes it as appropriate for collecting as it is for gift giving. Mint Edition books are only printed when a reader orders them, so natural resources are not wasted. We're proud that our books are never manufactured in excess and exist only in the exact quantity they need to be read and enjoyed.

Discover more of your favorite classics with Bookfinity™.

- Track your reading with custom book lists.
- Get great book recommendations for your personalized Reader Type.
- Add reviews for your favorite books.
- AND MUCH MORE!

Visit **bookfinity.com** and take the fun Reader Type quiz to get started.

Enjoy our classic and modern companion pairings!

Printed in the USA
CPSIA information can be obtained
at www.ICGtesting.com
JSHW022341140824
68134JS00019B/1625